ClaReNCE ™

ROSS RICHIE CEO & Founder • MATT GAGNON Editor-in-Chief • FILIP SABLIK President of Publishing & Marketing • STEPHEN CHRISTY President of Development • LANCE KREITER VP of Licensing & Merchandising
PHIL BARBARO VP of Finance • BRYCE CARLSON Managing Editor • MEL CAYLO Marketing Manager • SCOTT NEWMAN Production Design Manager • IRENE BRADISH Operations Manager
CHRISTINE DINH Brand Communications Manager • SIERRA HAHN Senior Editor • DAFNA PLEBAN Editor • SHANNON WATTERS Editor • ERIC HARBURN Editor • WHITNEY LEOPARD Associate Editor • JASMINE AMIRI Associate Editor
CHRIS ROSA Associate Editor • ALEX GALER Assistant Editor • CAMERON CHITTOCK Assistant Editor • MARY GUMPORT Assistant Editor • MATTHEW LEVINE Assistant Editor • KELSEY DIETERICH Production Designer
JILLIAN CRAB Production Designer • MICHELLE ANKLEY Production Design Assistant • GRACE PARK Production Design Assistant • AARON FERRARA Operations Coordinator • ELIZABETH LOUGHRIDGE Accounting Coordinator
JOSÉ MEZA Sales Assistant • JAMES ARRIOLA Mailroom Assistant • HOLLY AITCHISON Operations Assistant • STEPHANIE HOCUTT Marketing Assistant • SAM KUSEK Direct Market Representative

Written by
Liz Prince

Illustrated by
Evan Palmer

Colors by
Maarta Laiho

Letters by
Corey Breen

Short Stories

Written by
Derek Fridolfs

Illustrated by
JJ Harrison

Cover
JJ Harrison

Designer
Grace Park

Associate Editor
Whitney Leopard

Collection Assistant Editor
Alex Galer

Editor
Shannon Watters

With Special Thanks to Marisa Marionakis, Rick Blanco, Curtis Lelash, Conrad
Montgomery, Nicole Rivera, Meghan Bradley, Keith Mack, Eric Cookmeyer and the

Chapter One

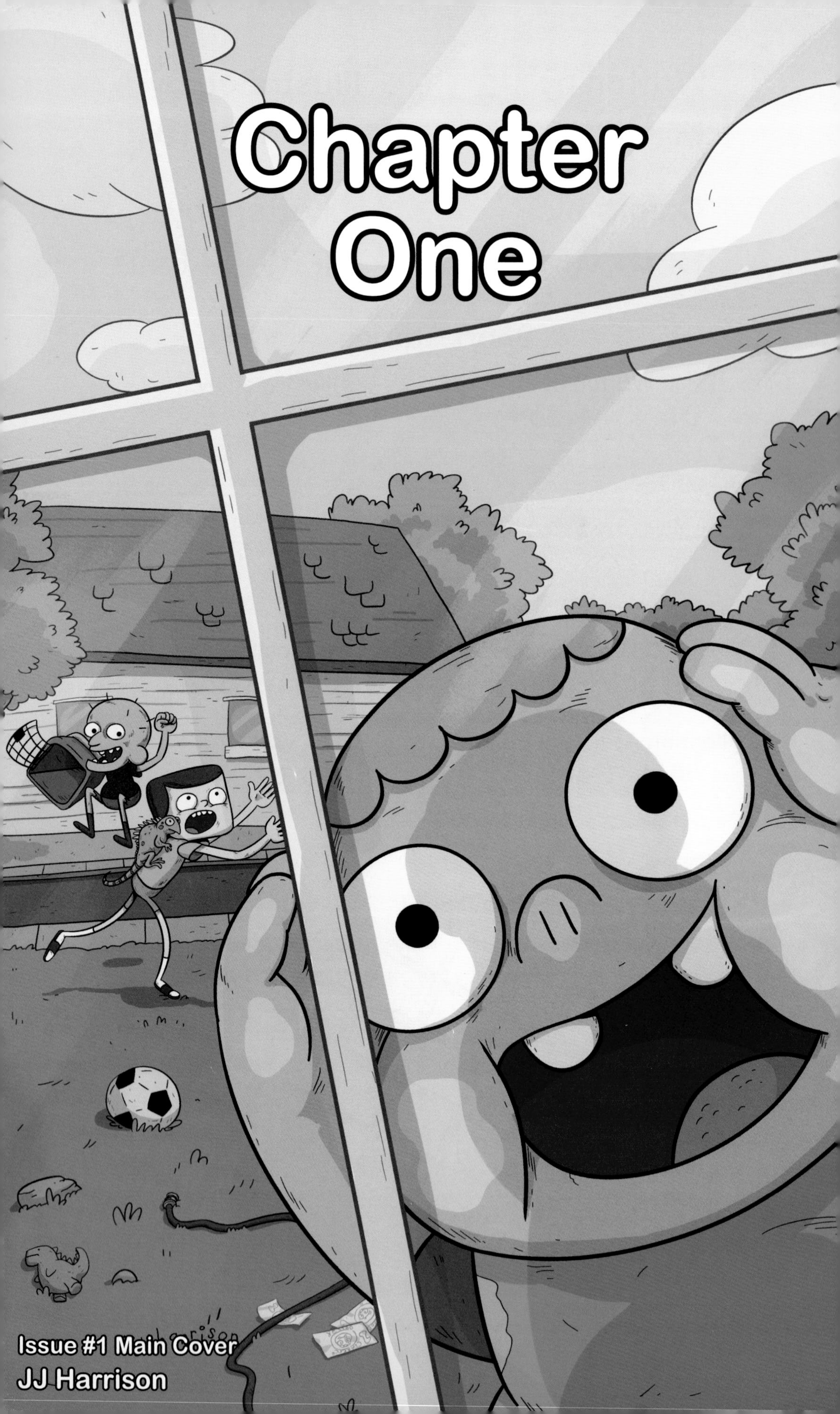

Issue #1 Main Cover
JJ Harrison

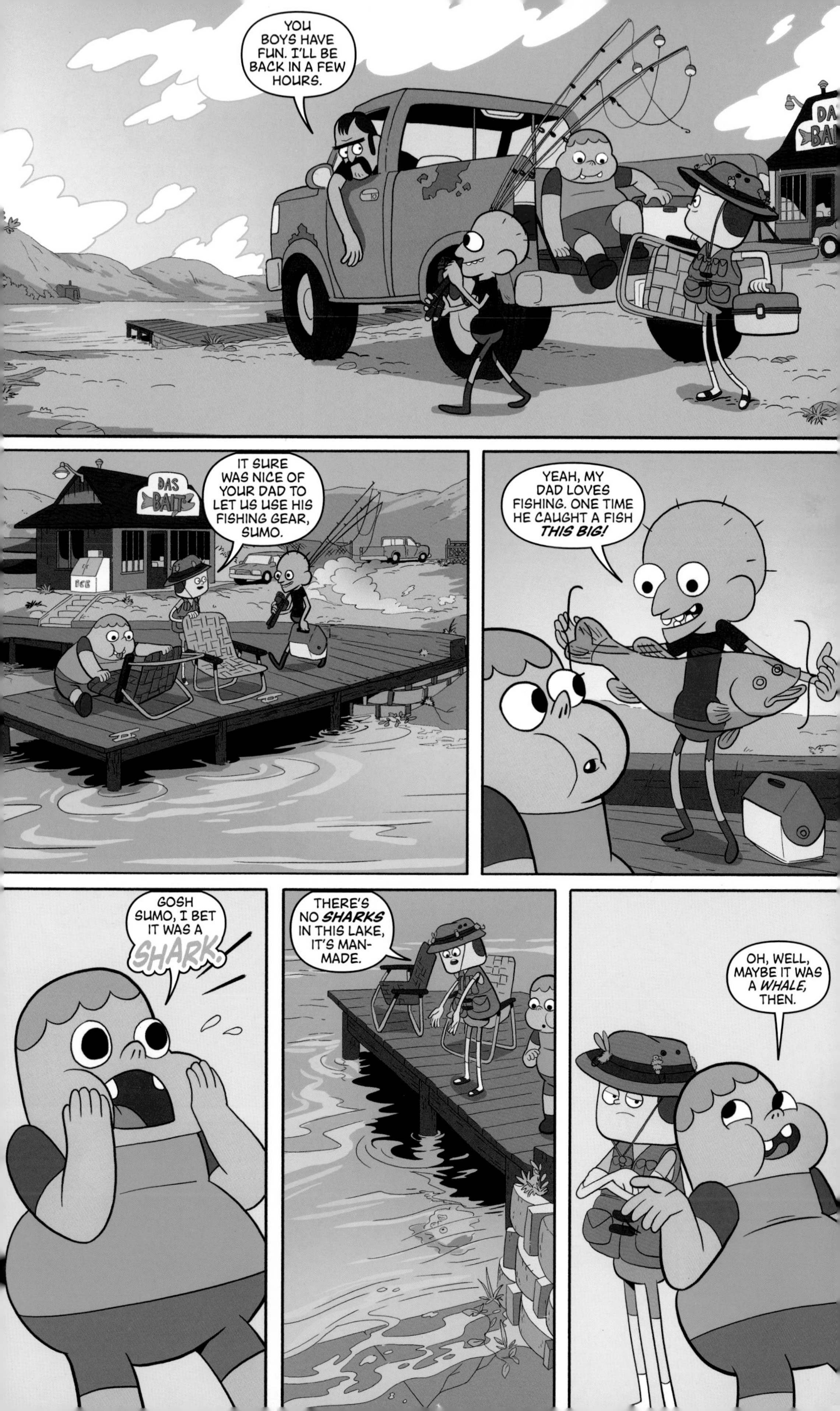
YOU BOYS HAVE FUN. I'LL BE BACK IN A FEW HOURS.
DAS BAIT
IT SURE WAS NICE OF YOUR DAD TO LET US USE HIS FISHING GEAR, SUMO.
YEAH, MY DAD LOVES FISHING. ONE TIME HE CAUGHT A FISH *THIS BIG!*
GOSH SUMO, I BET IT WAS A SHARK!
THERE'S NO *SHARKS* IN THIS LAKE, IT'S MAN-MADE.
OH, WELL, MAYBE IT WAS A *WHALE,* THEN.

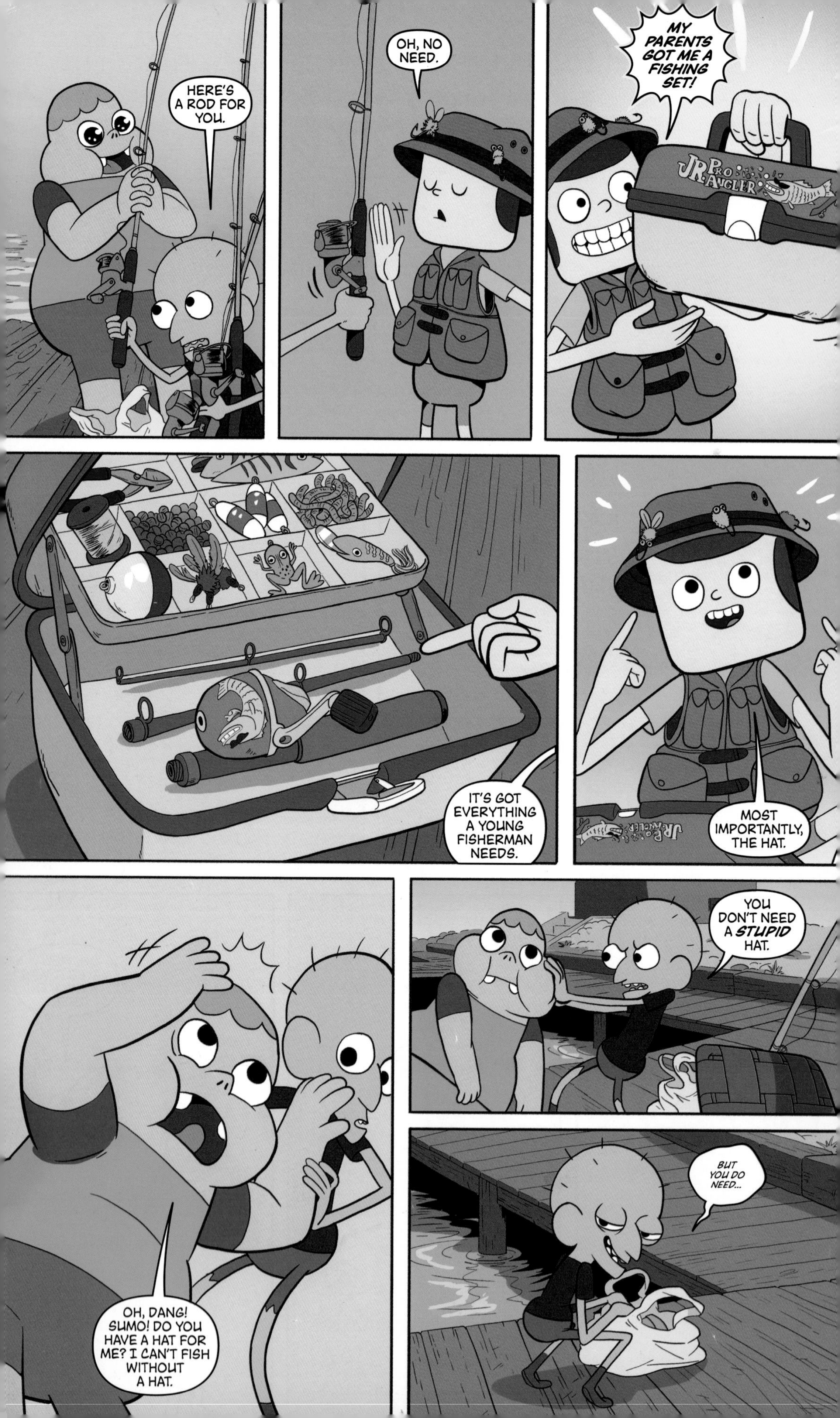
HERE'S A ROD FOR YOU.
OH, NO NEED.
MY PARENTS GOT ME A FISHING SET!
JR. PRO ANGLER
IT'S GOT EVERYTHING A YOUNG FISHERMAN NEEDS.
MOST IMPORTANTLY, THE HAT.
OH, DANG! SUMO! DO YOU HAVE A HAT FOR ME? I CAN'T FISH WITHOUT A HAT.
YOU DON'T NEED A *STUPID* HAT.
BUT YOU DO NEED...

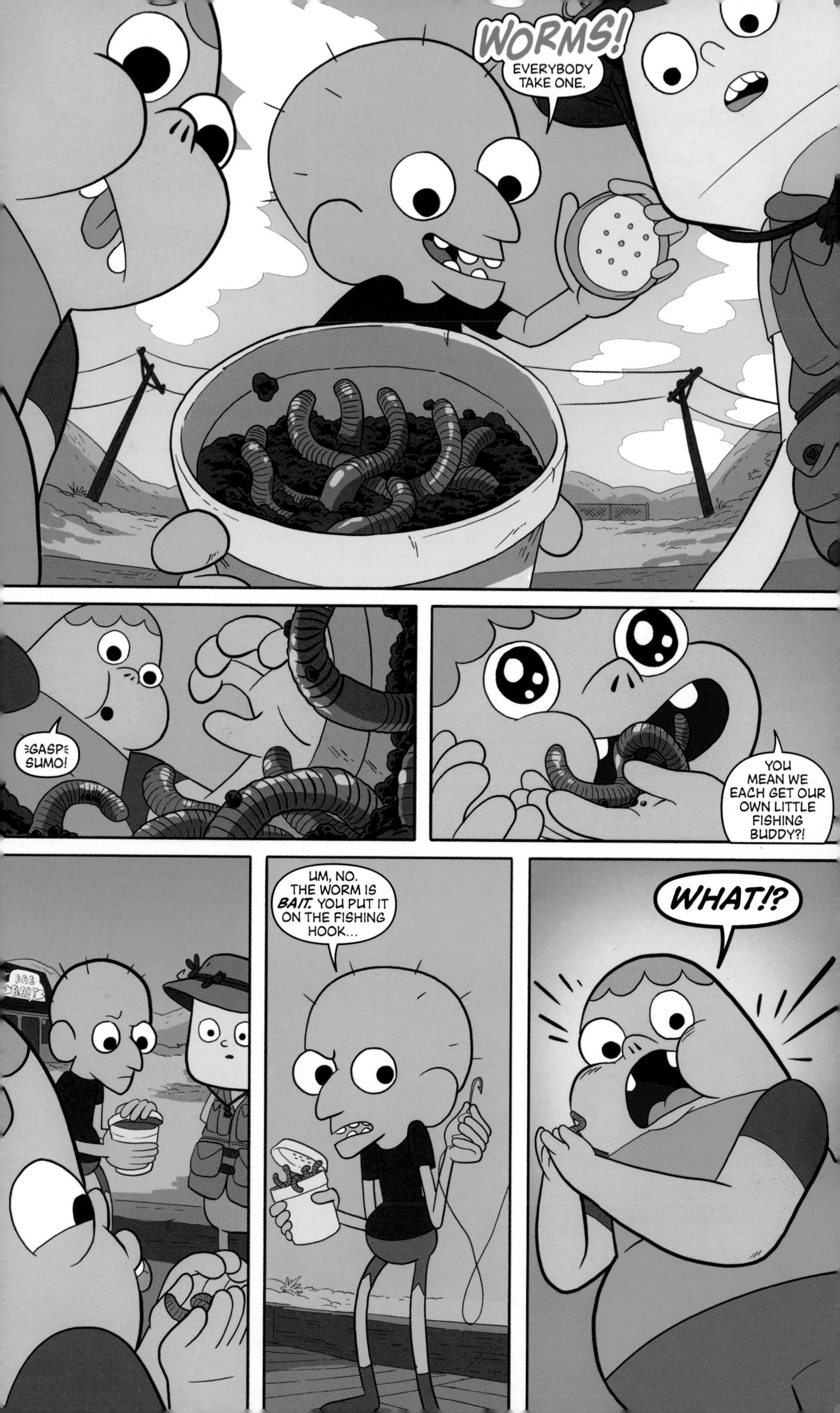
WORMS!
EVERYBODY TAKE ONE.
GASP SUMO!
YOU MEAN WE EACH GET OUR OWN LITTLE FISHING BUDDY?!
UM, NO. THE WORM IS *BAIT.* YOU PUT IT ON THE FISHING HOOK...
WHAT!?

YOU CAN'T JUST PUT A HOOK...

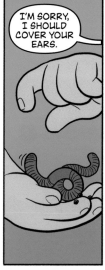

I'M SORRY, I SHOULD COVER YOUR EARS.

YOU CAN'T JUST PUT A HOOK THROUGH OUR LITTLE WORMY FRIENDS!

BUT THAT'S HOW YOU GO FISHING.

WELL, IN THAT CASE...

HEY!

I'LL SAVE YOU!

DAS BAIT

GO! RUN BE FREE!

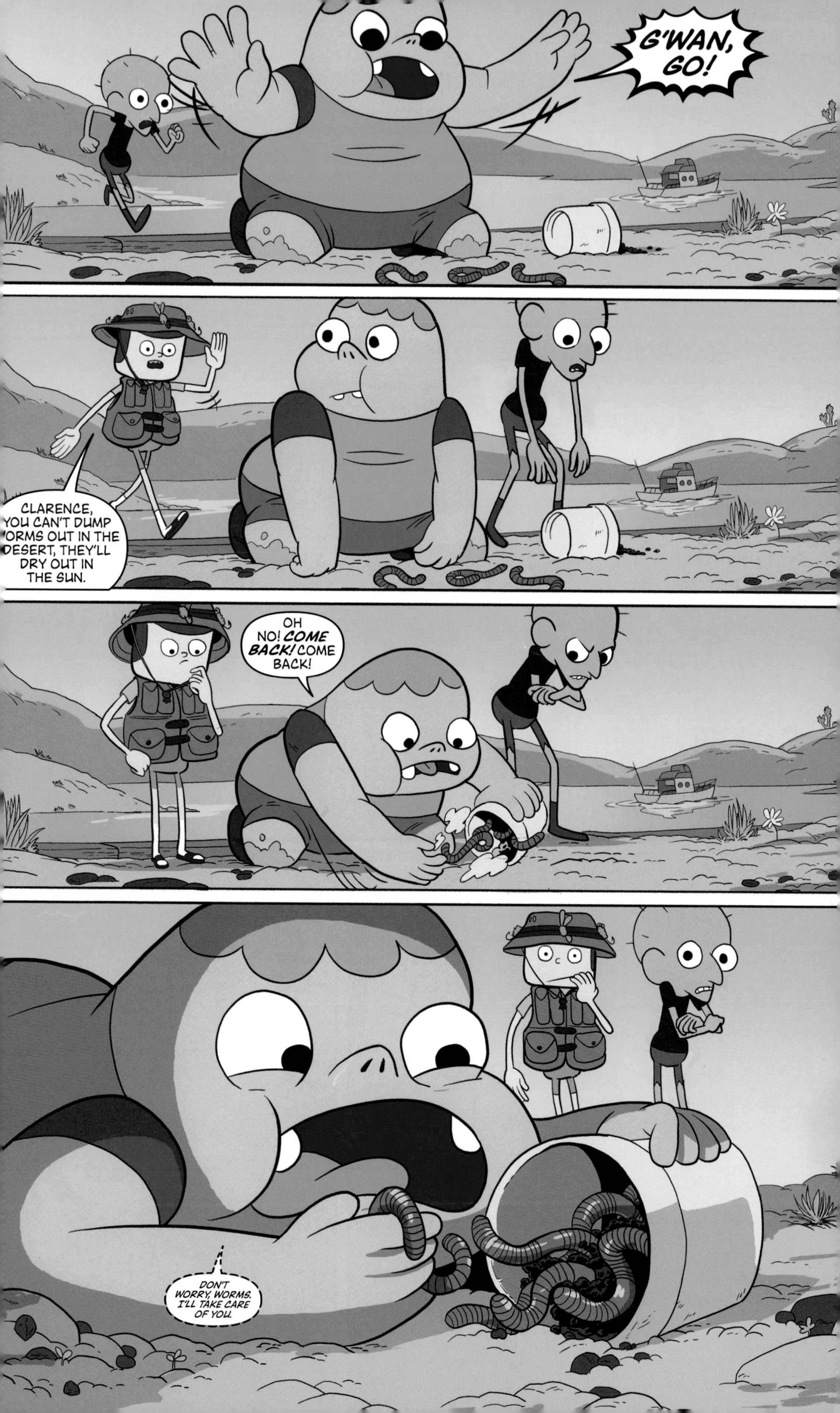
G'WAN, GO!
CLARENCE, YOU CAN'T DUMP ORMS OUT IN THE DESERT, THEY'LL DRY OUT IN THE SUN.
OH NO! COME BACK! COME BACK!
DON'T WORRY, WORMS. I'LL TAKE CARE OF YOU.

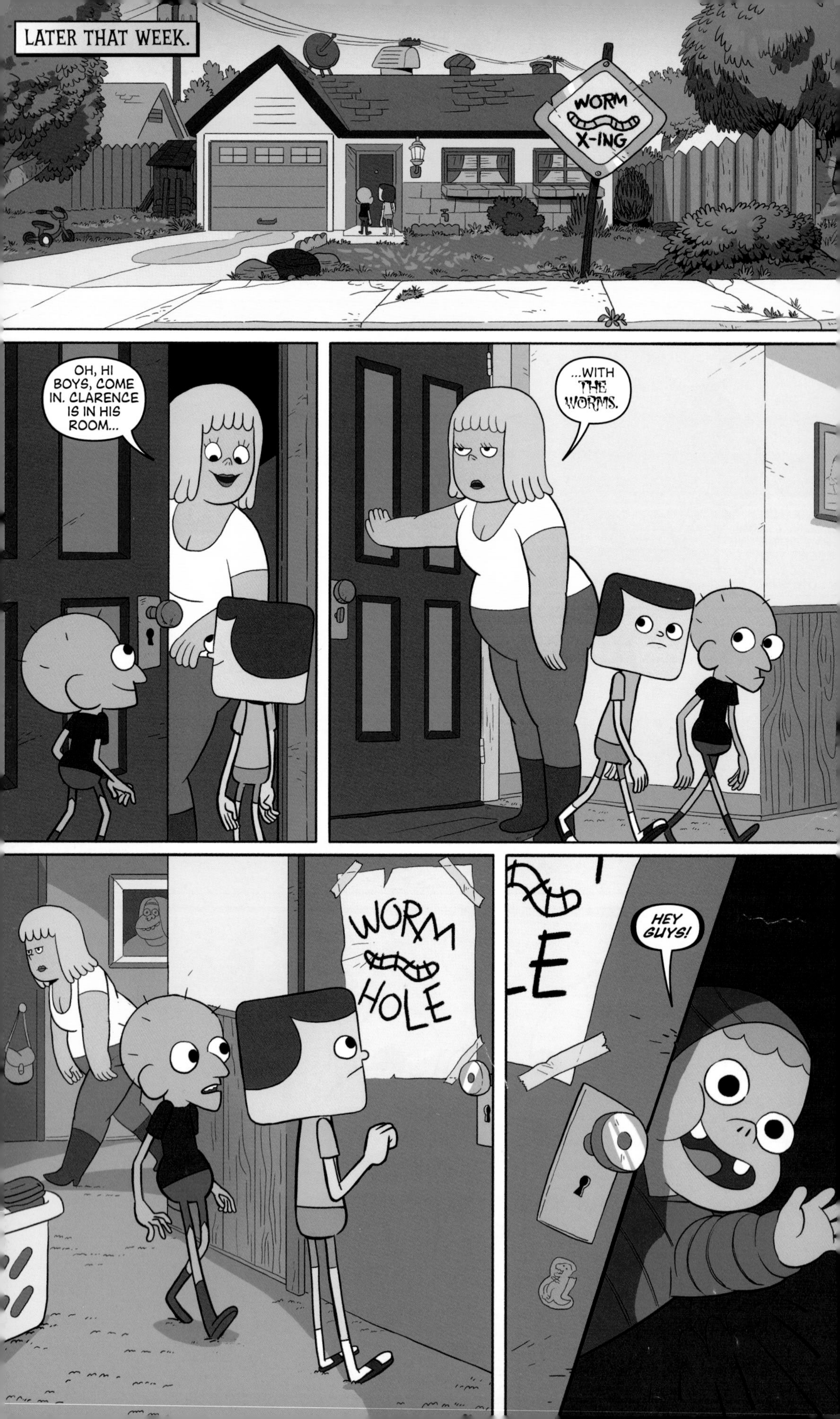
LATER THAT WEEK.
WORM X-ING
OH, HI BOYS, COME IN. CLARENCE IS IN HIS ROOM...
...WITH THE WORMS.
WORM HOLE
HEY GUYS!

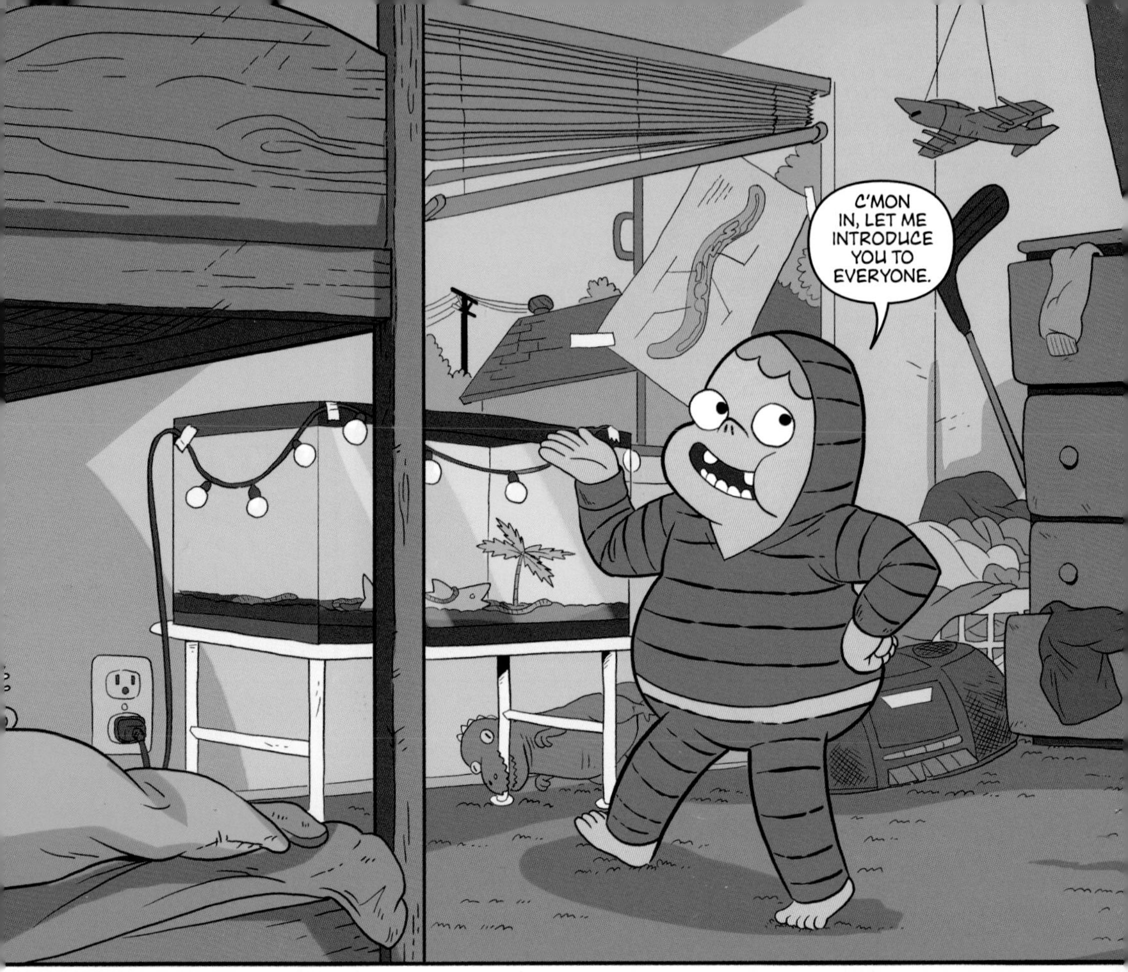
C'MON IN, LET ME INTRODUCE YOU TO EVERYONE.

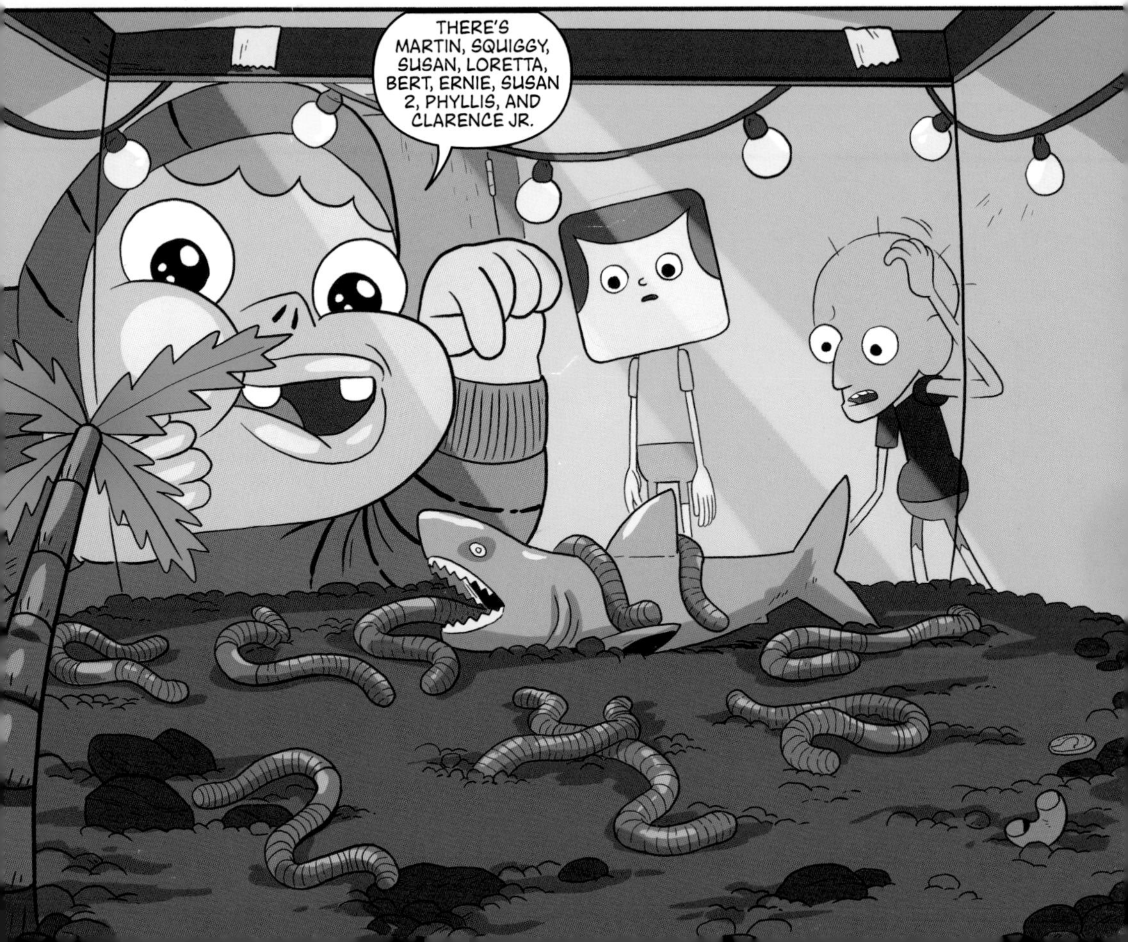
THERE'S MARTIN, SQUIGGY, SUSAN, LORETTA, BERT, ERNIE, SUSAN 2, PHYLLIS, AND CLARENCE JR.

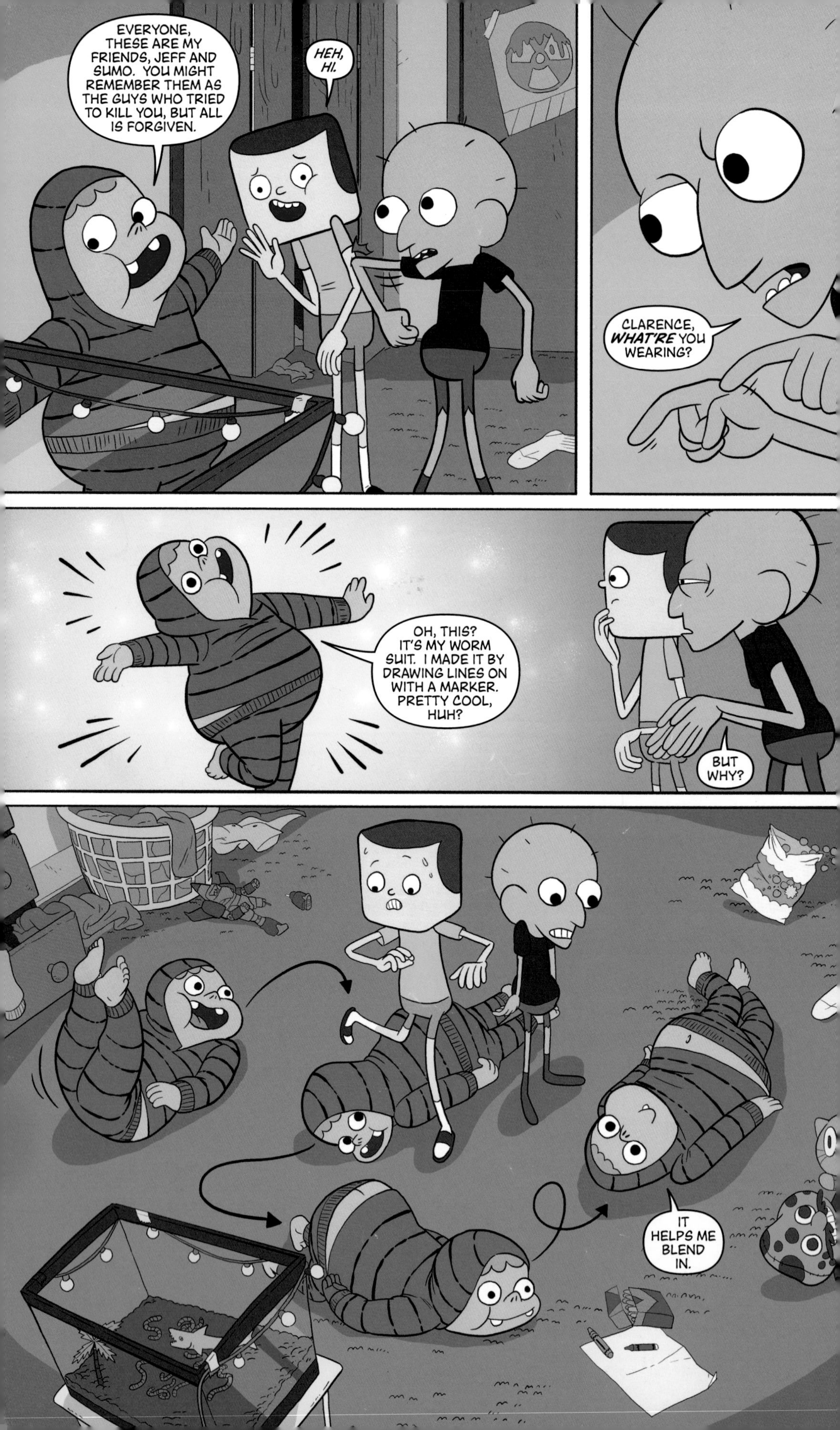
EVERYONE, THESE ARE MY FRIENDS, JEFF AND SUMO. YOU MIGHT REMEMBER THEM AS THE GUYS WHO TRIED TO KILL YOU, BUT ALL IS FORGIVEN.
HEH, HI.
CLARENCE, *WHAT'RE* YOU WEARING?
OH, THIS? IT'S MY WORM SUIT. I MADE IT BY DRAWING LINES ON WITH A MARKER. PRETTY COOL, HUH?
BUT WHY?
IT HELPS ME BLEND IN.

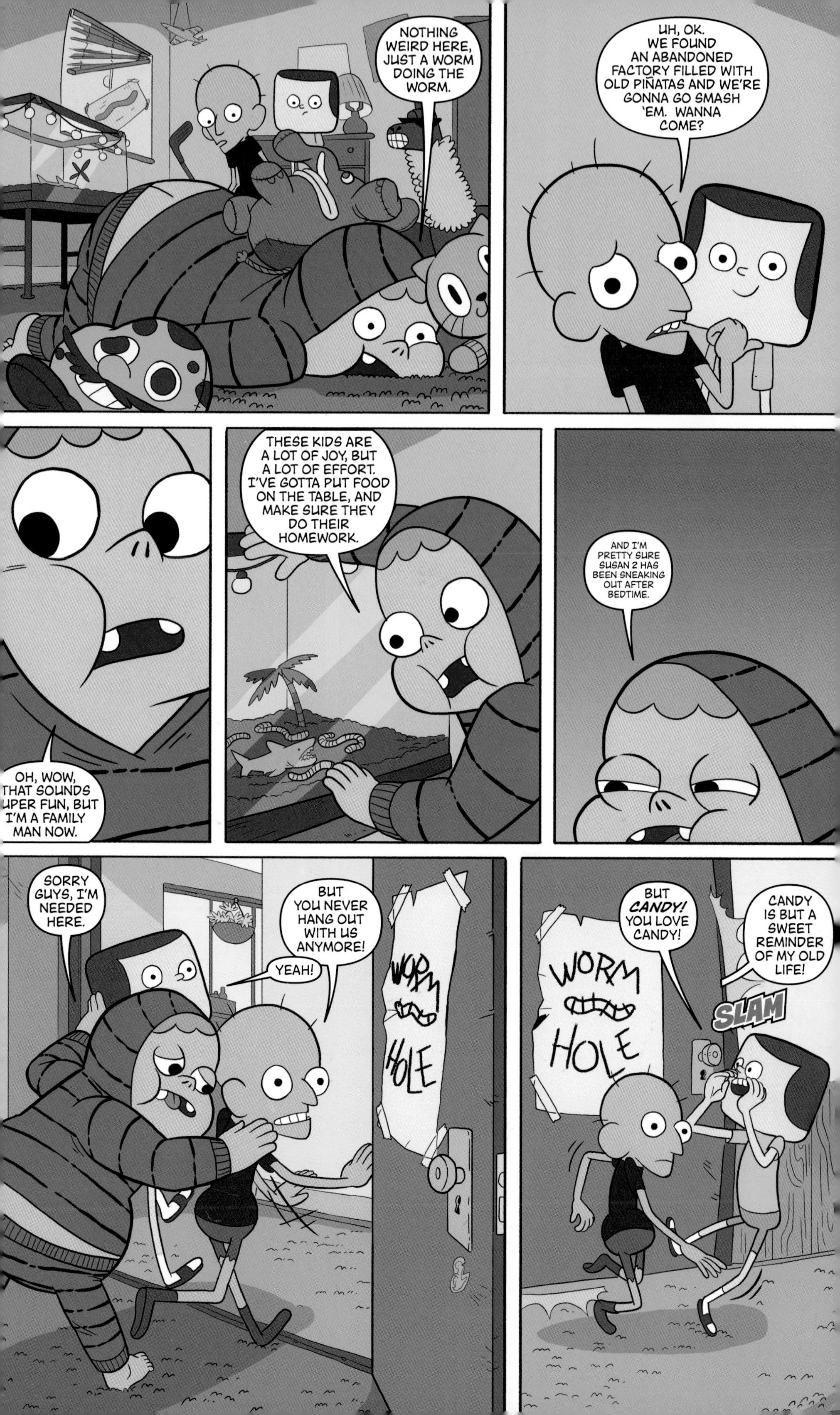
NOTHING WEIRD HERE, JUST A WORM DOING THE WORM.
UH, OK. WE FOUND AN ABANDONED FACTORY FILLED WITH OLD PIÑATAS AND WE'RE GONNA GO SMASH 'EM. WANNA COME?
OH, WOW, THAT SOUNDS UPER FUN, BUT I'M A FAMILY MAN NOW.
THESE KIDS ARE A LOT OF JOY, BUT A LOT OF EFFORT. I'VE GOTTA PUT FOOD ON THE TABLE, AND MAKE SURE THEY DO THEIR HOMEWORK.
AND I'M PRETTY SURE SUSAN 2 HAS BEEN SNEAKING OUT AFTER BEDTIME.
SORRY GUYS, I'M NEEDED HERE.
BUT YOU NEVER HANG OUT WITH US ANYMORE!
YEAH!
WORM HOLE
BUT CANDY! YOU LOVE CANDY!
CANDY IS BUT A SWEET REMINDER OF MY OLD LIFE!
WORM HOLE
SLAM

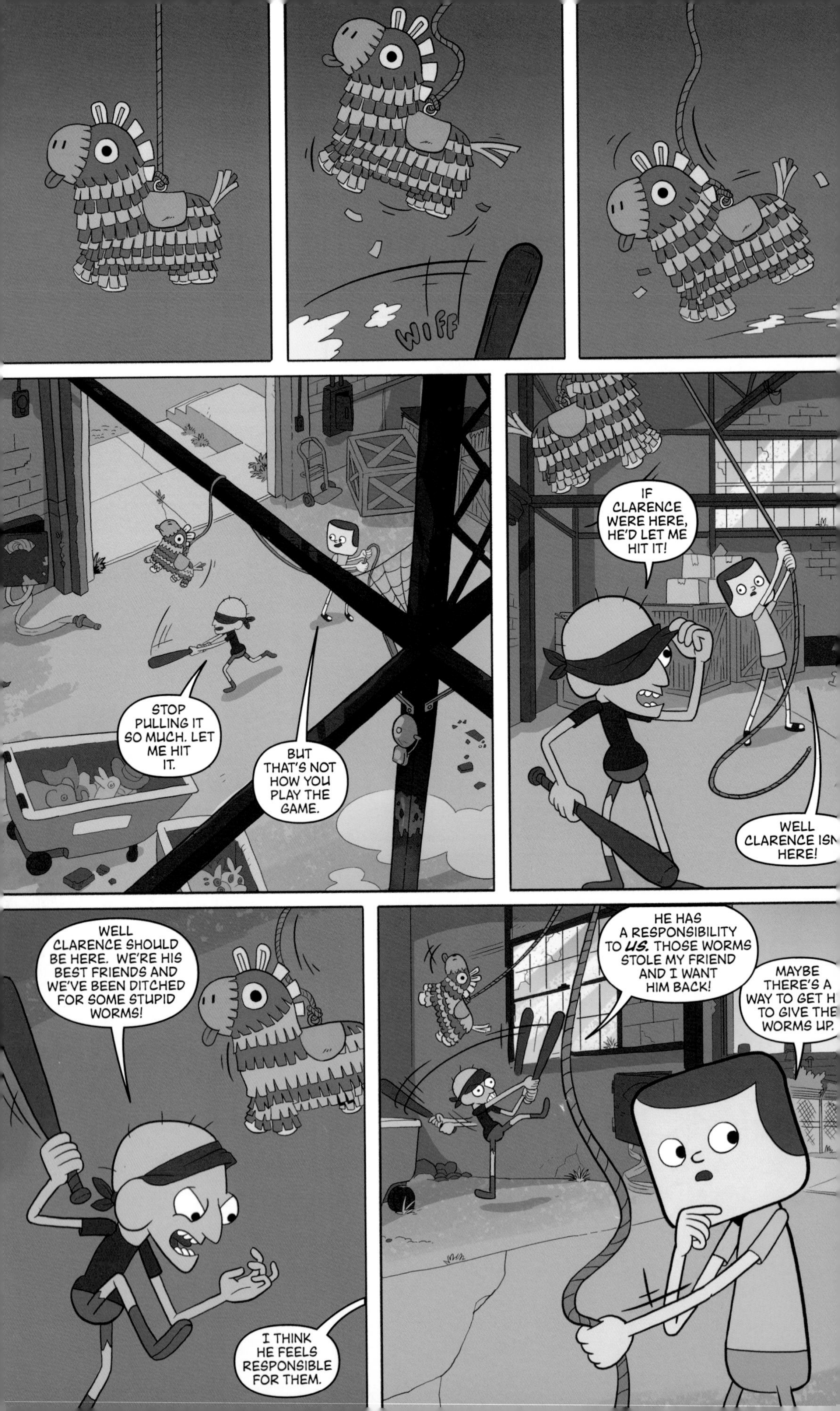
WIFF
STOP PULLING IT SO MUCH. LET ME HIT IT.
BUT THAT'S NOT HOW YOU PLAY THE GAME.
IF CLARENCE WERE HERE, HE'D LET ME HIT IT!
WELL CLARENCE ISN
HERE!
WELL CLARENCE SHOULD BE HERE. WE'RE HIS BEST FRIENDS AND WE'VE BEEN DITCHED FOR SOME STUPID WORMS!
I THINK HE FEELS RESPONSIBLE FOR THEM.
HE HAS A RESPONSIBILITY TO *US.* THOSE WORMS STOLE MY FRIEND AND I WANT HIM BACK!
MAYBE THERE'S A WAY TO GET H
TO GIVE THE
WORMS UP.

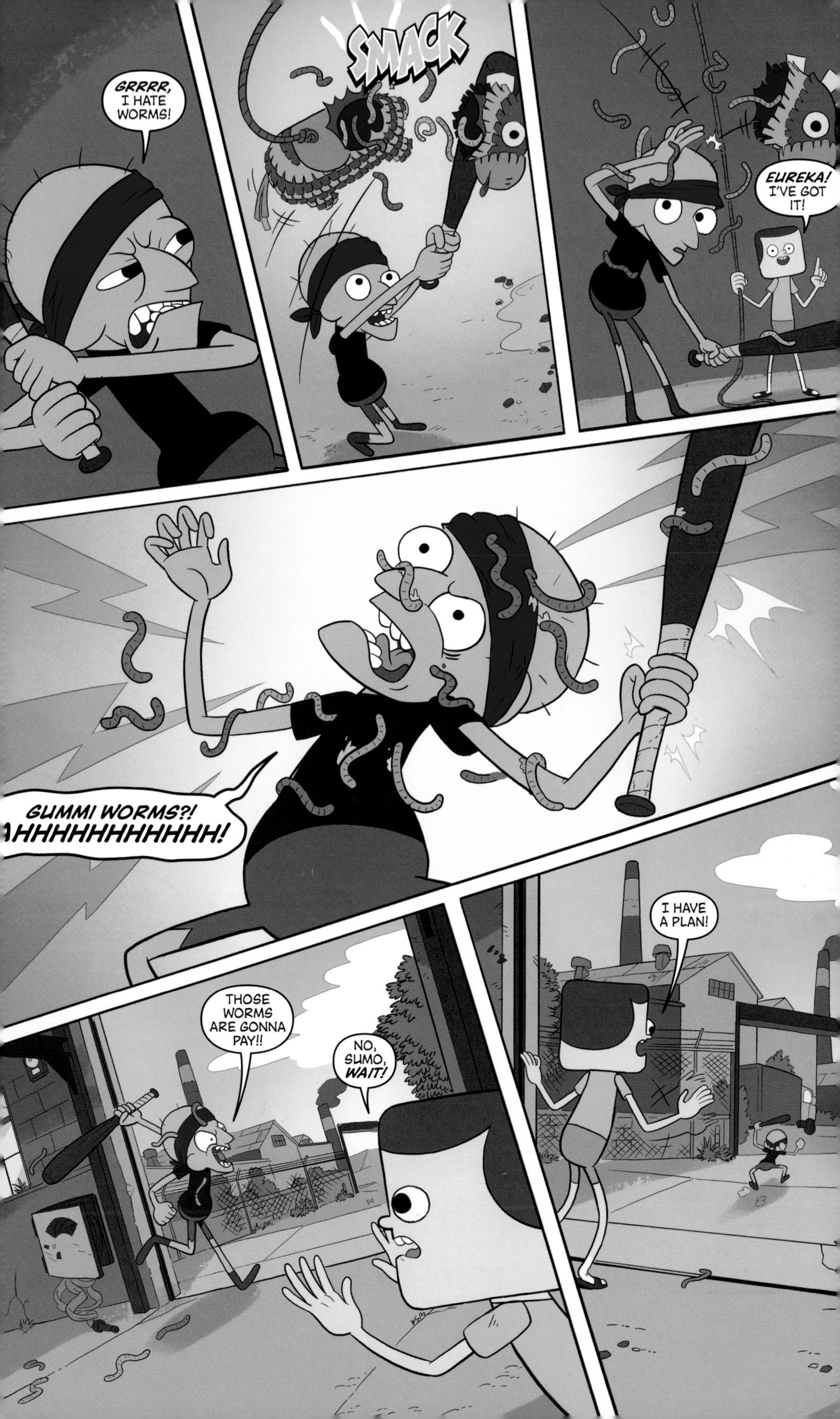
GRRRR, I HATE WORMS!
SMACK
EUREKA! I'VE GOT IT!
GUMMI WORMS?! AHHHHHHHHHH!
THOSE WORMS ARE GONNA PAY!!
NO, SUMO, WAIT!
I HAVE A PLAN!

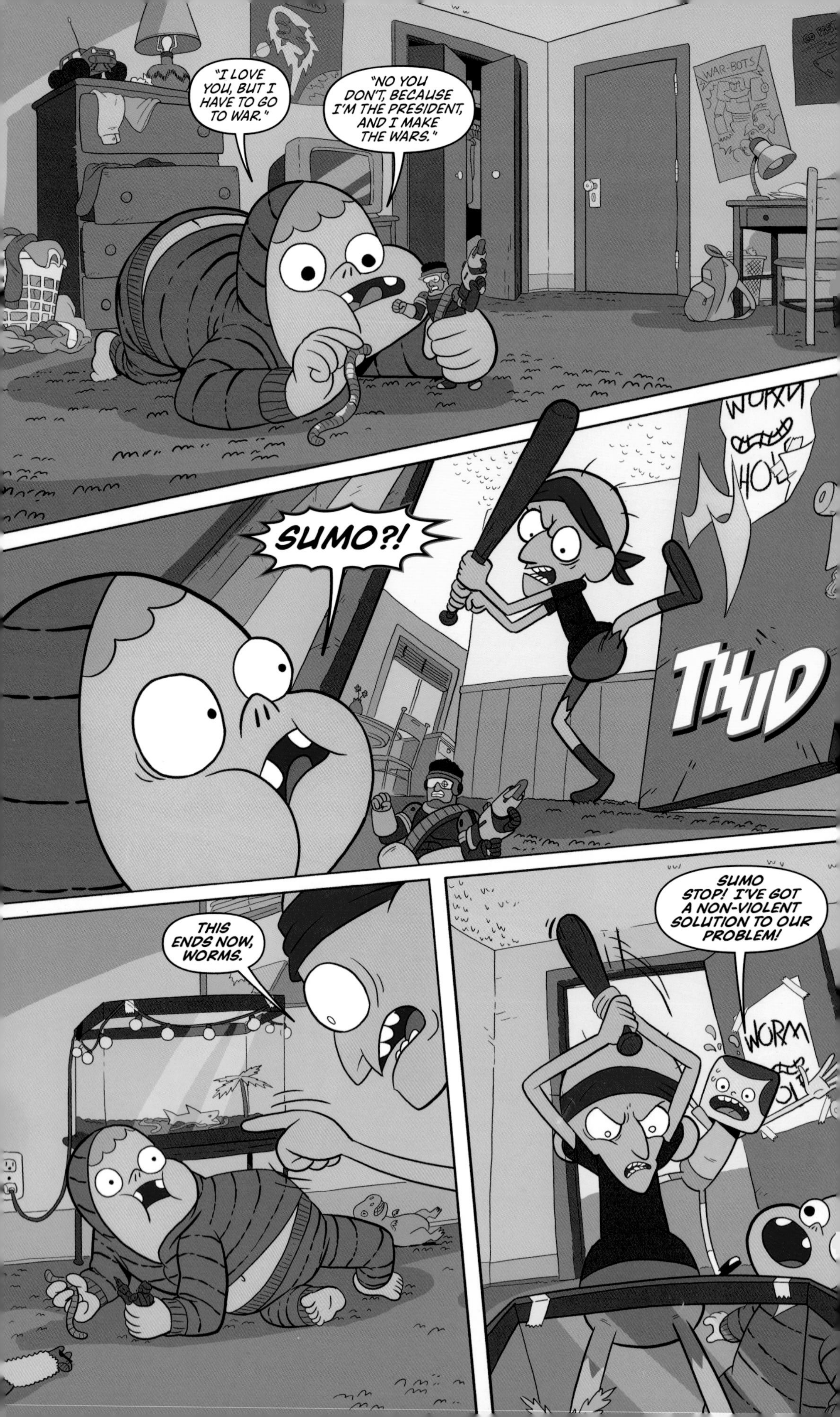
"I LOVE YOU, BUT I HAVE TO GO TO WAR."
"NO YOU DON'T, BECAUSE I'M THE PRESIDENT, AND I MAKE THE WARS."
WAR-BOTS
SUMO?!
THUD
THIS ENDS NOW, WORMS.
SUMO STOP! I'VE GOT A NON-VIOLENT SOLUTION TO OUR PROBLEM!

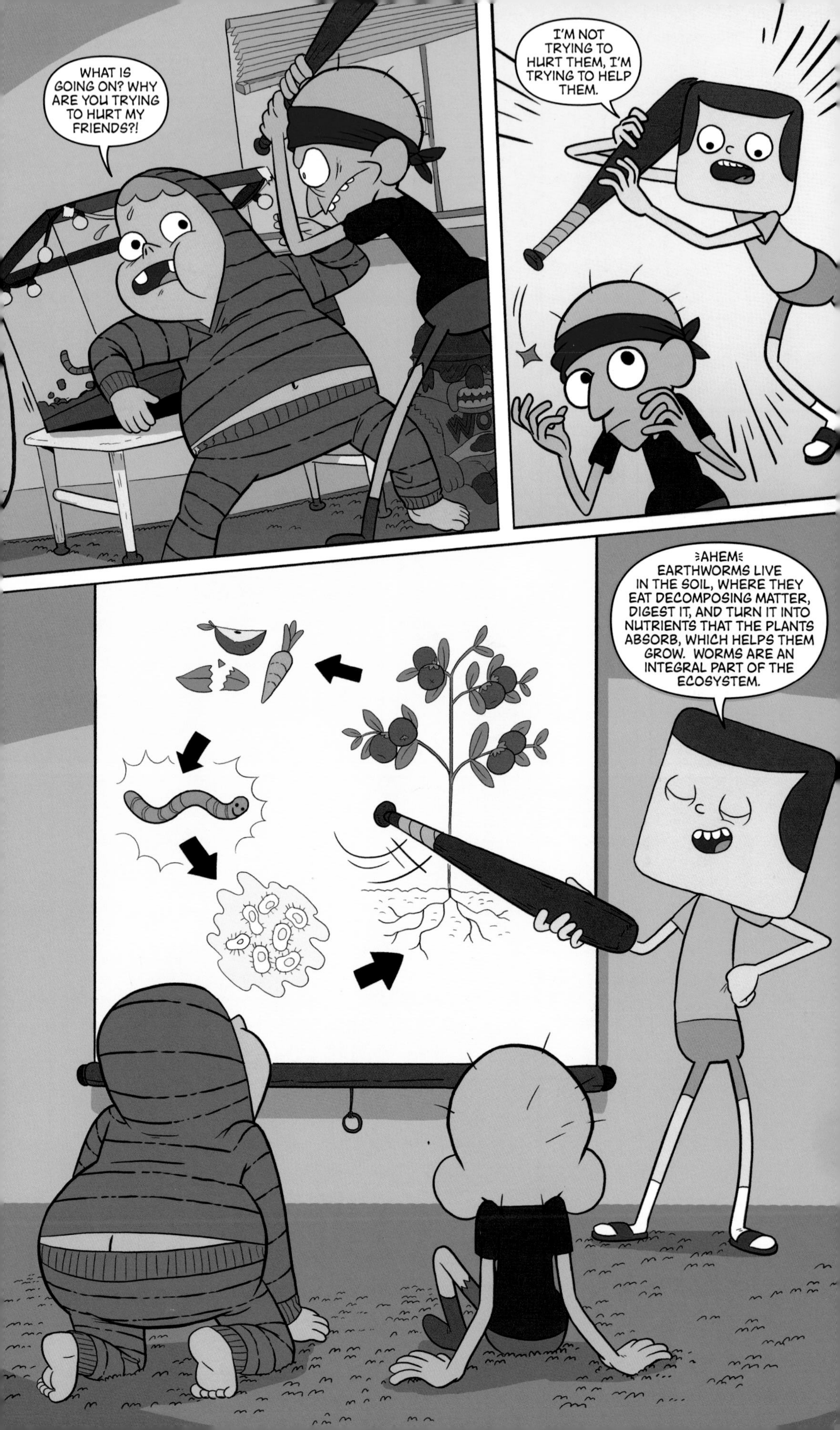
WHAT IS GOING ON? WHY ARE YOU TRYING TO HURT MY FRIENDS?!
I'M NOT TRYING TO HURT THEM, I'M TRYING TO HELP THEM.
AHEM
EARTHWORMS LIVE IN THE SOIL, WHERE THEY EAT DECOMPOSING MATTER, DIGEST IT, AND TURN IT INTO NUTRIENTS THAT THE PLANTS ABSORB, WHICH HELPS THEM GROW. WORMS ARE AN INTEGRAL PART OF THE ECOSYSTEM.

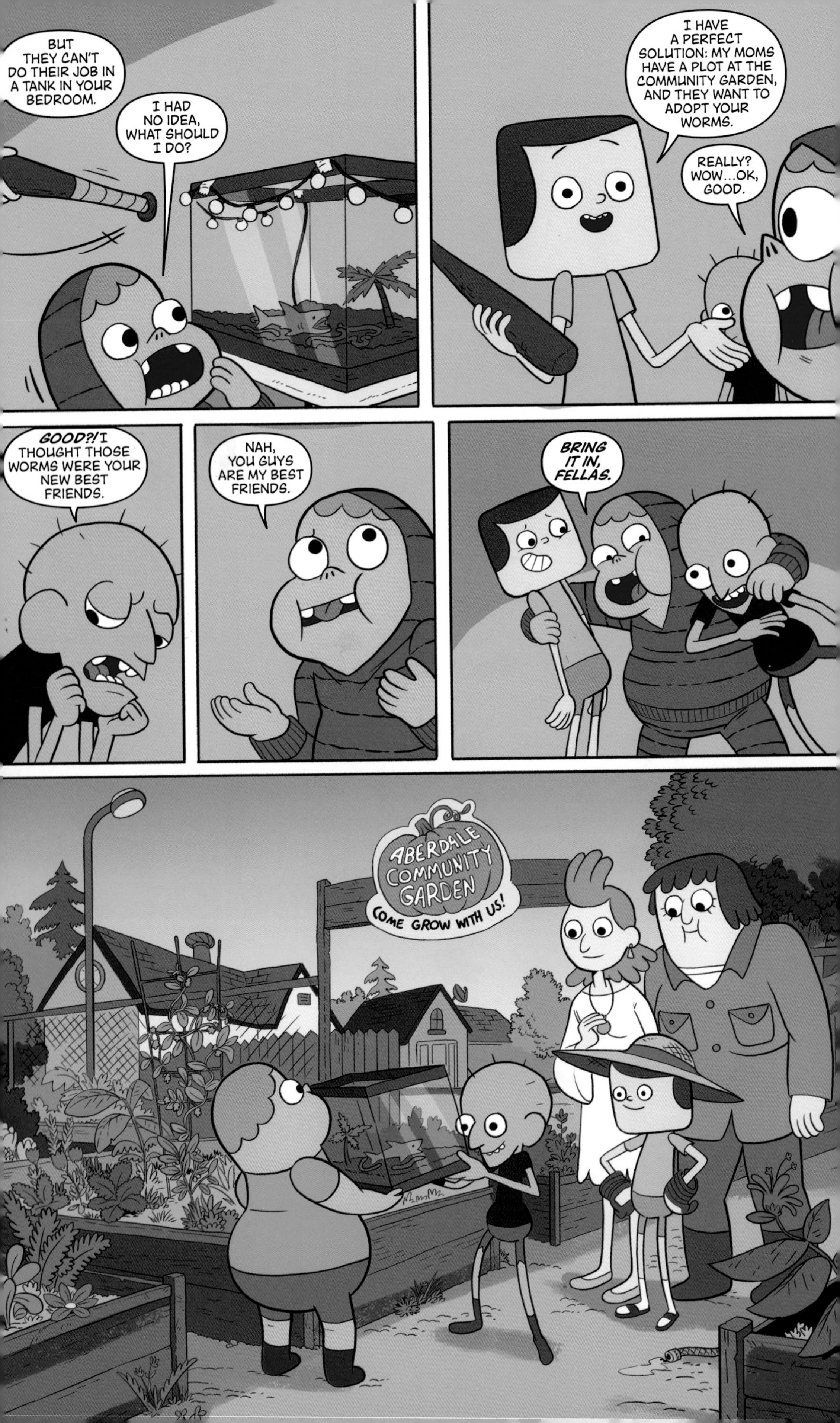
BUT THEY CAN'T DO THEIR JOB IN A TANK IN YOUR BEDROOM.
I HAD NO IDEA, WHAT SHOULD I DO?
I HAVE A PERFECT SOLUTION: MY MOMS HAVE A PLOT AT THE COMMUNITY GARDEN, AND THEY WANT TO ADOPT YOUR WORMS.
REALLY? WOW...OK, GOOD.
GOOD?! I THOUGHT THOSE WORMS WERE YOUR NEW BEST FRIENDS.
NAH, YOU GUYS ARE MY BEST FRIENDS.
BRING IT IN, FELLAS.
ABERDALE COMMUNITY GARDEN
COME GROW WITH US!

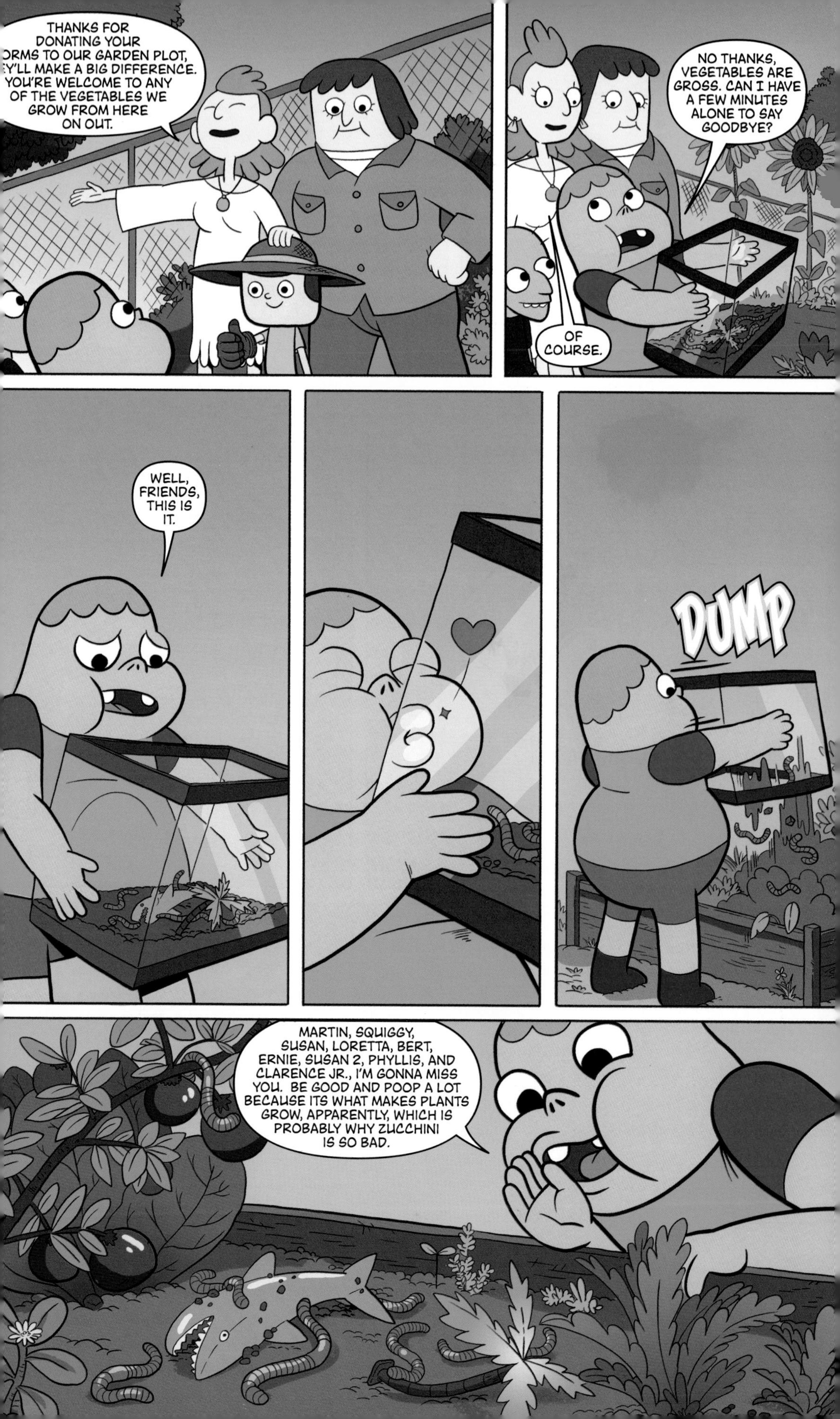
THANKS FOR DONATING YOUR ORMS TO OUR GARDEN PLOT, EY'LL MAKE A BIG DIFFERENCE. YOU'RE WELCOME TO ANY OF THE VEGETABLES WE GROW FROM HERE ON OUT.
NO THANKS, VEGETABLES ARE GROSS. CAN I HAVE A FEW MINUTES ALONE TO SAY GOODBYE?
OF COURSE.
WELL, FRIENDS, THIS IS IT.
DUMP
MARTIN, SQUIGGY, SUSAN, LORETTA, BERT, ERNIE, SUSAN 2, PHYLLIS, AND CLARENCE JR., I'M GONNA MISS YOU. BE GOOD AND POOP A LOT BECAUSE ITS WHAT MAKES PLANTS GROW, APPARENTLY, WHICH IS PROBABLY WHY ZUCCHINI IS SO BAD.

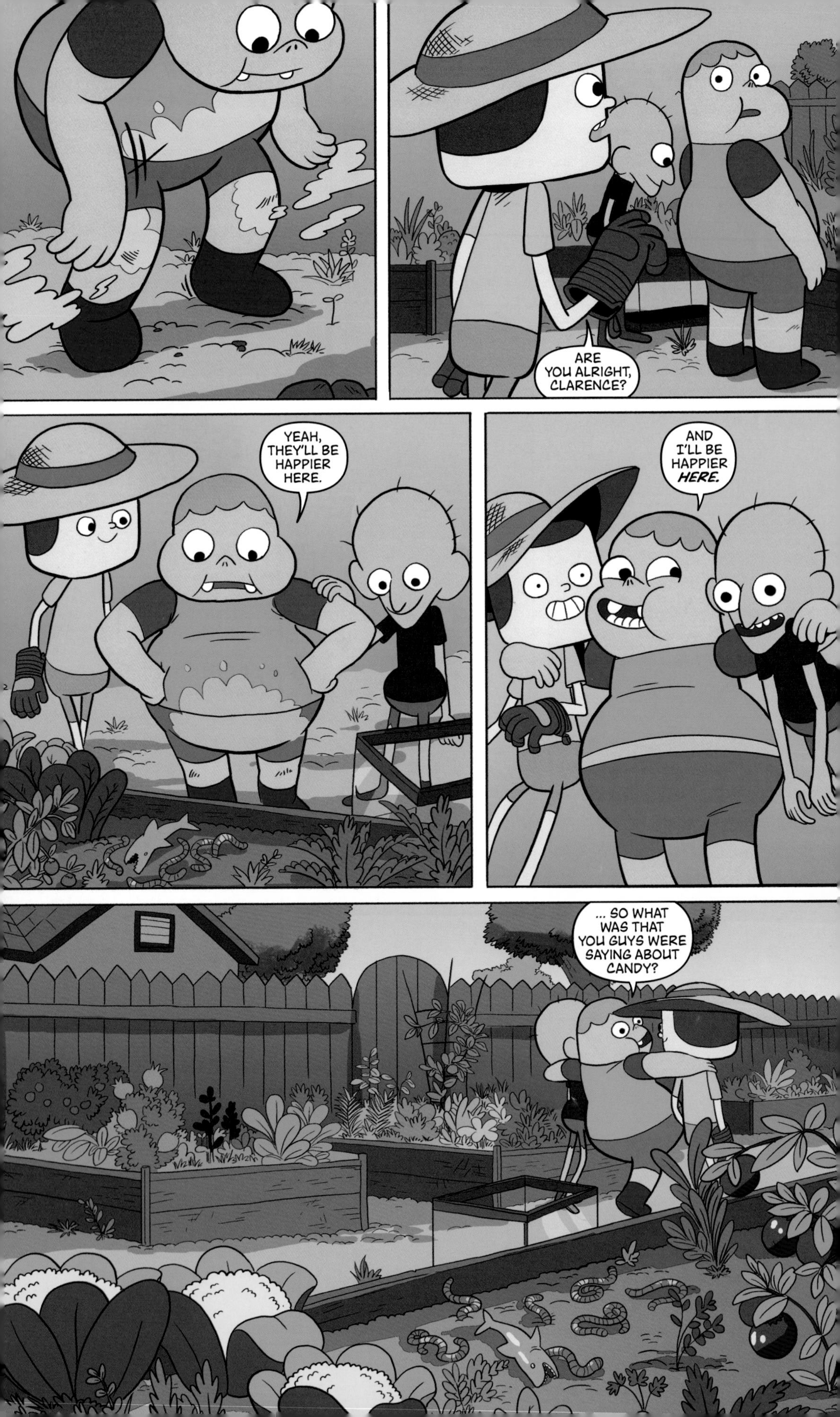
ARE YOU ALRIGHT, CLARENCE?
YEAH, THEY'LL BE HAPPIER HERE.
AND I'LL BE HAPPIER *HERE.*
... SO WHAT WAS THAT YOU GUYS WERE SAYING ABOUT CANDY?

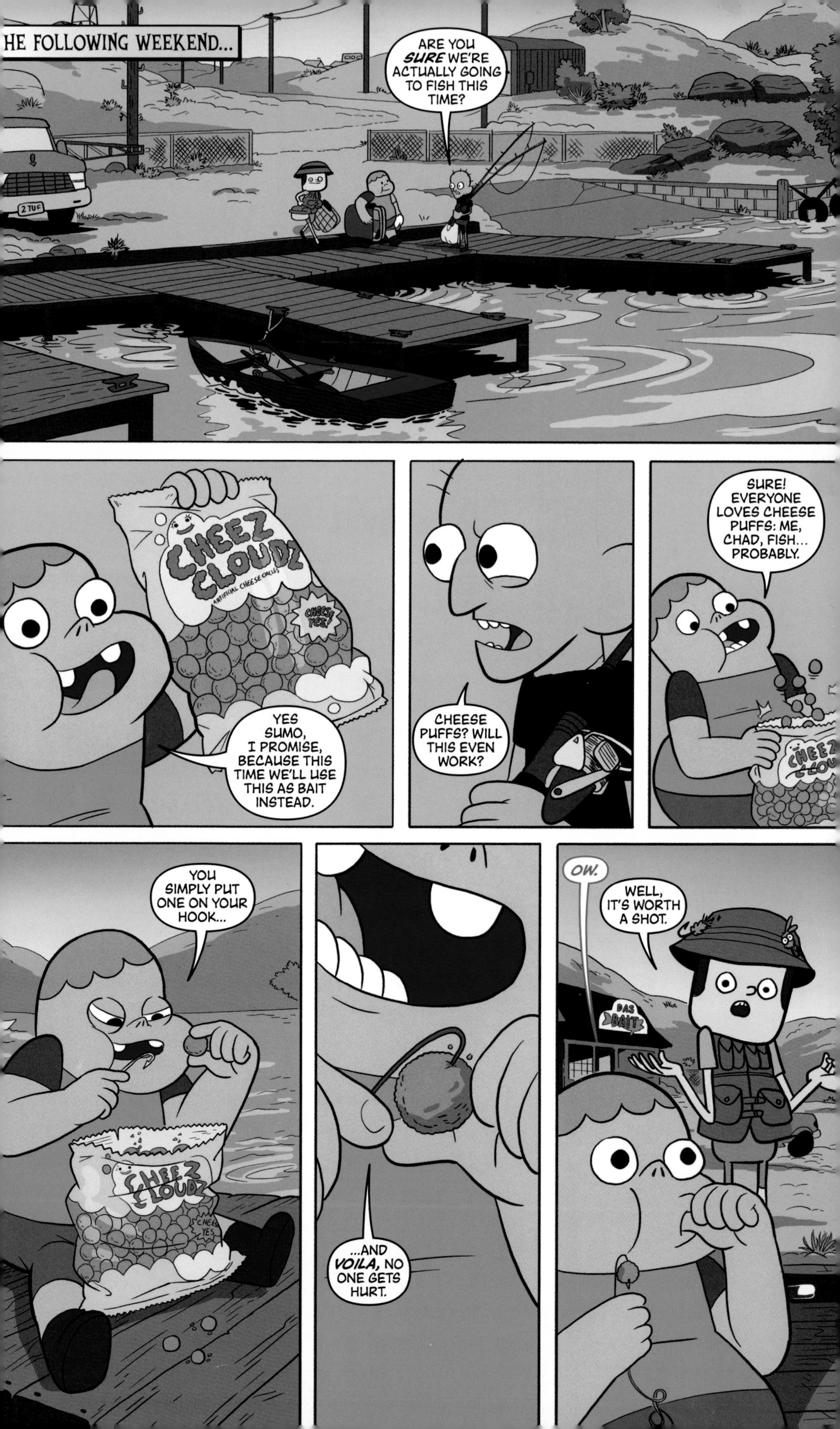
HE FOLLOWING WEEKEND...
ARE YOU SURE WE'RE ACTUALLY GOING TO FISH THIS TIME?
2 TUF
CHEEZ CLOUDZ
ARTIFICIAL CHEESE CIRCLES
CHEESE YES!
YES SUMO, I PROMISE, BECAUSE THIS TIME WE'LL USE THIS AS BAIT INSTEAD.
CHEESE PUFFS? WILL THIS EVEN WORK?
SURE! EVERYONE LOVES CHEESE PUFFS: ME, CHAD, FISH... PROBABLY.
YOU SIMPLY PUT ONE ON YOUR HOOK...
...AND VOILA, NO ONE GETS HURT.
OW.
WELL, IT'S WORTH A SHOT.
DAS BAIT

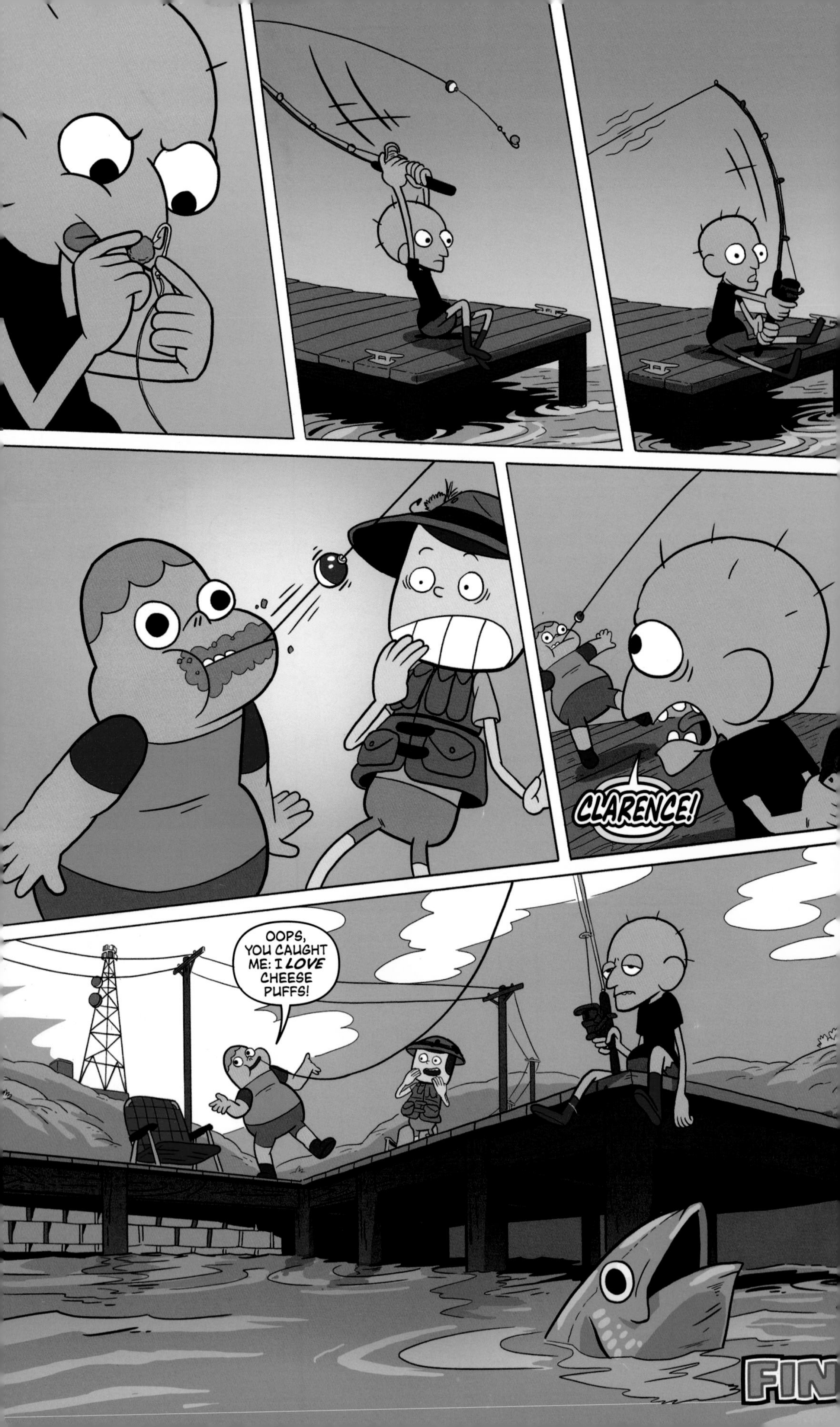
CLARENCE!
OOPS, YOU CAUGHT ME: I *LOVE* CHEESE PUFFS!
FIN

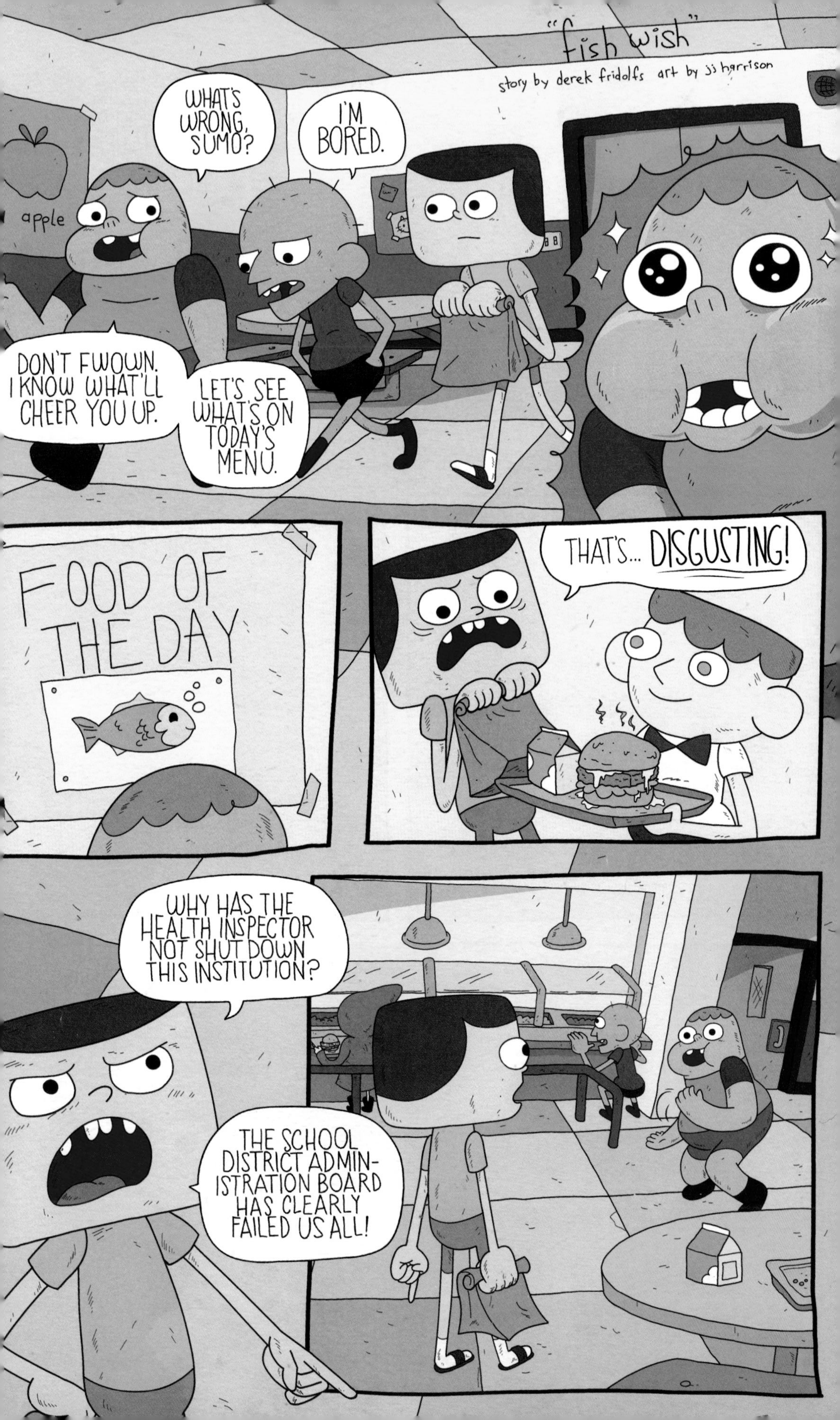
"fish wish"
story by derek fridolfs art by jj harrison
apple
WHAT'S WRONG, SUMO?
I'M BORED.
DON'T FWOWN. I KNOW WHAT'LL CHEER YOU UP.
LET'S SEE WHAT'S ON TODAY'S MENU.
FOOD OF THE DAY
THAT'S... DISGUSTING!
WHY HAS THE HEALTH INSPECTOR NOT SHUT DOWN THIS INSTITUTION?
THE SCHOOL DISTRICT ADMIN-ISTRATION BOARD HAS CLEARLY FAILED US ALL!

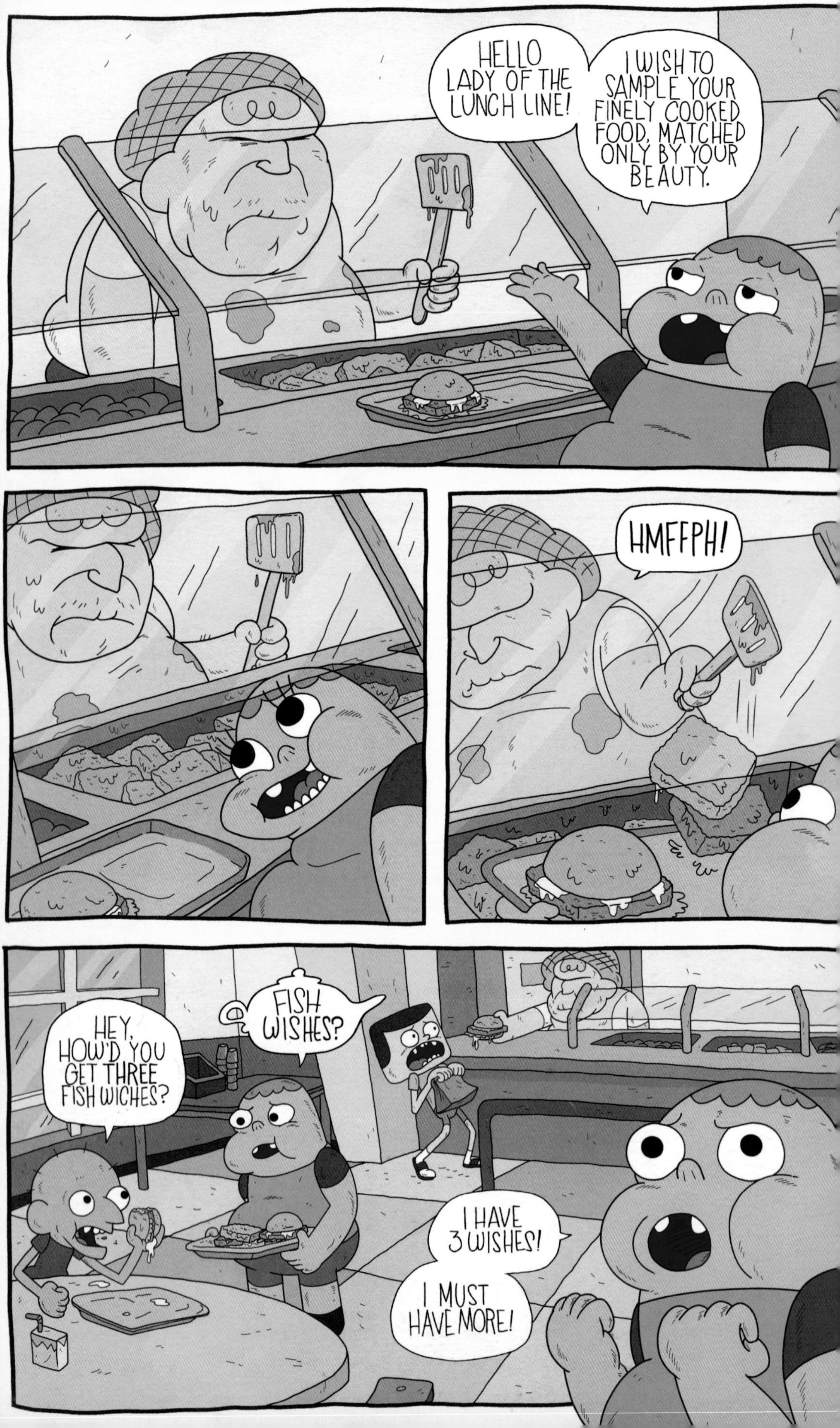
HELLO LADY OF THE LUNCH LINE!
I WISH TO SAMPLE YOUR FINELY COOKED FOOD, MATCHED ONLY BY YOUR BEAUTY.
HMFFPH!
HEY, HOW'D YOU GET THREE FISH WICHES?
FISH WISHES?
I HAVE 3 WISHES!
I MUST HAVE MORE!

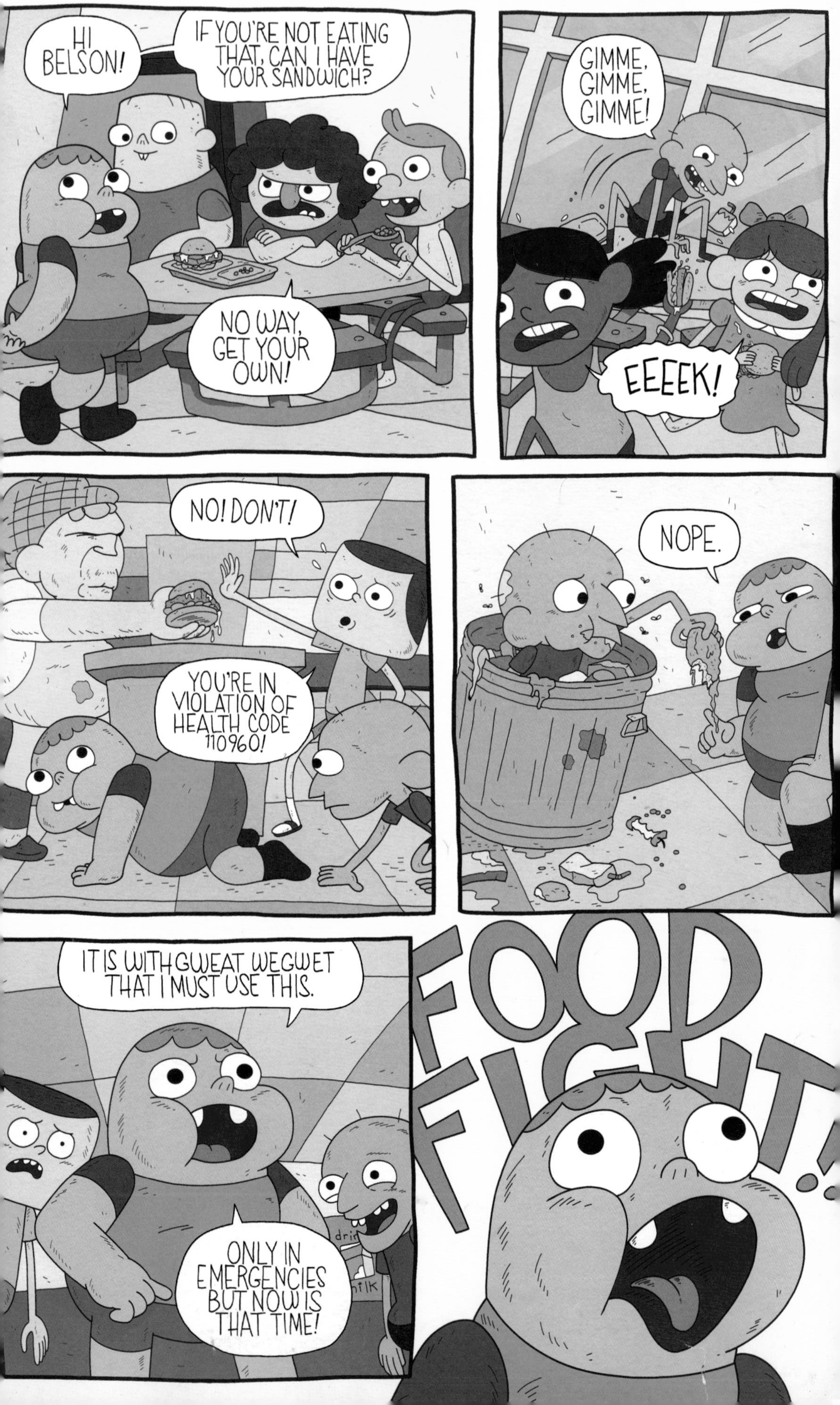
HI BELSON!
IF YOU'RE NOT EATING THAT, CAN I HAVE YOUR SANDWICH?
NO WAY, GET YOUR OWN!
GIMME, GIMME, GIMME!
EEEEK!
NO! DON'T!
YOU'RE IN VIOLATION OF HEALTH CODE 110960!
NOPE.
IT IS WITH GWEAT WEGWET THAT I MUST USE THIS.
ONLY IN EMERGENCIES BUT NOW IS THAT TIME!
FOOD FIGHT!!

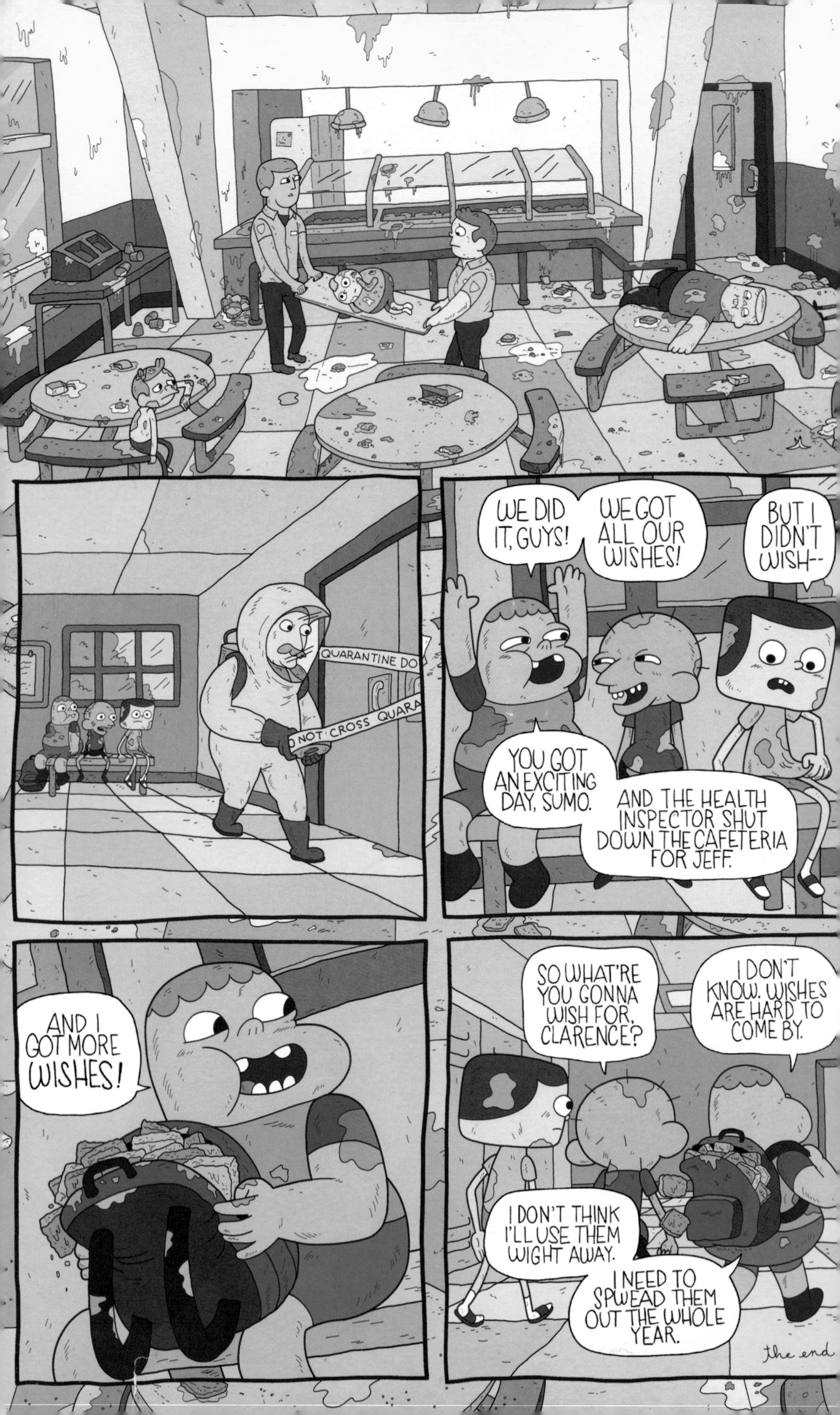
QUARANTINE DO
NOT CROSS QUARA
WE DID IT, GUYS!
WE GOT ALL OUR WISHES!
BUT I DIDN'T WISH--
YOU GOT AN EXCITING DAY, SUMO.
AND THE HEALTH INSPECTOR SHUT DOWN THE CAFETERIA FOR JEFF.
AND I GOT MORE WISHES!
SO WHAT'RE YOU GONNA WISH FOR, CLARENCE?
I DON'T KNOW. WISHES ARE HARD TO COME BY.
I DON'T THINK I'LL USE THEM WIGHT AWAY.
I NEED TO SPWEAD THEM OUT THE WHOLE YEAR.
the end

Chapter Two

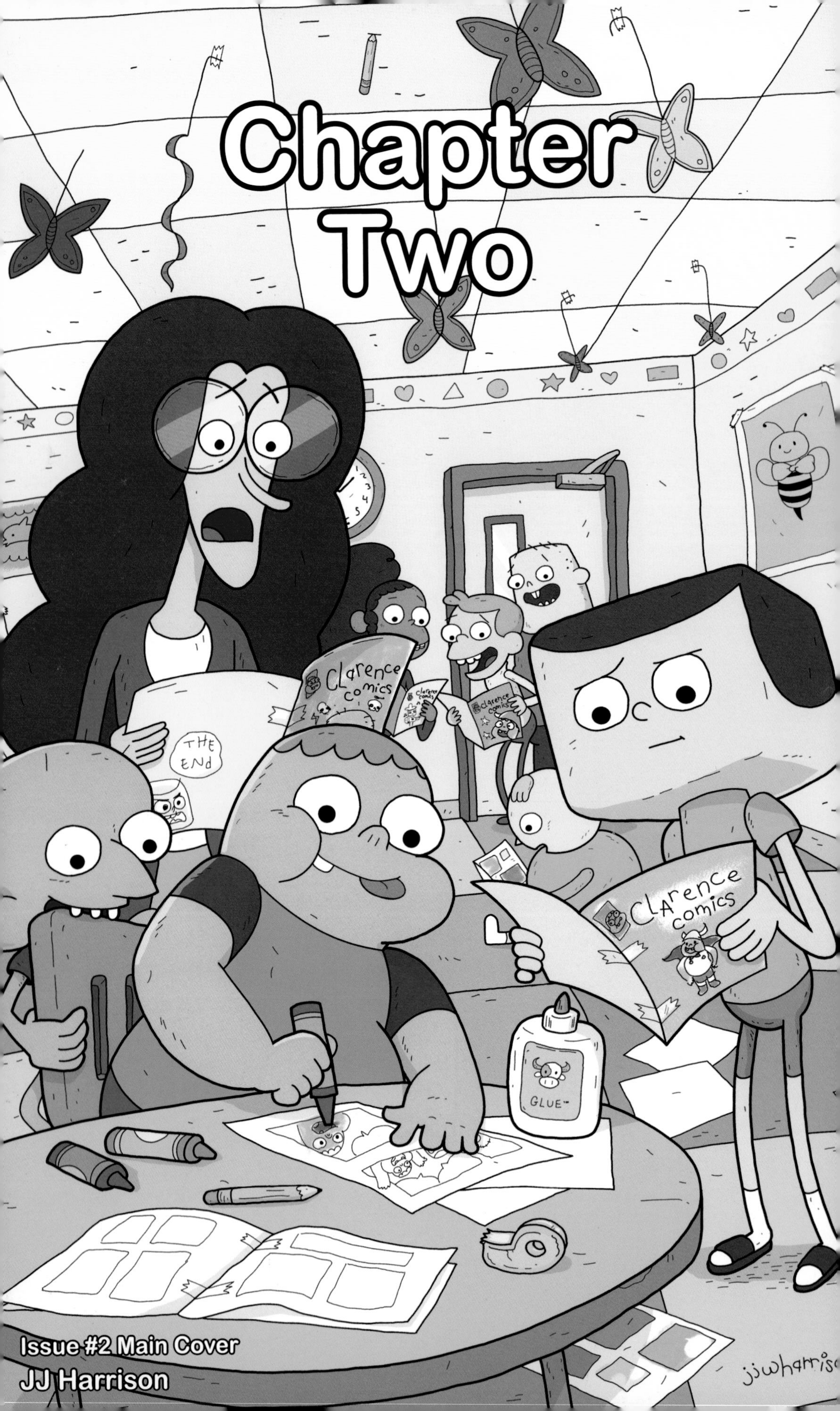
THE ENd
Clarence comics
Clarence comics
Clarence comics
GLUE™
jjwharrison

Issue #2 Main Cover
JJ Harrison

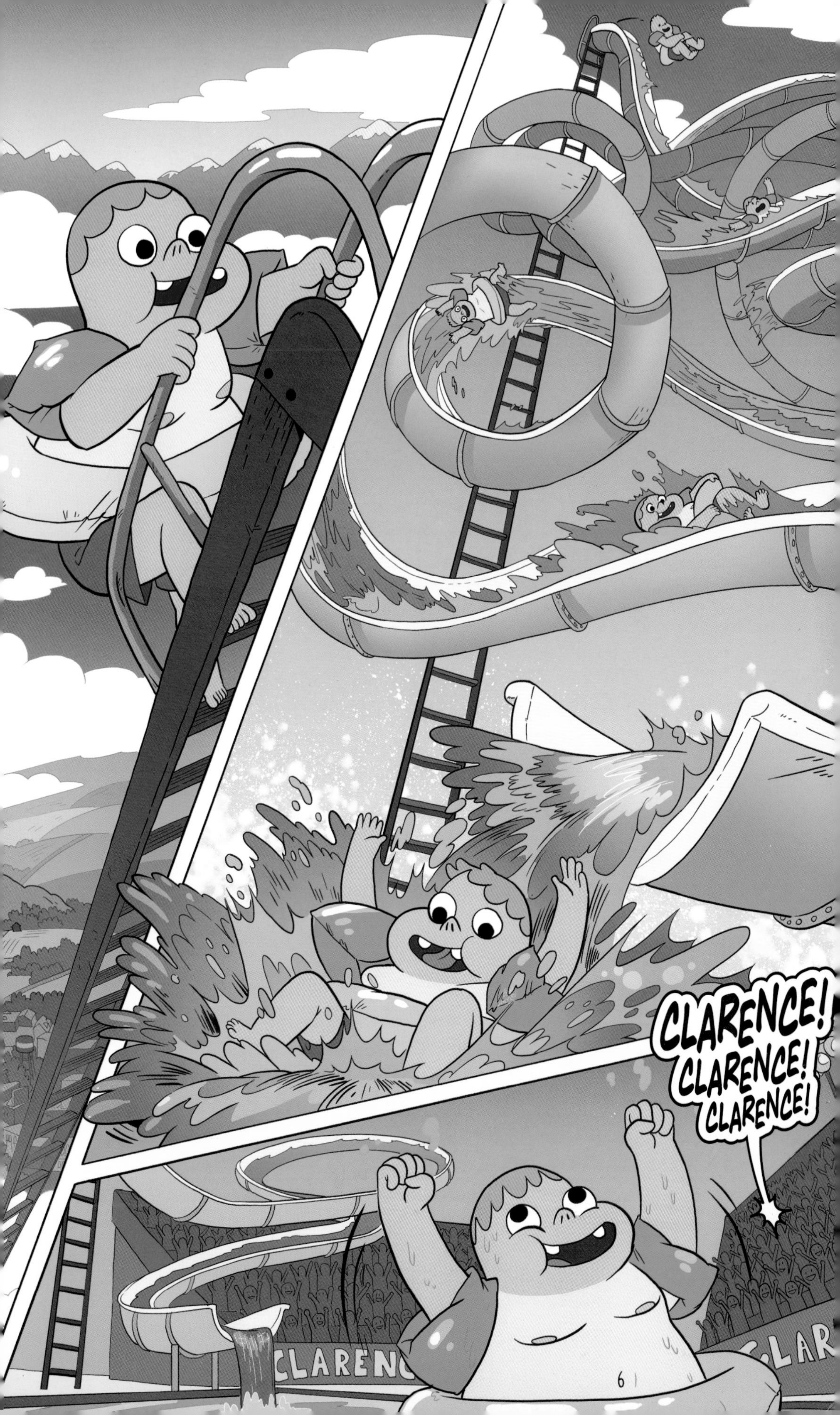
CLARENCE! CLARENCE! CLARENCE!
CLARENC
CLAR

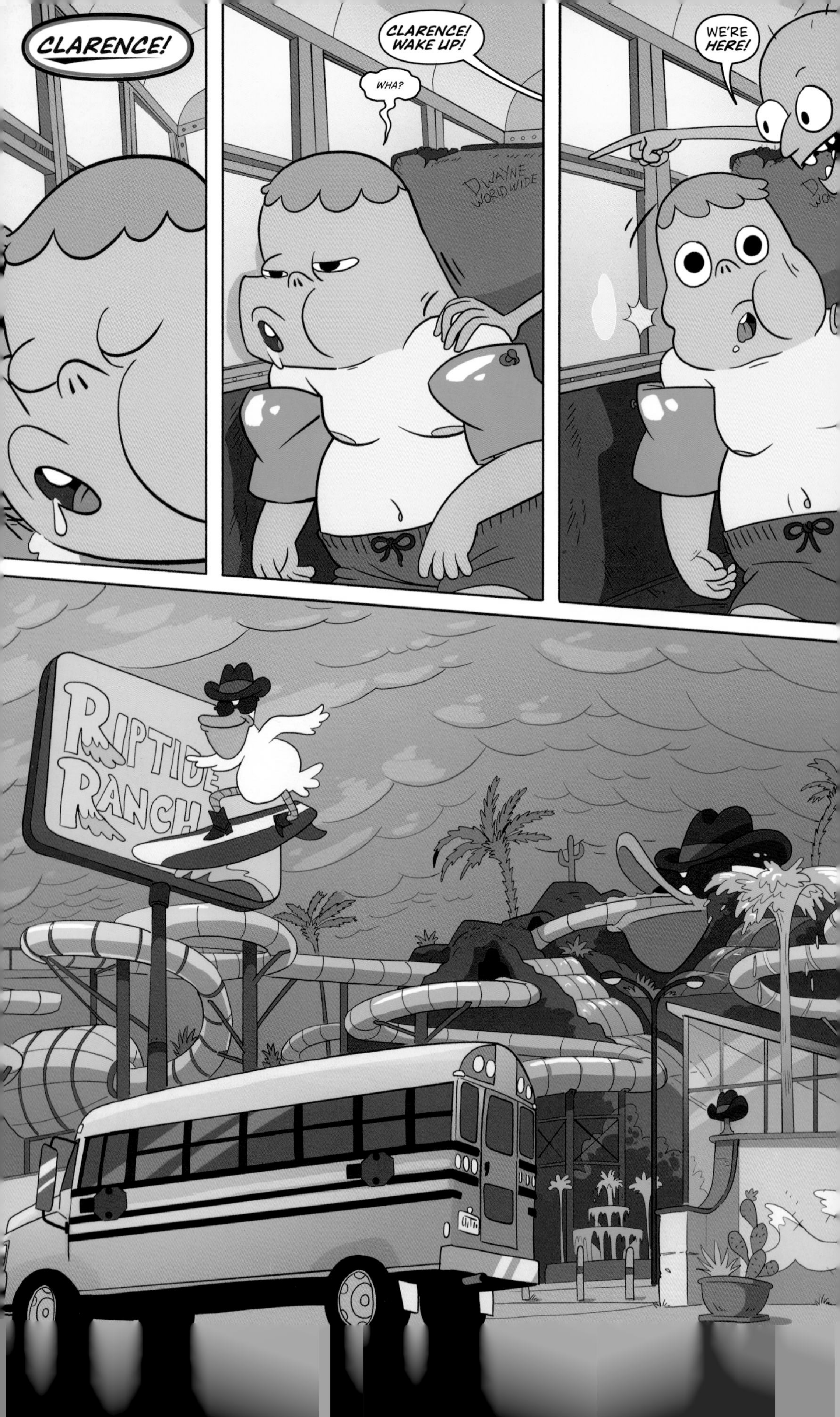
CLARENCE!
CLARENCE! WAKE UP!
WHA?
DWAYNE WORLDWIDE
WE'RE HERE!
RIPTIDE RANCH

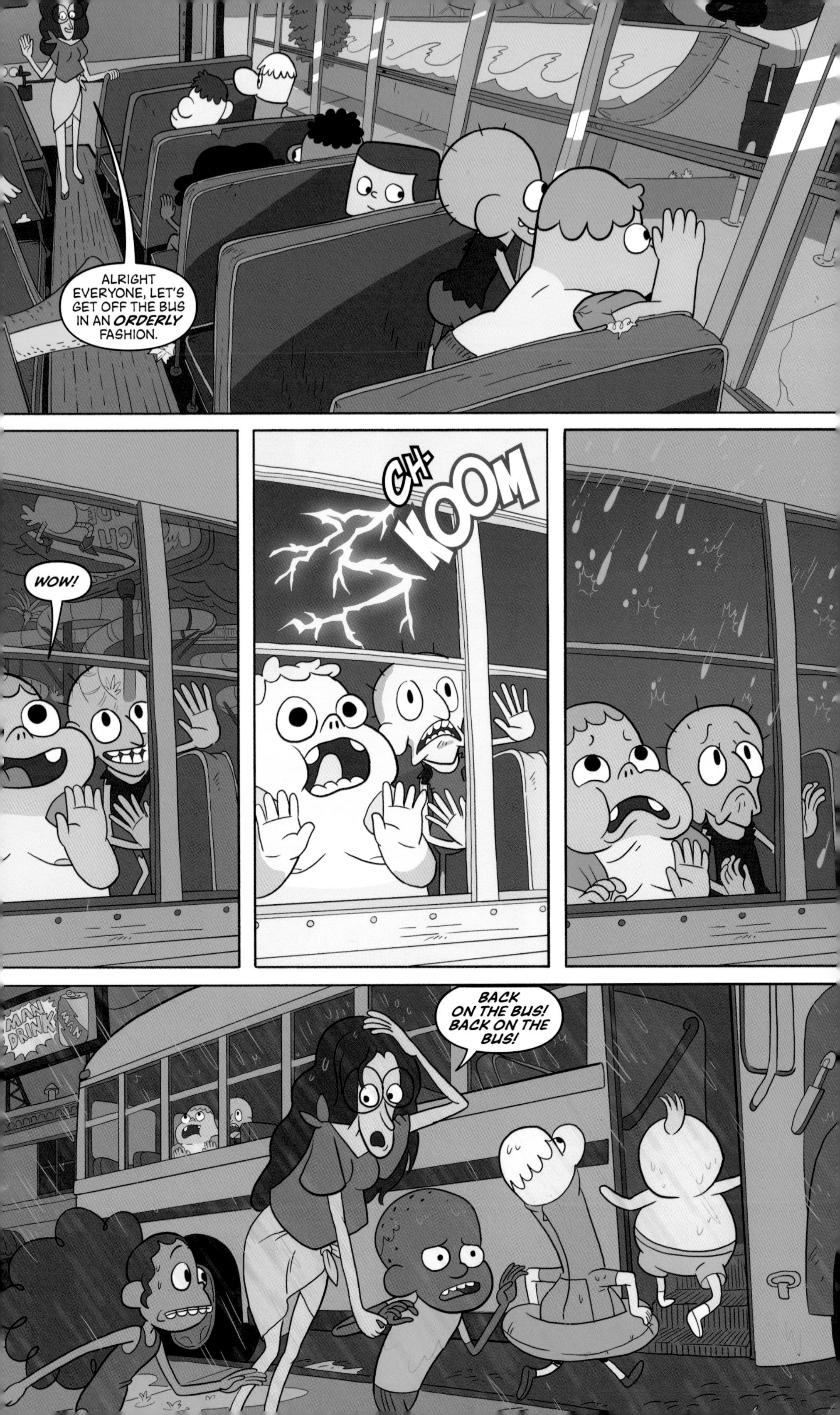
ALRIGHT EVERYONE, LET'S GET OFF THE BUS IN AN *ORDERLY* FASHION.
WOW!
CH-KOOM
BACK ON THE BUS! BACK ON THE BUS!
MAN DRINK

I'M *SO* SORRY, CLASS, I DON'T THINK THIS STORM IS GOING TO LET UP.

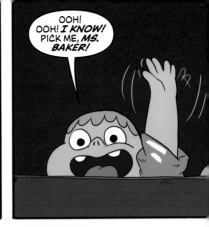

OOH! OOH! *I KNOW!* PICK ME, *MS. BAKER!*

THAT WASN'T A QUESTION, CLARENCE.

BUT, IT DOESN'T MATTER IF IT'S RAINING AT THE WATER PARK BECAUSE WE'RE GONNA GET WET ANYWAY.

YOU *CAN'T GO SWIMMING* IN A *THUNDERSTORM.*

MY *MOM* WOULD LET ME.

CLARENCE! NO I WOULDN'T!

MOM! WHY ARE YOU AT SCHOOL!?

WE'RE NOT AT *SCHOOL*, WE'RE ON A FIELD TRIP AND I VOLUNTEERED TO BE A CHAPERONE, REMEMBER?

OH, *RIGHT.* YOU'RE BEING MOM FOR THE WHOLE CLASS TODAY.

WHAT DO WE DO NOW?

WE CAN'T TAKE THEM BACK TO SCHOOL. TODAY IS THE DAY THEY CLEAN OUT THE CUBBIES.

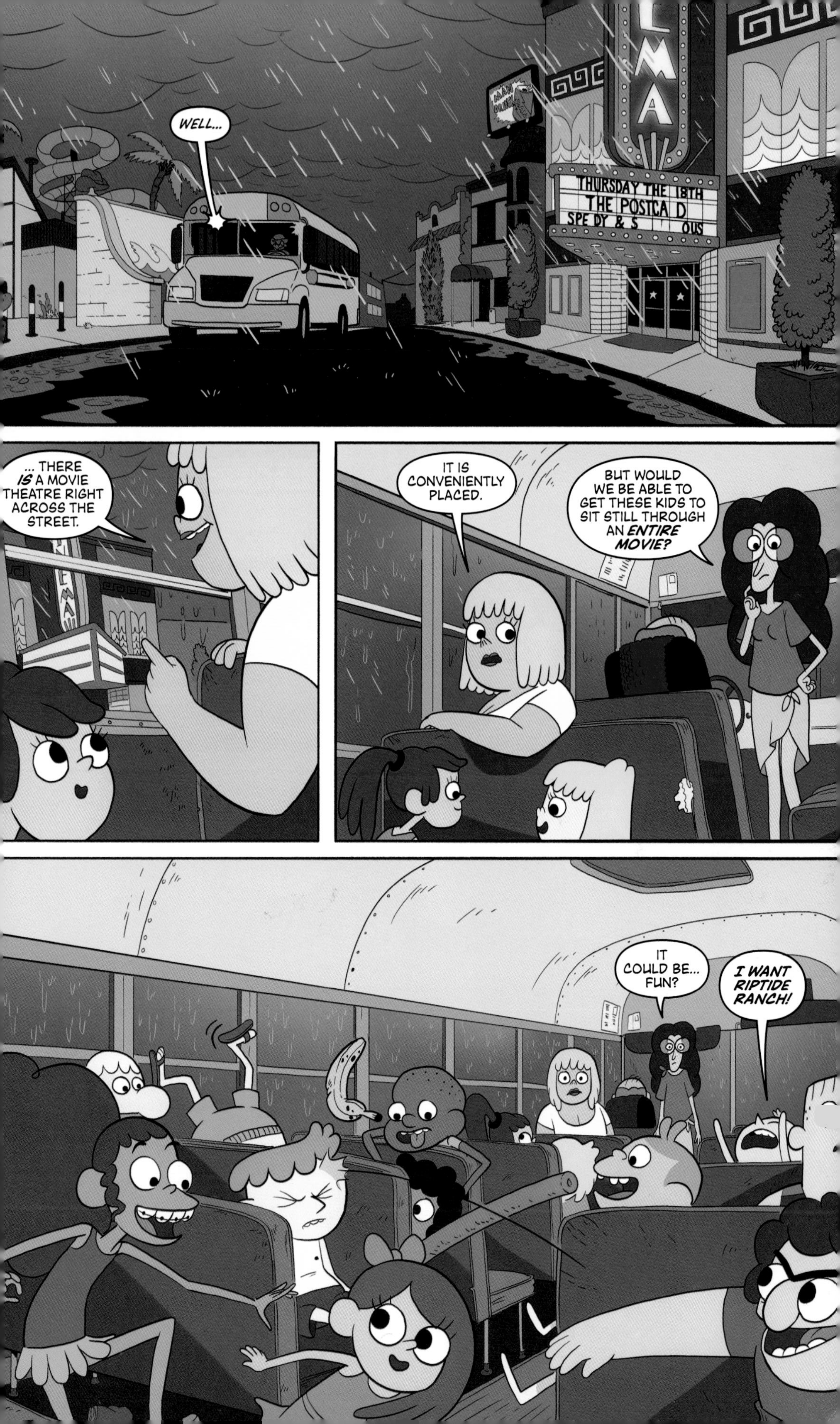
WELL...
THURSDAY THE 18TH
THE POSTCA D
SPE DY & S OUS
... THERE IS A MOVIE THEATRE RIGHT ACROSS THE STREET.
IT IS CONVENIENTLY PLACED.
BUT WOULD WE BE ABLE TO GET THESE KIDS TO SIT STILL THROUGH AN ENTIRE MOVIE?
IT COULD BE... FUN?
I WANT RIPTIDE RANCH!

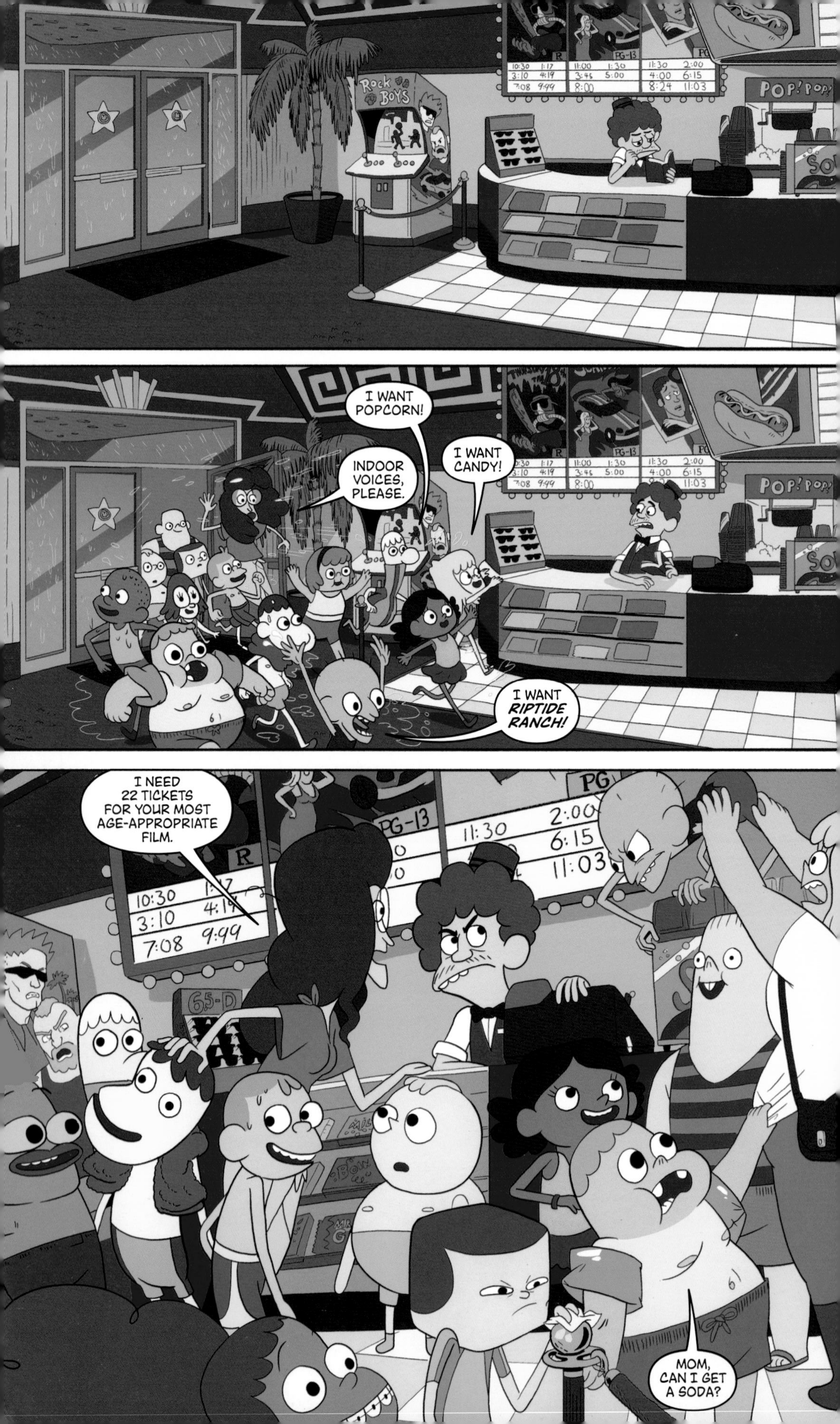
Rock BOYS
R
PG-13
PG
10:30 1:17
3:10 4:19
7:08 9:99
11:00 1:30
3:45 5:00
8:00
11:30 2:00
4:00 6:15
8:24 11:03
POP! POP!
I WANT POPCORN!
INDOOR VOICES, PLEASE.
I WANT CANDY!
I WANT *RIPTIDE RANCH!*
I NEED 22 TICKETS FOR YOUR MOST AGE-APPROPRIATE FILM.
MOM, CAN I GET A SODA?

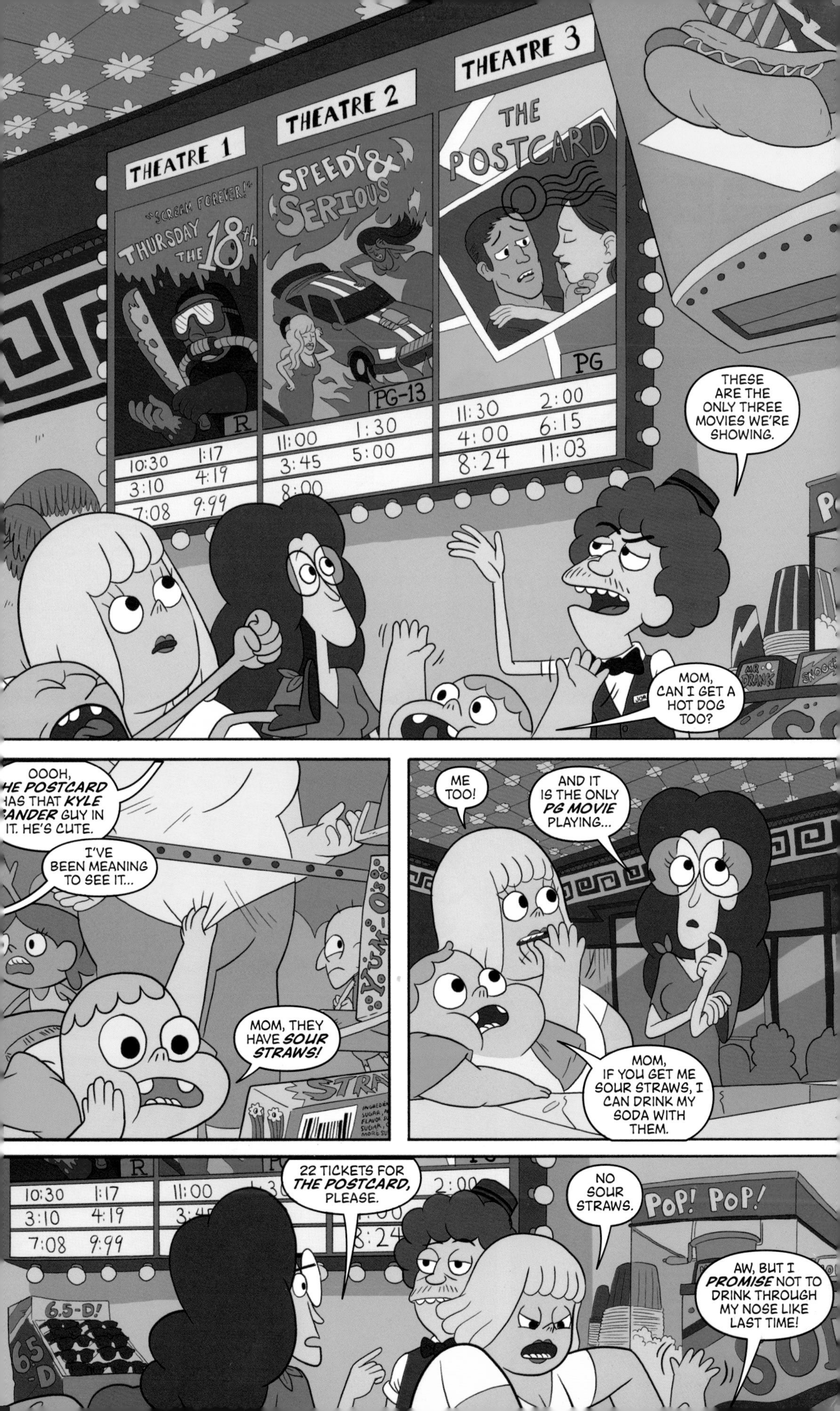
THEATRE 1
THEATRE 2
THEATRE 3
"SCREAM FOREVER!"
THURSDAY THE 18th
R
10:30 1:17
3:10 4:19
7:08 9:99
SPEEDY & SERIOUS
PG-13
11:00 1:30
3:45 5:00
8:00
THE POSTCARD
PG
11:30 2:00
4:00 6:15
8:24 11:03
THESE ARE THE ONLY THREE MOVIES WE'RE SHOWING.
MOM, CAN I GET A HOT DOG TOO?
OOOH, HE POSTCARD HAS THAT KYLE ANDER GUY IN IT. HE'S CUTE.
I'VE BEEN MEANING TO SEE IT...
YUM-O'S
MOM, THEY HAVE SOUR STRAWS!
ME TOO!
AND IT IS THE ONLY PG MOVIE PLAYING...
MOM, IF YOU GET ME SOUR STRAWS, I CAN DRINK MY SODA WITH THEM.
22 TICKETS FOR THE POSTCARD, PLEASE.
NO SOUR STRAWS.
POP! POP!
6.5-D!
AW, BUT I PROMISE NOT TO DRINK THROUGH MY NOSE LIKE LAST TIME!

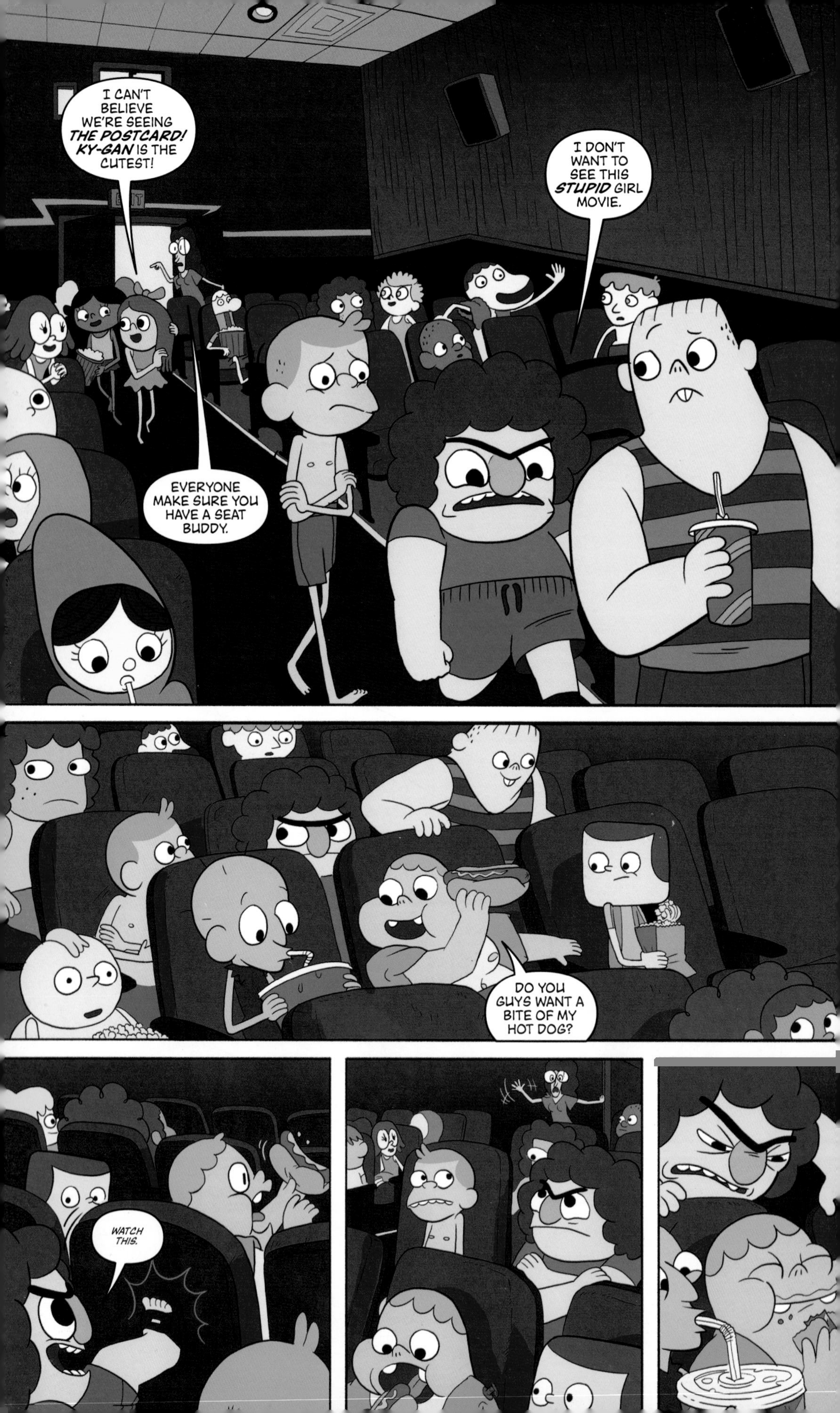
I CAN'T BELIEVE WE'RE SEEING THE POSTCARD! KY-GAN IS THE CUTEST!
I DON'T WANT TO SEE THIS STUPID GIRL MOVIE.
EVERYONE MAKE SURE YOU HAVE A SEAT BUDDY.
DO YOU GUYS WANT A BITE OF MY HOT DOG?
WATCH THIS.

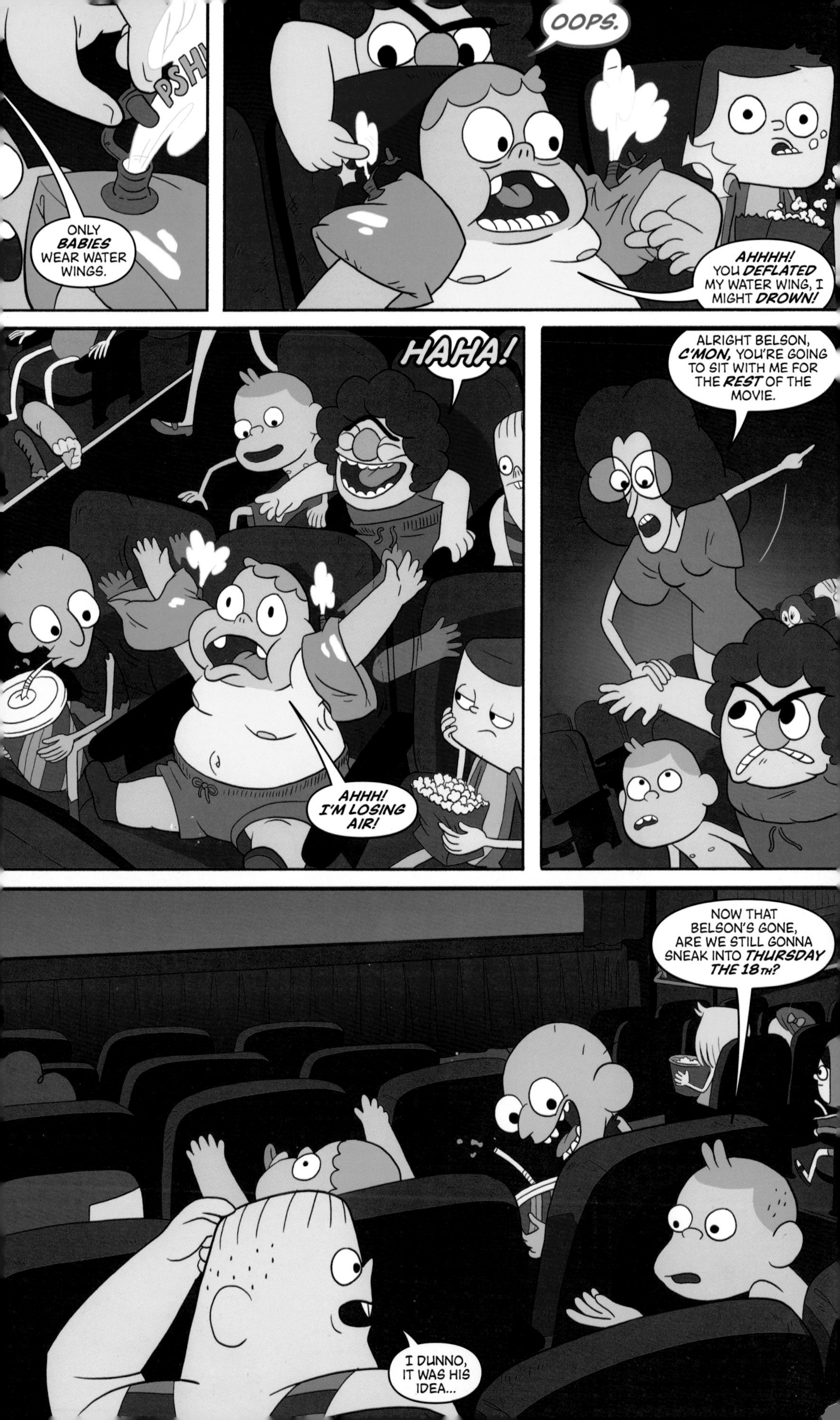
PSHH
ONLY BABIES WEAR WATER WINGS.
OOPS.
AHHHH! YOU DEFLATED MY WATER WING, I MIGHT DROWN!
HAHA!
AHHH! I'M LOSING AIR!
ALRIGHT BELSON, C'MON, YOU'RE GOING TO SIT WITH ME FOR THE REST OF THE MOVIE.
NOW THAT BELSON'S GONE, ARE WE STILL GONNA SNEAK INTO THURSDAY THE 18TH?
I DUNNO, IT WAS HIS IDEA...

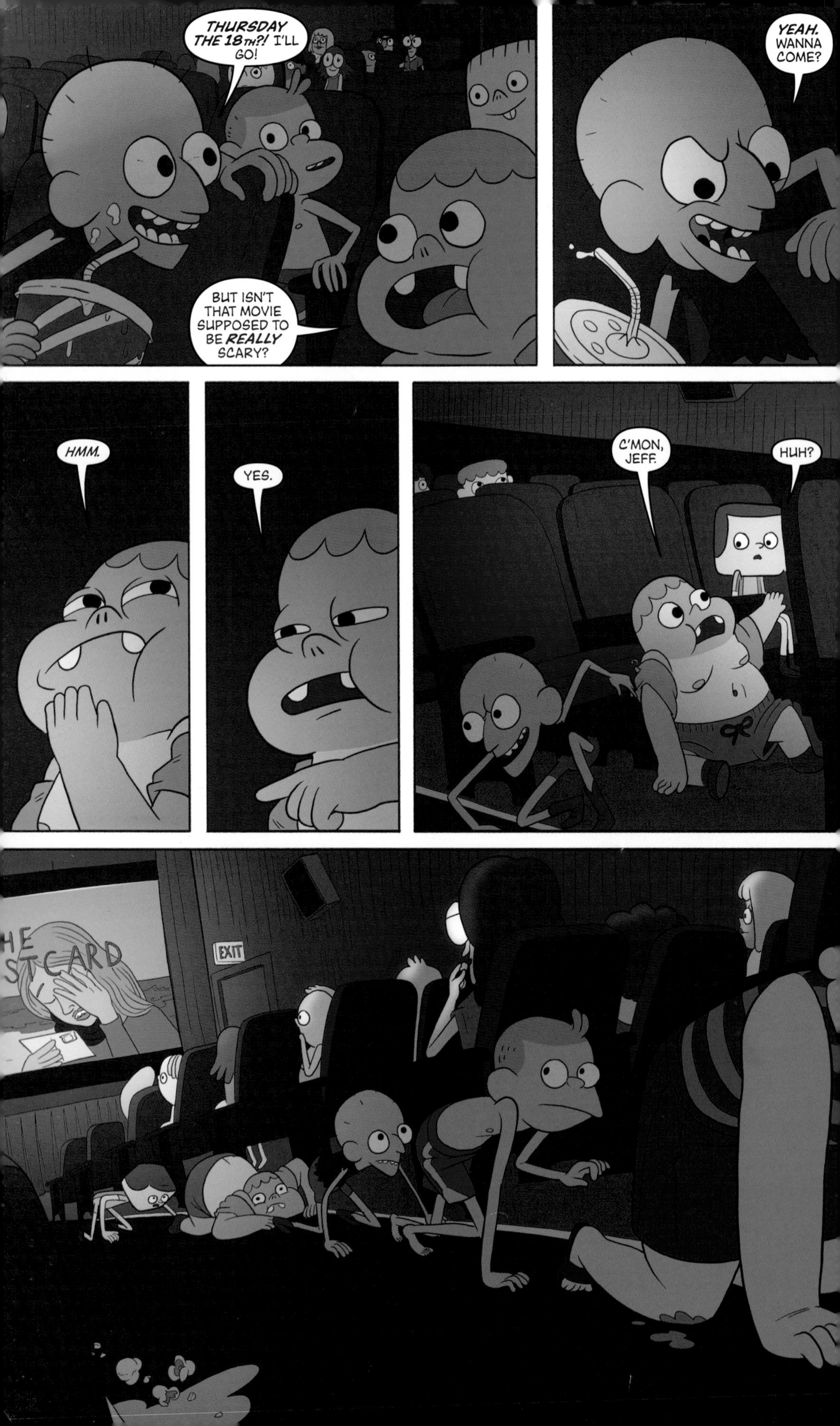
THURSDAY THE 18TH?! I'LL GO!
BUT ISN'T THAT MOVIE SUPPOSED TO BE REALLY SCARY?
YEAH. WANNA COME?
HMM.
YES.
C'MON, JEFF.
HUH?

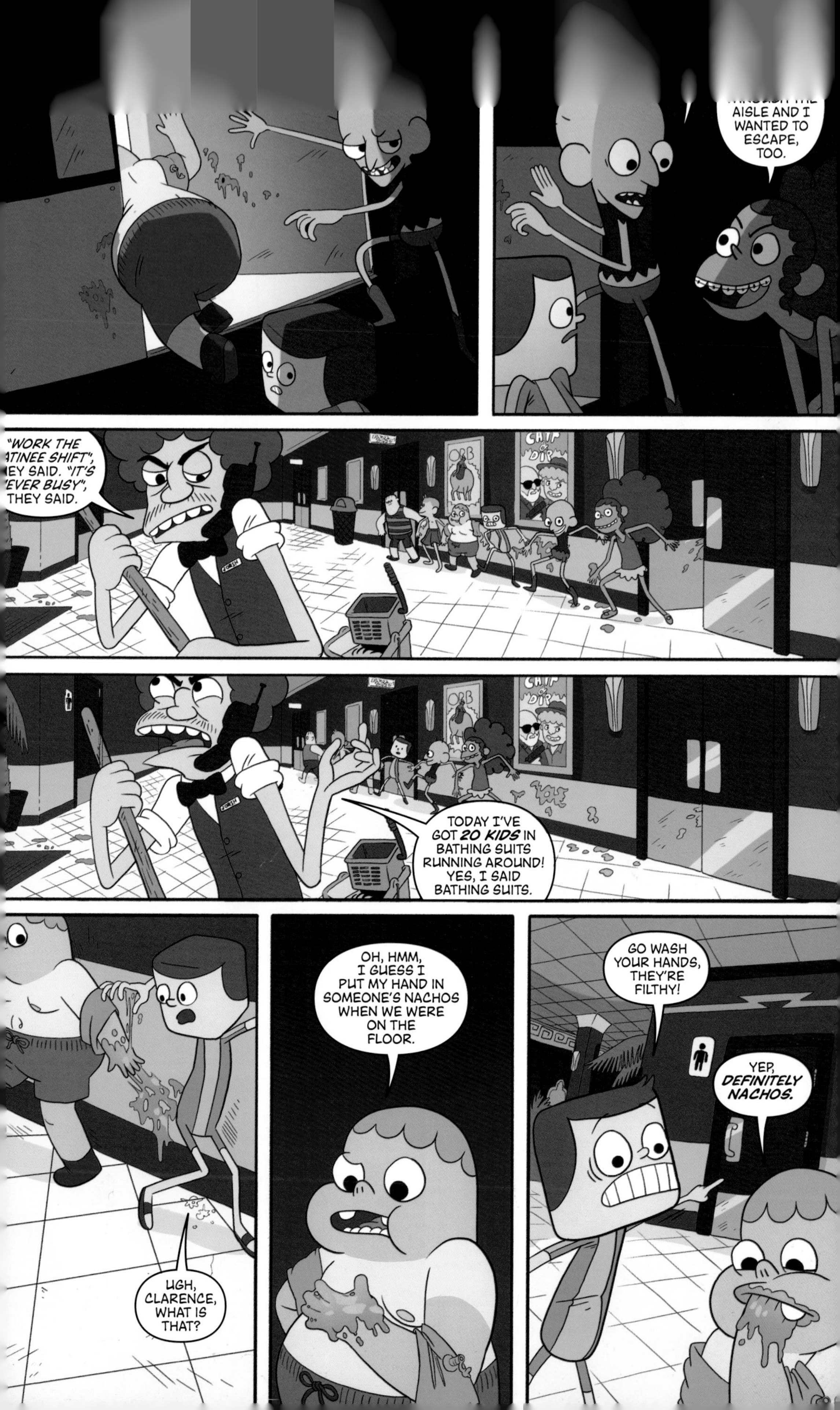

AISLE AND I WANTED TO ESCAPE, TOO.
"WORK THE
ATINEE SHIFT",
EY SAID. "IT'S
EVER BUSY",
THEY SAID.
CHIP DIP
ORB
TODAY I'VE GOT **20 KIDS** IN BATHING SUITS RUNNING AROUND! YES, I SAID BATHING SUITS.
UGH, CLARENCE, WHAT IS THAT?
OH, HMM, I GUESS I PUT MY HAND IN SOMEONE'S NACHOS WHEN WE WERE ON THE FLOOR.
GO WASH YOUR HANDS, THEY'RE FILTHY!
YEP, ***DEFINITELY NACHOS.***

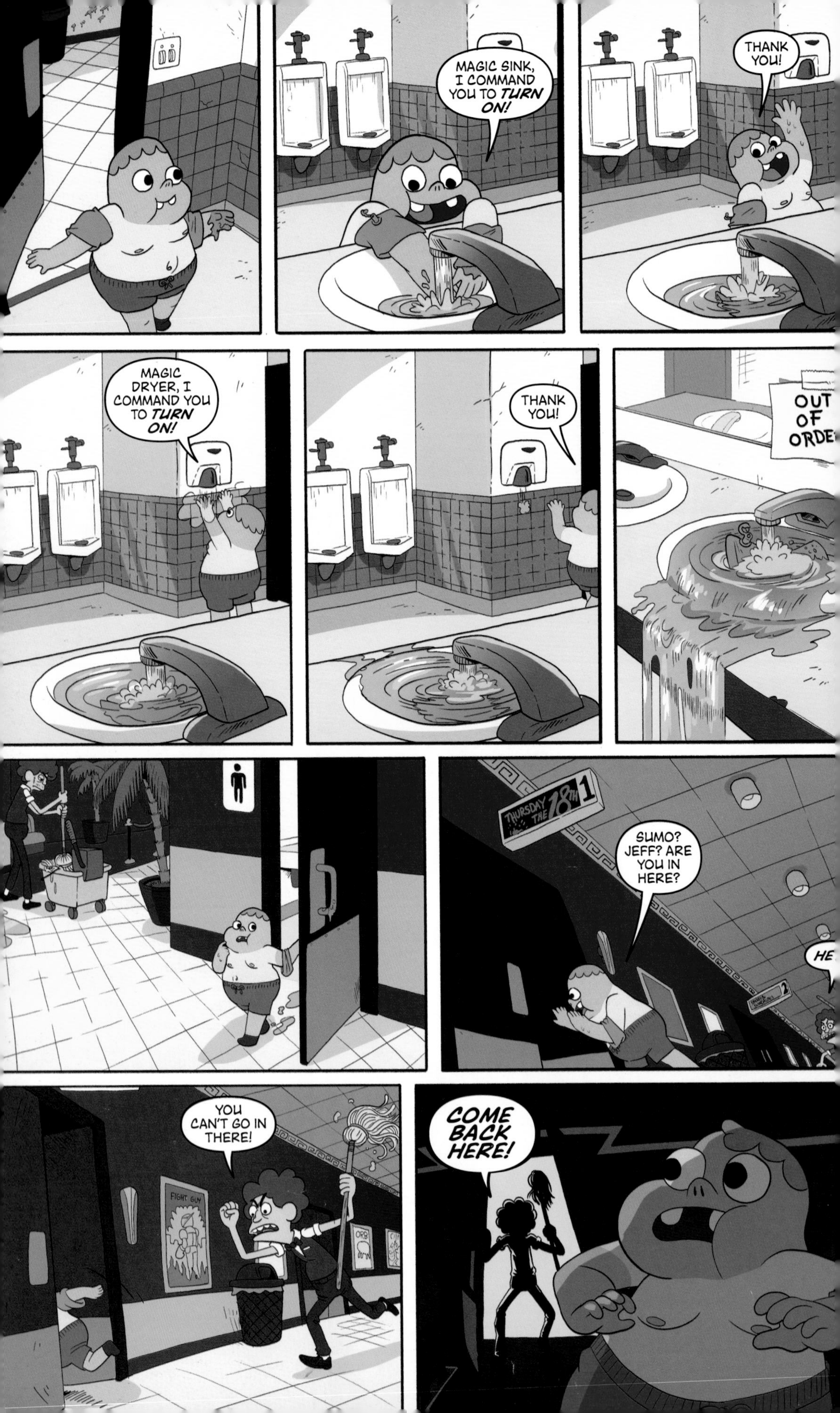
MAGIC SINK, I COMMAND YOU TO *TURN ON!*
THANK YOU!
MAGIC DRYER, I COMMAND YOU TO *TURN ON!*
THANK YOU!
OUT OF ORDE
THURSDAY THE 18TH
1
SUMO? JEFF? ARE YOU IN HERE?
HE
FIGHT GUY
ORB
YOU CAN'T GO IN THERE!
COME BACK HERE!

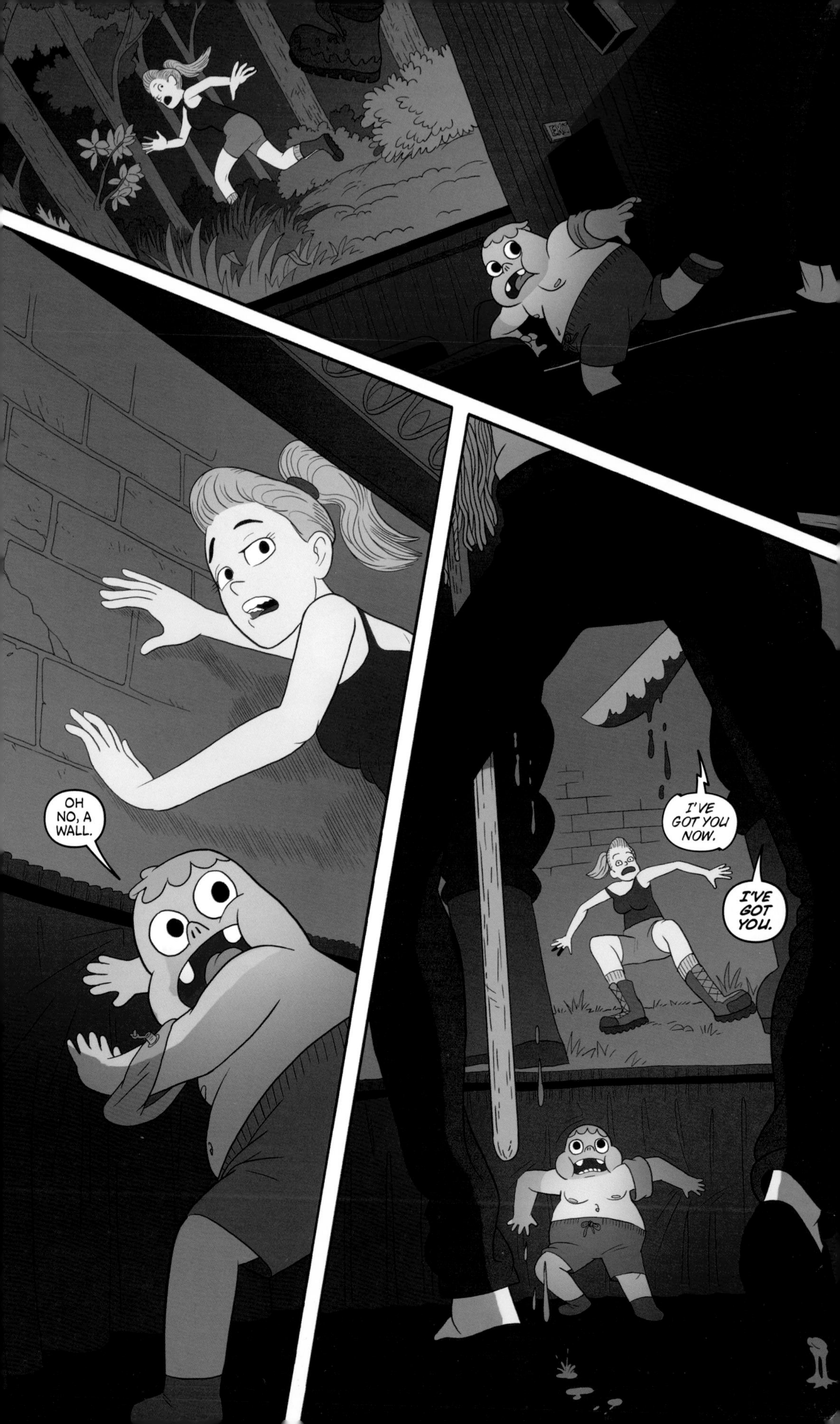
OH NO, A WALL.
I'VE GOT YOU NOW.
I'VE GOT YOU.

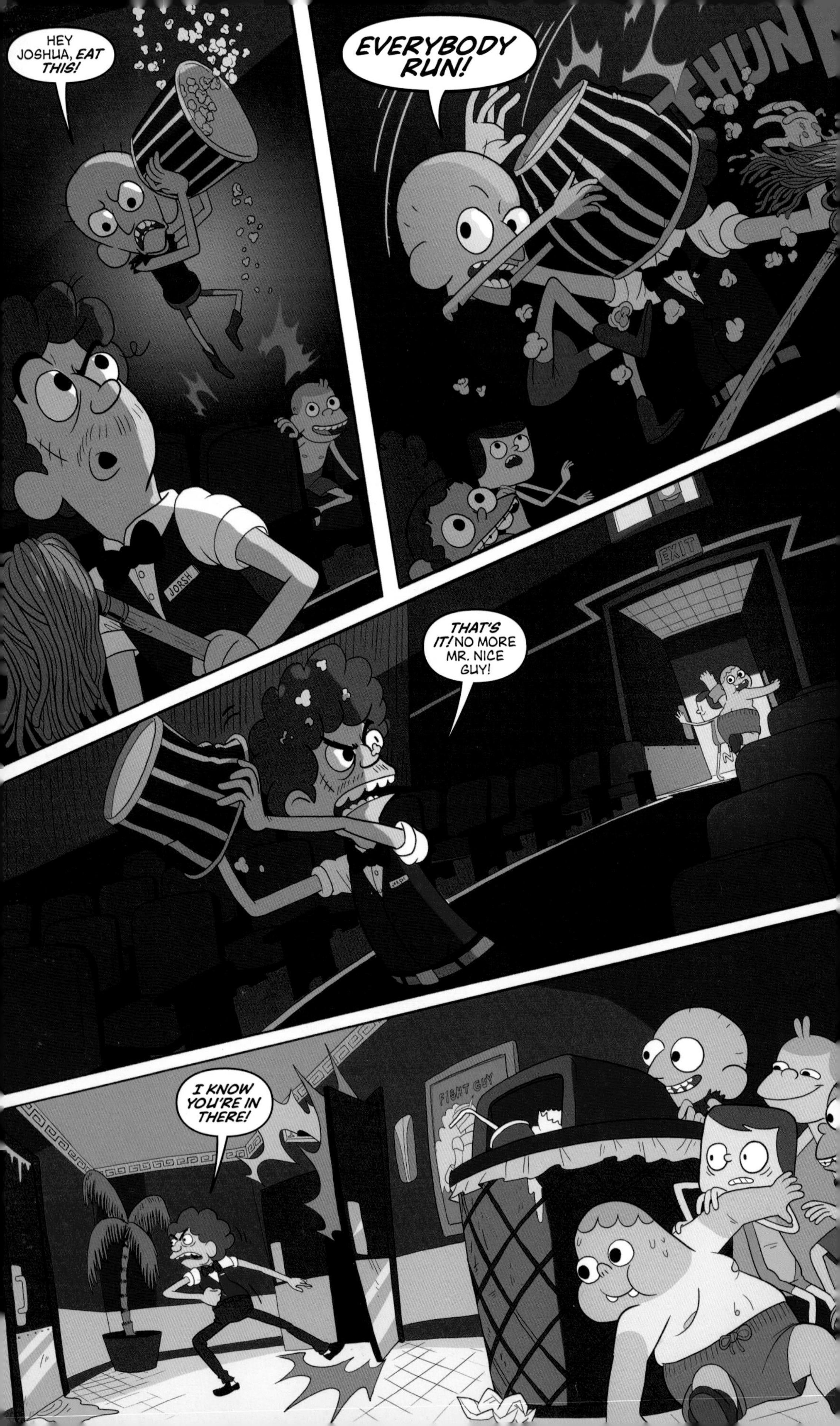
HEY JOSHUA, EAT THIS!
EVERYBODY RUN!
THUN
JORSH
EXIT
THAT'S IT! NO MORE MR. NICE GUY!
I KNOW YOU'RE IN THERE!
FIGHT GUY

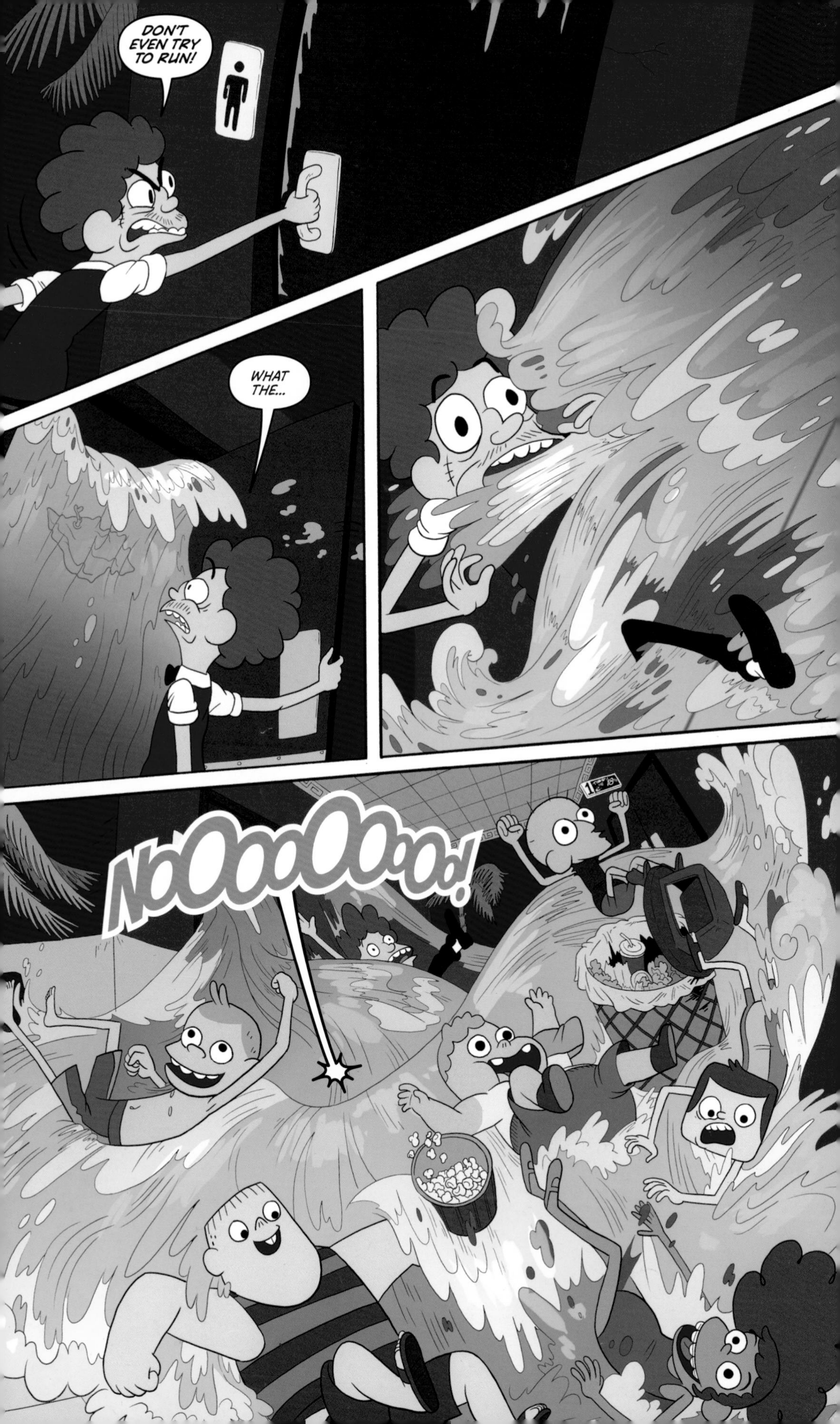
DON'T EVEN TRY TO RUN!
WHAT THE...
NOOOOOOooo!

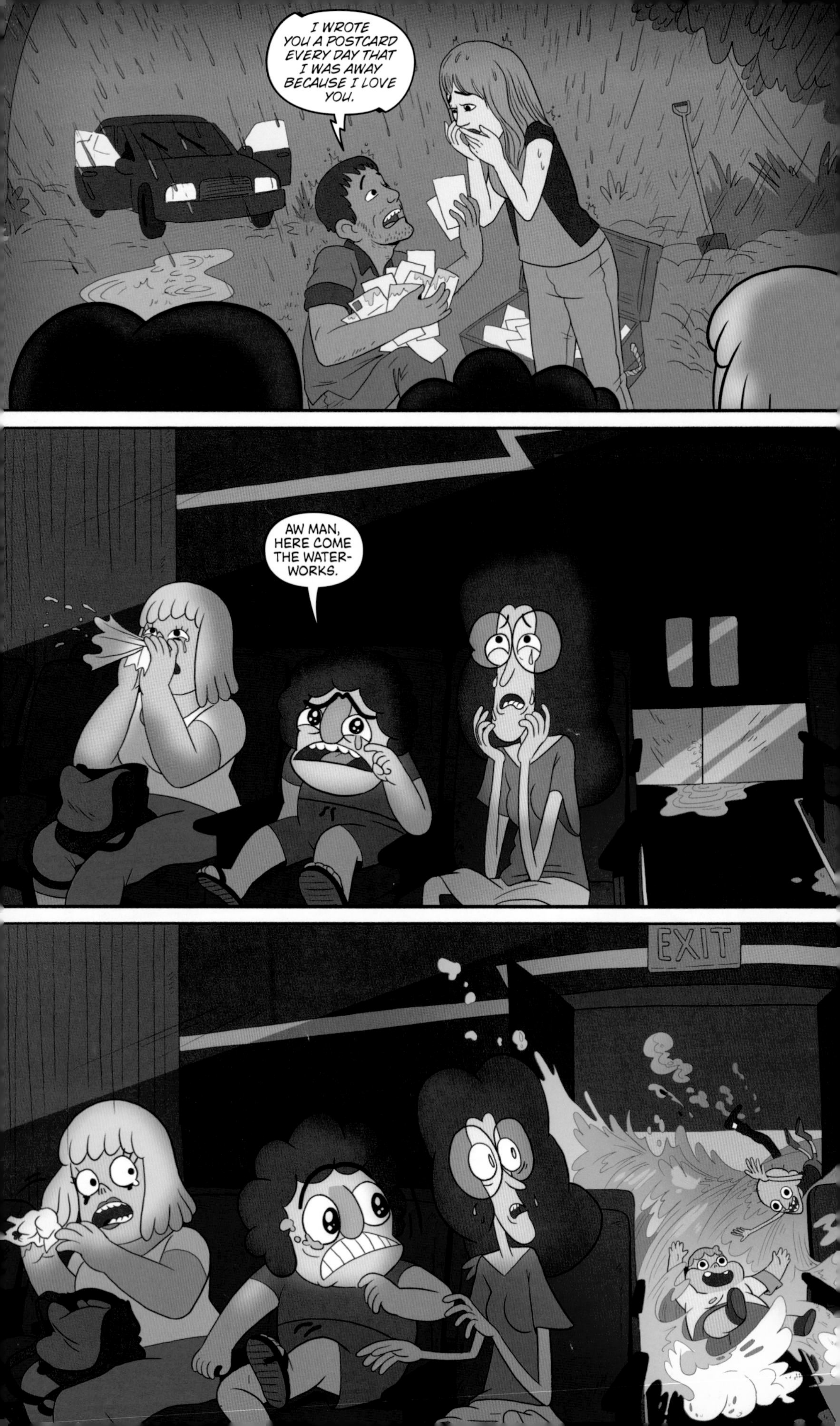
I WROTE YOU A POSTCARD EVERY DAY THAT I WAS AWAY BECAUSE I LOVE YOU.
AW MAN, HERE COME THE WATER-WORKS.
EXIT

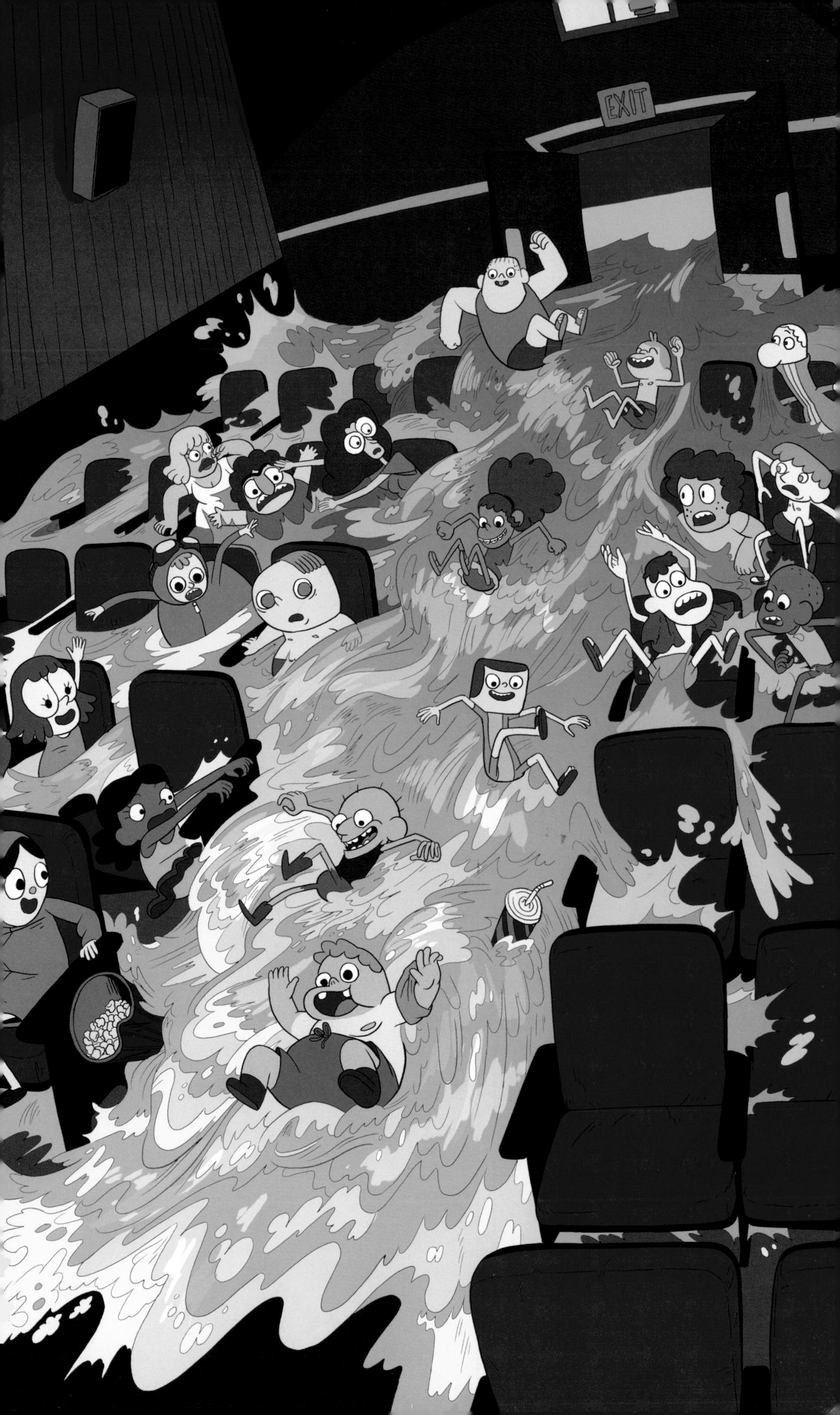
EXIT

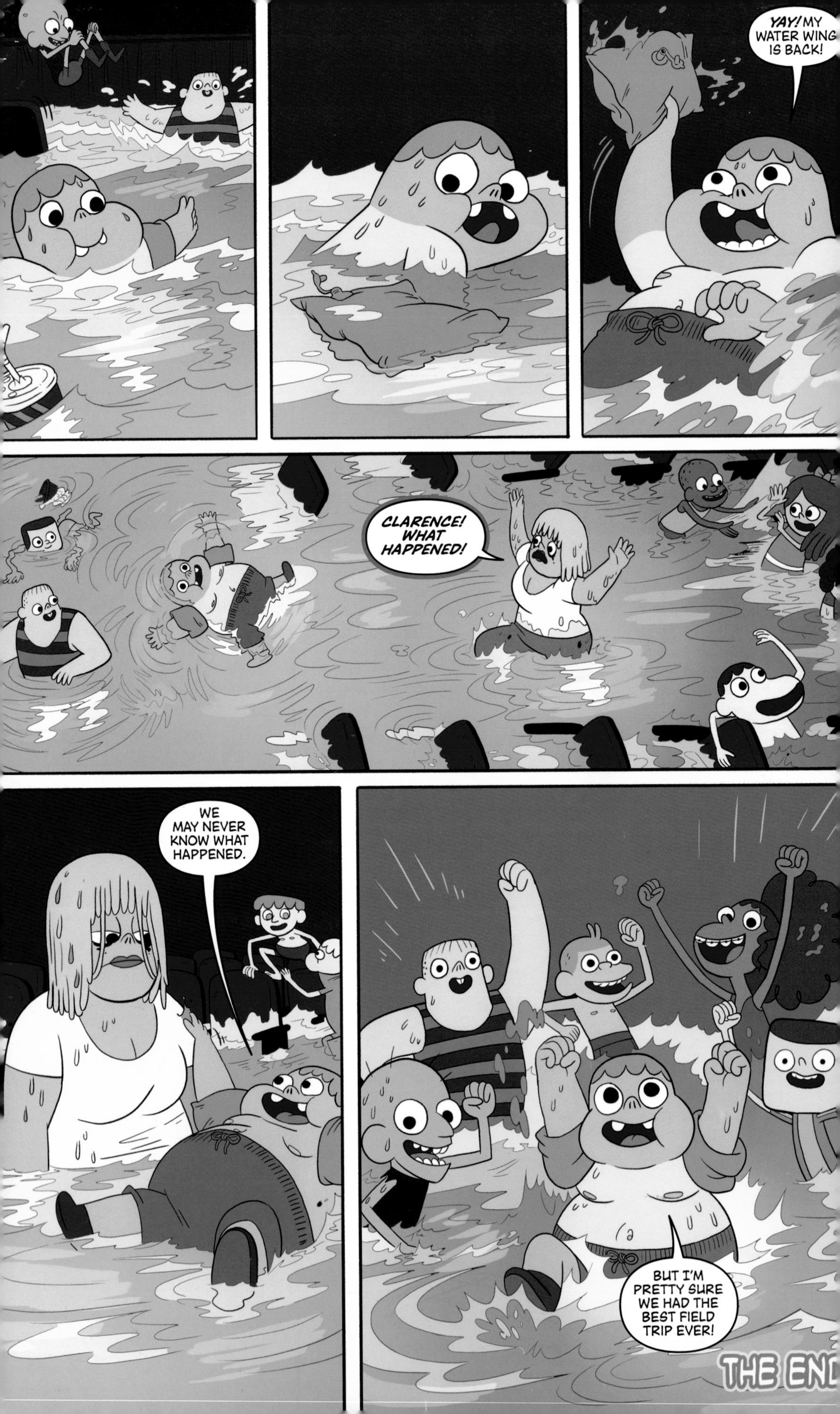
YAY! MY WATER WING IS BACK!
CLARENCE! WHAT HAPPENED!
WE MAY NEVER KNOW WHAT HAPPENED.
BUT I'M PRETTY SURE WE HAD THE BEST FIELD TRIP EVER!
THE END

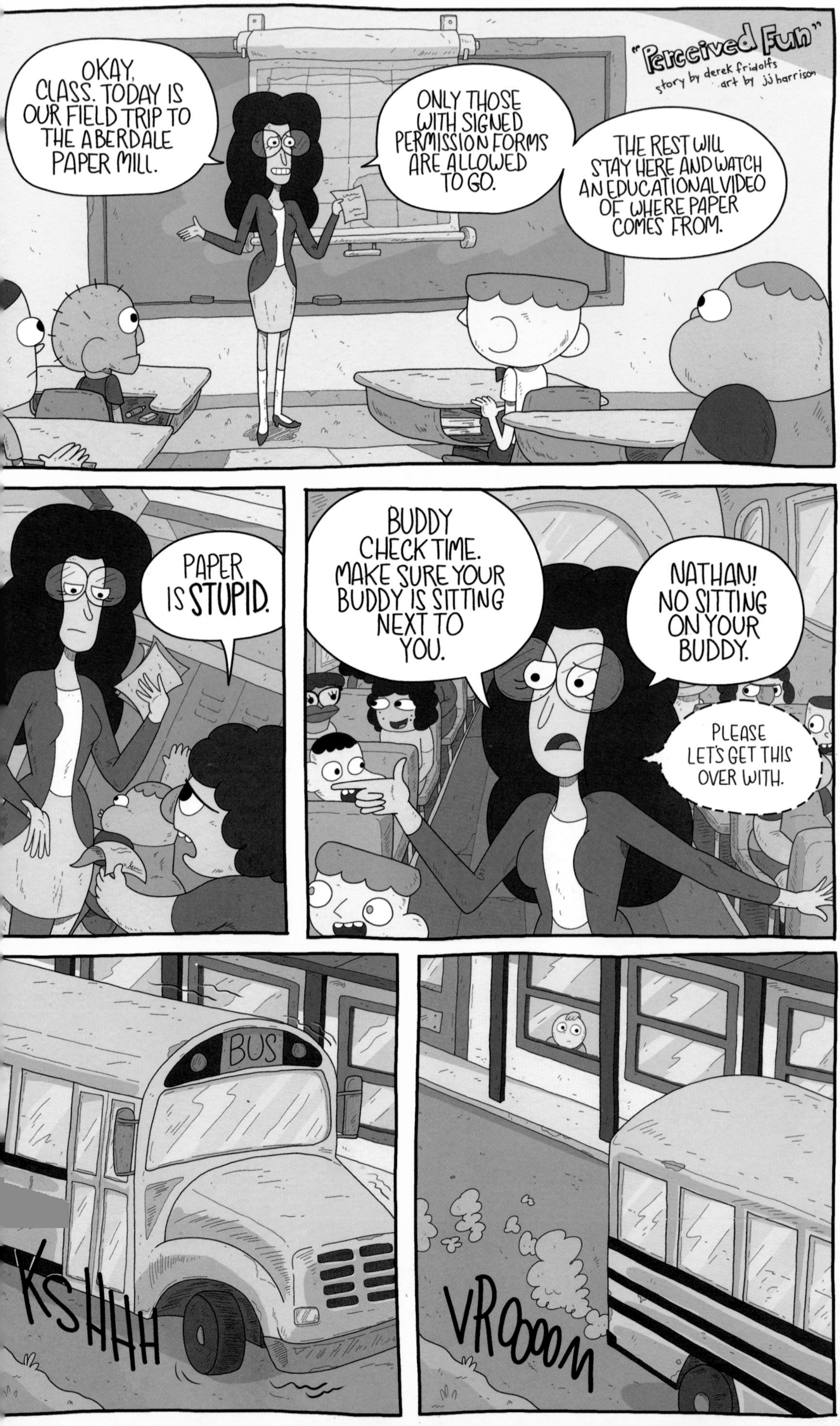
"Perceived Fun"
story by derek fridolfs
art by jj harrison
OKAY, CLASS. TODAY IS OUR FIELD TRIP TO THE ABERDALE PAPER MILL.
ONLY THOSE WITH SIGNED PERMISSION FORMS ARE ALLOWED TO GO.
THE REST WILL STAY HERE AND WATCH AN EDUCATIONAL VIDEO OF WHERE PAPER COMES FROM.
PAPER IS STUPID.
BUDDY CHECK TIME. MAKE SURE YOUR BUDDY IS SITTING NEXT TO YOU.
NATHAN! NO SITTING ON YOUR BUDDY.
PLEASE LET'S GET THIS OVER WITH.
BUS
KSHHH
VROOOOM

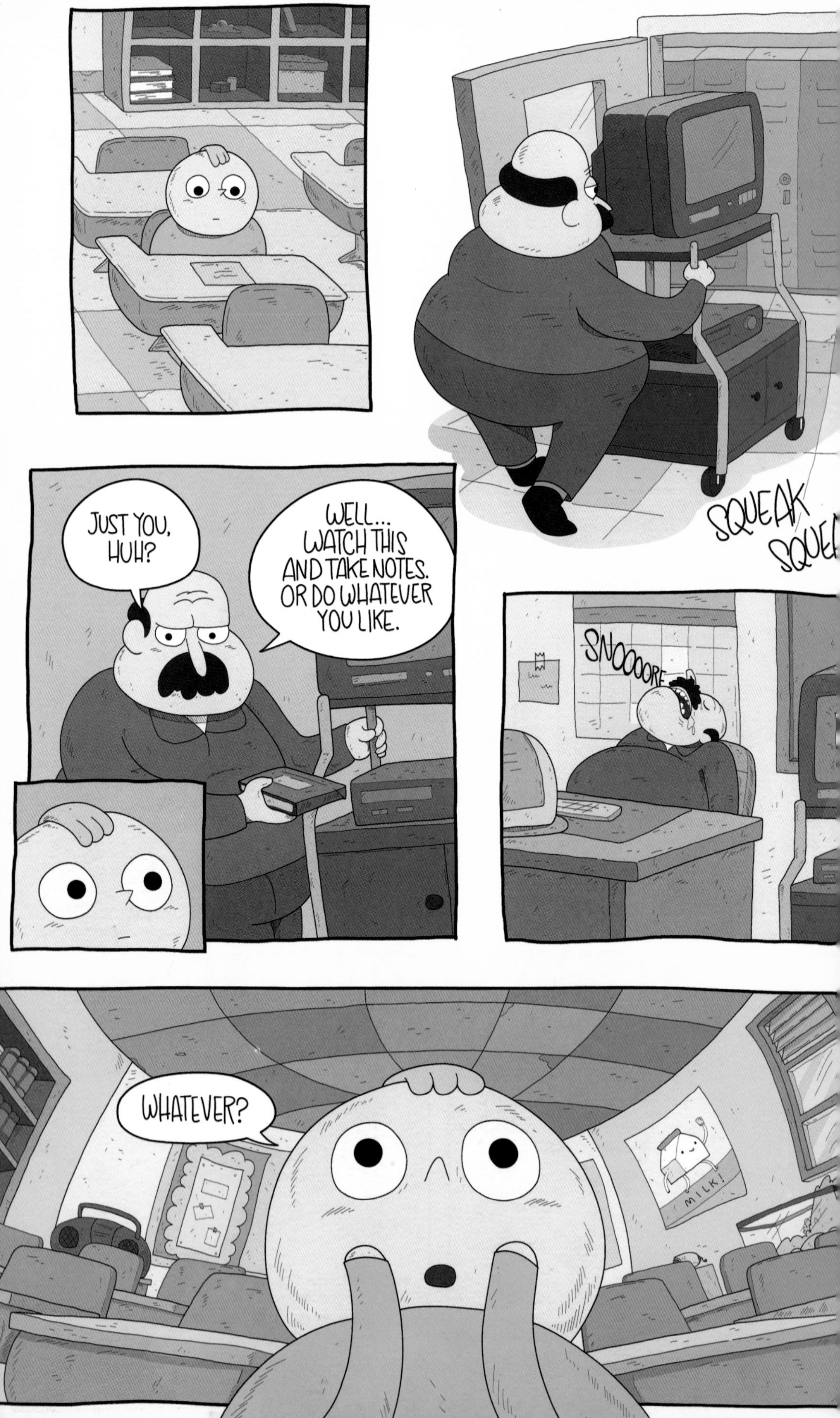
SQUEAK
SQUEA
JUST YOU, HUH?
WELL... WATCH THIS AND TAKE NOTES. OR DO WHATEVER YOU LIKE.
SNOOOORE
WHATEVER?
MILK!

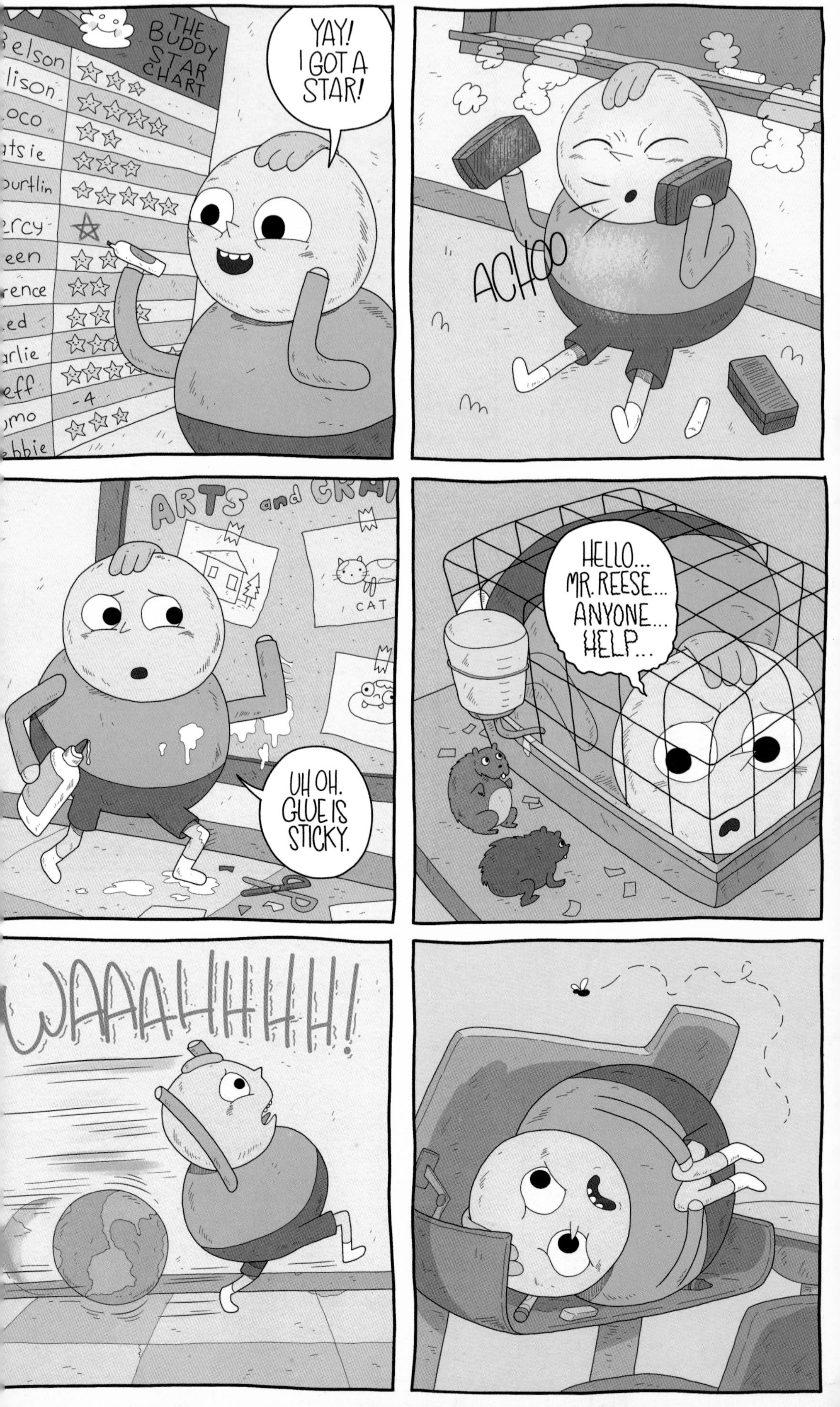
THE BUDDY STAR CHART
YAY! I GOT A STAR!
ACHOO
ARTS and CRA
CAT
UH OH. GLUE IS STICKY.
HELLO... MR. REESE... ANYONE... HELP...
WAAAHHHH!

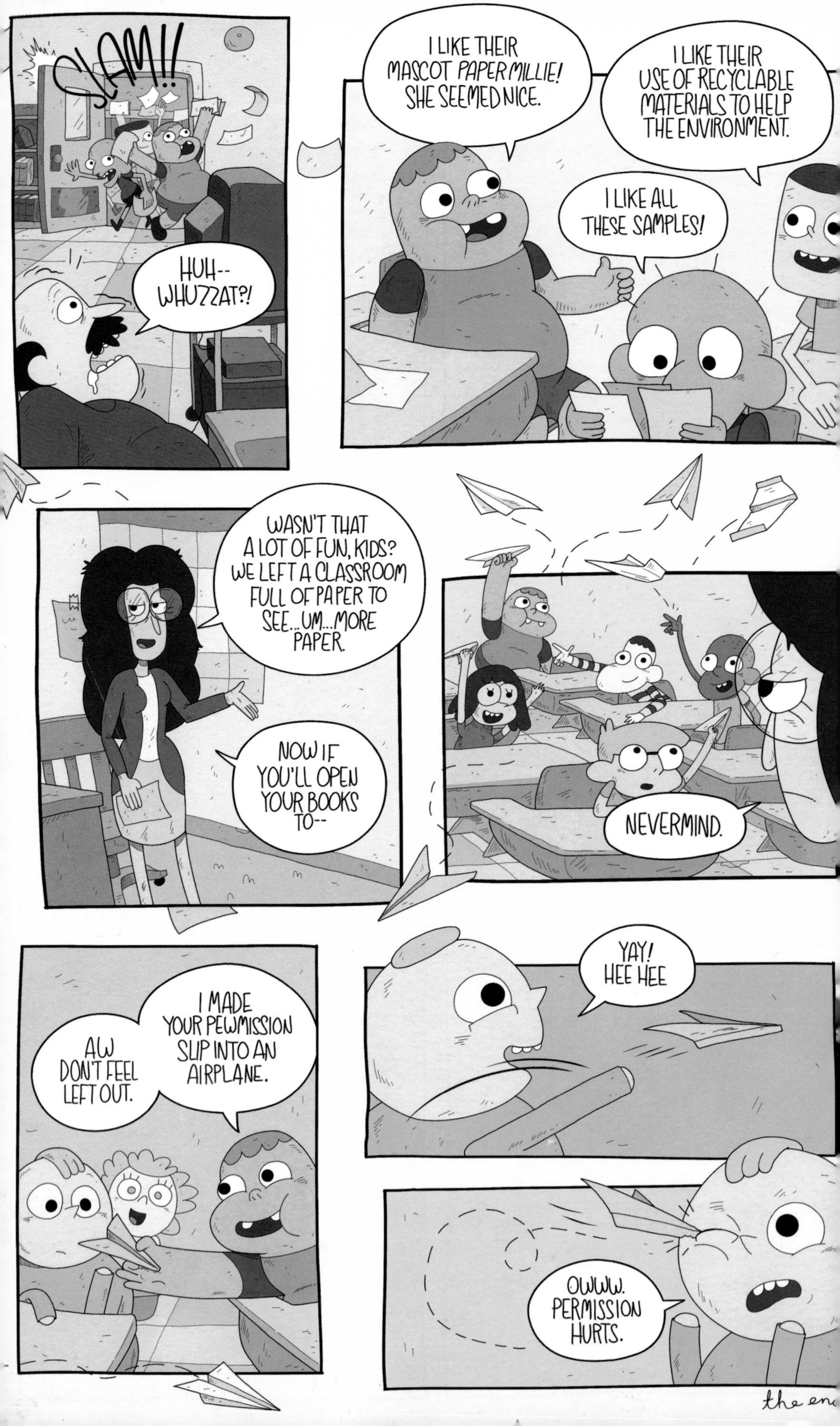
SLAM!!
HUH-- WHUZZAT?!
I LIKE THEIR MASCOT PAPER MILLIE! SHE SEEMED NICE.
I LIKE THEIR USE OF RECYCLABLE MATERIALS TO HELP THE ENVIRONMENT.
I LIKE ALL THESE SAMPLES!
WASN'T THAT A LOT OF FUN, KIDS? WE LEFT A CLASSROOM FULL OF PAPER TO SEE...UM...MORE PAPER.
NOW IF YOU'LL OPEN YOUR BOOKS TO--
NEVERMIND.
AW DON'T FEEL LEFT OUT.
I MADE YOUR PEWMISSION SLIP INTO AN AIRPLANE.
YAY! HEE HEE
OWWW. PERMISSION HURTS.
the end

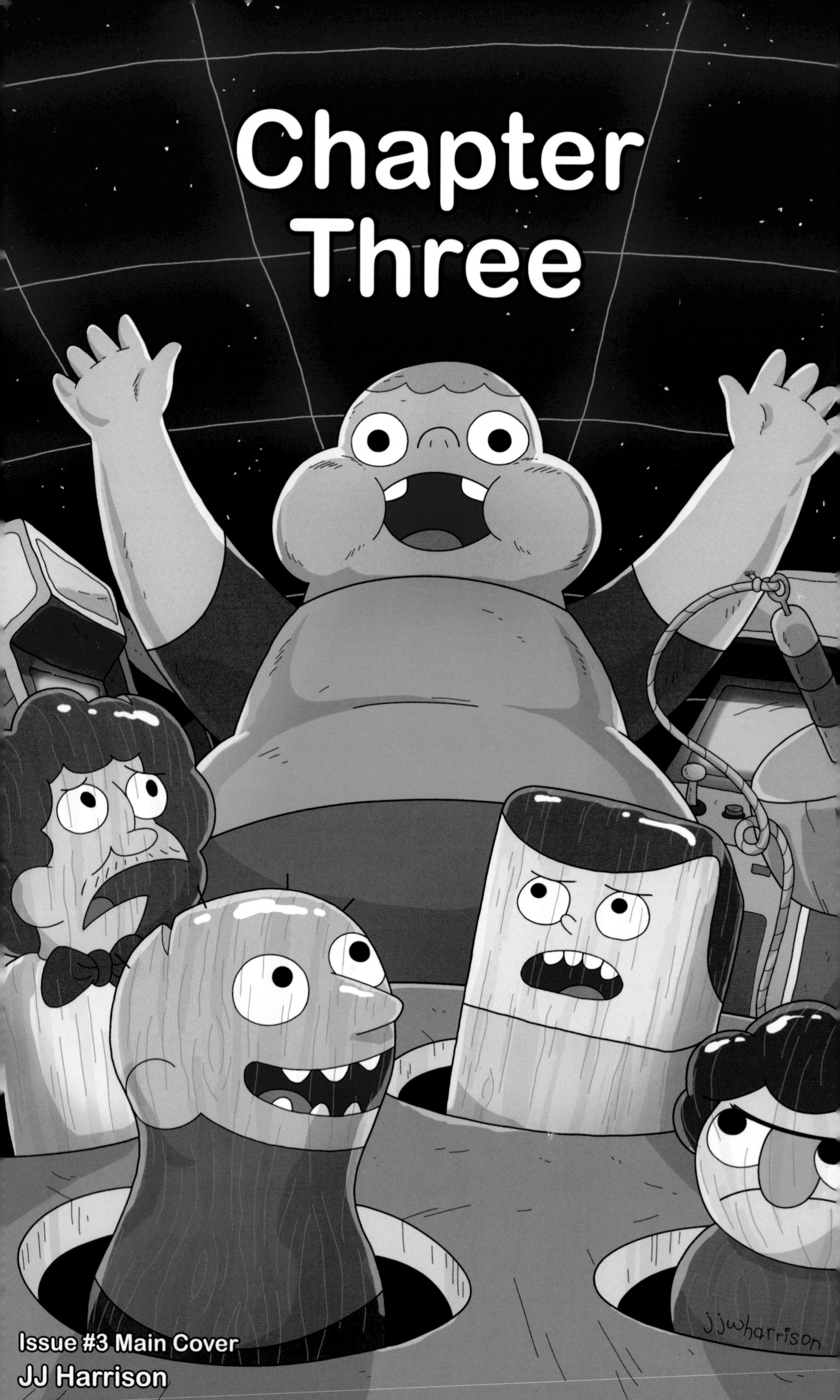
Chapter
Three
jjwharrison

Issue #3 Main Cover
JJ Harrison

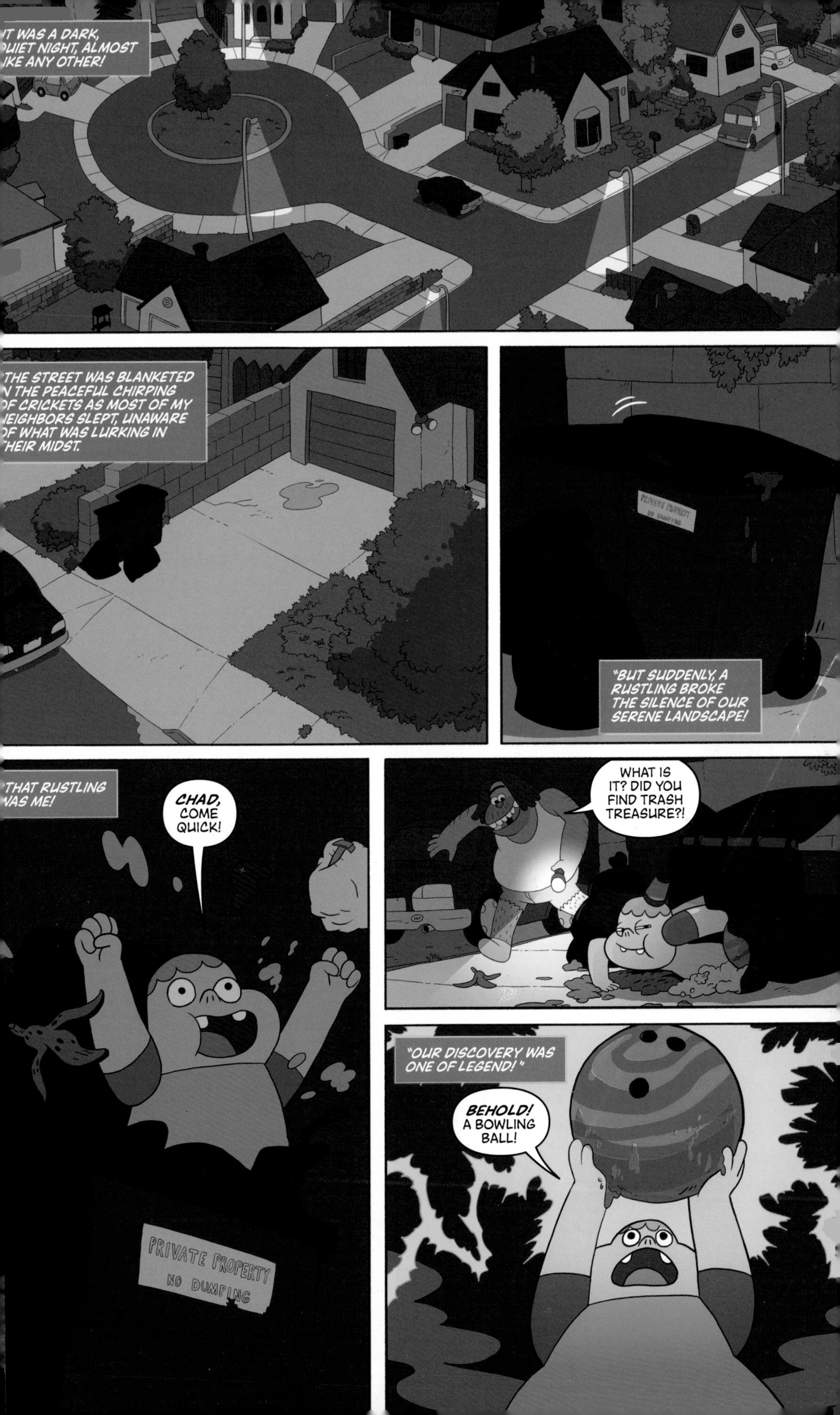
IT WAS A DARK, QUIET NIGHT, ALMOST LIKE ANY OTHER!
THE STREET WAS BLANKETED IN THE PEACEFUL CHIRPING OF CRICKETS AS MOST OF MY NEIGHBORS SLEPT, UNAWARE OF WHAT WAS LURKING IN THEIR MIDST.
PRIVATE PROPERTY NO DUMPING
"BUT SUDDENLY, A RUSTLING BROKE THE SILENCE OF OUR SERENE LANDSCAPE!
THAT RUSTLING WAS ME!
CHAD, COME QUICK!
PRIVATE PROPERTY NO DUMPING
WHAT IS IT? DID YOU FIND TRASH TREASURE?!
"OUR DISCOVERY WAS ONE OF LEGEND!"
BEHOLD! A BOWLING BALL!

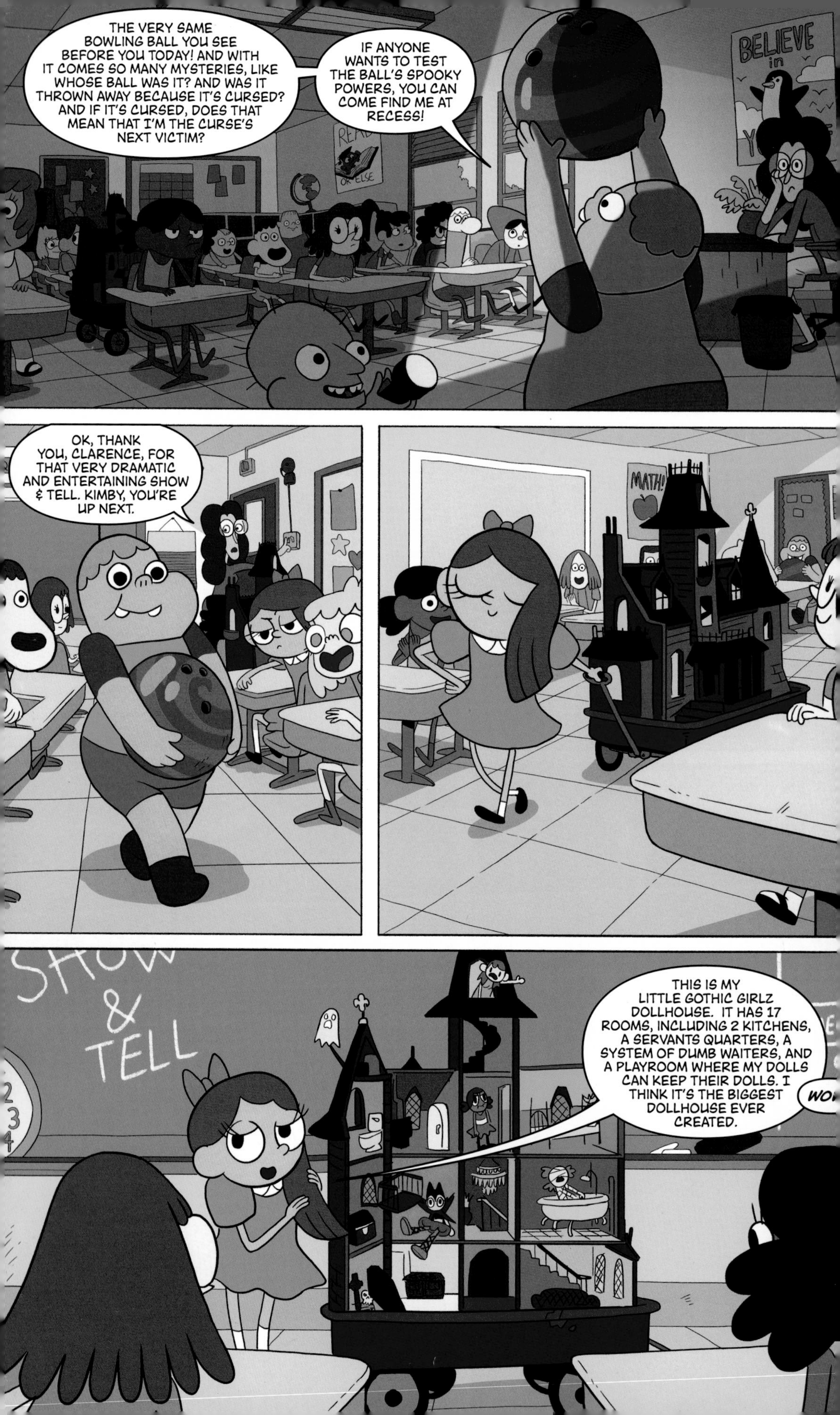
THE VERY SAME BOWLING BALL YOU SEE BEFORE YOU TODAY! AND WITH IT COMES SO MANY MYSTERIES, LIKE WHOSE BALL WAS IT? AND WAS IT THROWN AWAY BECAUSE IT'S CURSED? AND IF IT'S CURSED, DOES THAT MEAN THAT I'M THE CURSE'S NEXT VICTIM?
IF ANYONE WANTS TO TEST THE BALL'S SPOOKY POWERS, YOU CAN COME FIND ME AT RECESS!
BELIEVE in
OK, THANK YOU, CLARENCE, FOR THAT VERY DRAMATIC AND ENTERTAINING SHOW & TELL. KIMBY, YOU'RE UP NEXT.
MATH!
SHOW & TELL
THIS IS MY LITTLE GOTHIC GIRLZ DOLLHOUSE. IT HAS 17 ROOMS, INCLUDING 2 KITCHENS, A SERVANTS QUARTERS, A SYSTEM OF DUMB WAITERS, AND A PLAYROOM WHERE MY DOLLS CAN KEEP THEIR DOLLS. I THINK IT'S THE BIGGEST DOLLHOUSE EVER CREATED.

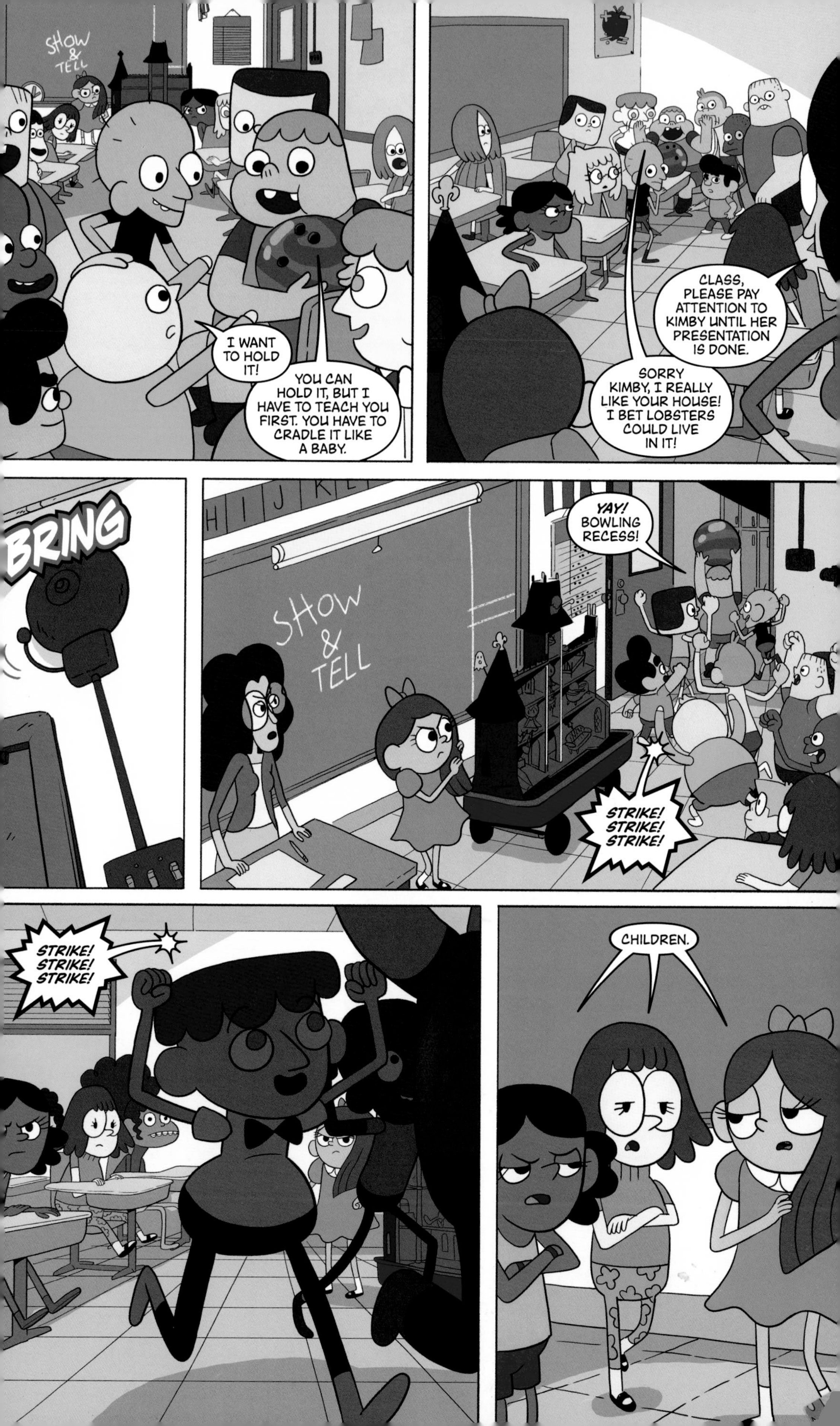
SHOW & TELL
I WANT TO HOLD IT!
YOU CAN HOLD IT, BUT I HAVE TO TEACH YOU FIRST. YOU HAVE TO CRADLE IT LIKE A BABY.
CLASS, PLEASE PAY ATTENTION TO KIMBY UNTIL HER PRESENTATION IS DONE.
SORRY KIMBY, I REALLY LIKE YOUR HOUSE! I BET LOBSTERS COULD LIVE IN IT!
BRING
SHOW & TELL
YAY! BOWLING RECESS!
STRIKE! STRIKE! STRIKE!
STRIKE! STRIKE! STRIKE!
CHILDREN.

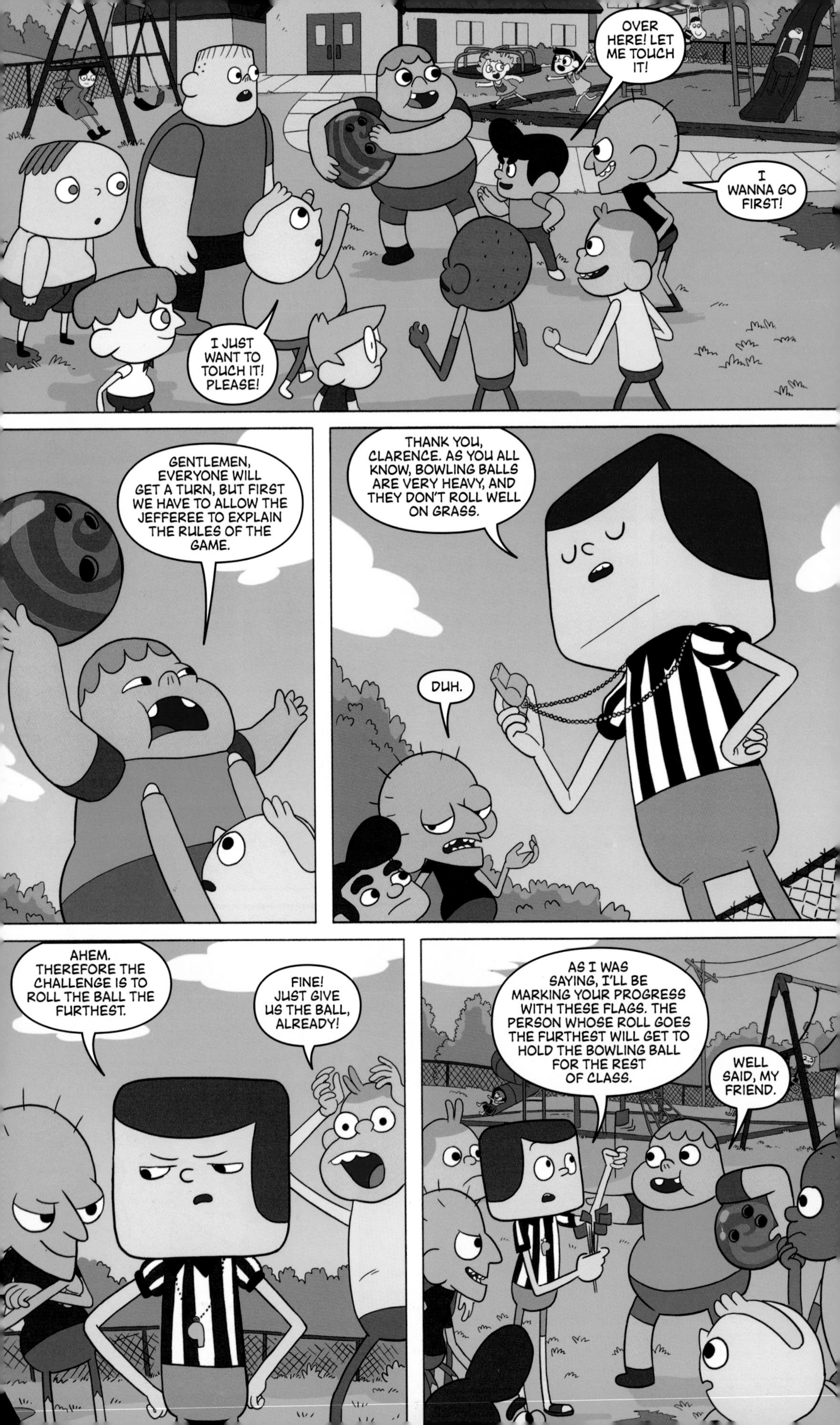
OVER HERE! LET ME TOUCH IT!
I WANNA GO FIRST!
I JUST WANT TO TOUCH IT! PLEASE!
GENTLEMEN, EVERYONE WILL GET A TURN, BUT FIRST WE HAVE TO ALLOW THE JEFFEREE TO EXPLAIN THE RULES OF THE GAME.
THANK YOU, CLARENCE. AS YOU ALL KNOW, BOWLING BALLS ARE VERY HEAVY, AND THEY DON'T ROLL WELL ON GRASS.
DUH.
AHEM. THEREFORE THE CHALLENGE IS TO ROLL THE BALL THE FURTHEST.
FINE! JUST GIVE US THE BALL, ALREADY!
AS I WAS SAYING, I'LL BE MARKING YOUR PROGRESS WITH THESE FLAGS. THE PERSON WHOSE ROLL GOES THE FURTHEST WILL GET TO HOLD THE BOWLING BALL FOR THE REST OF CLASS.
WELL SAID, MY FRIEND.

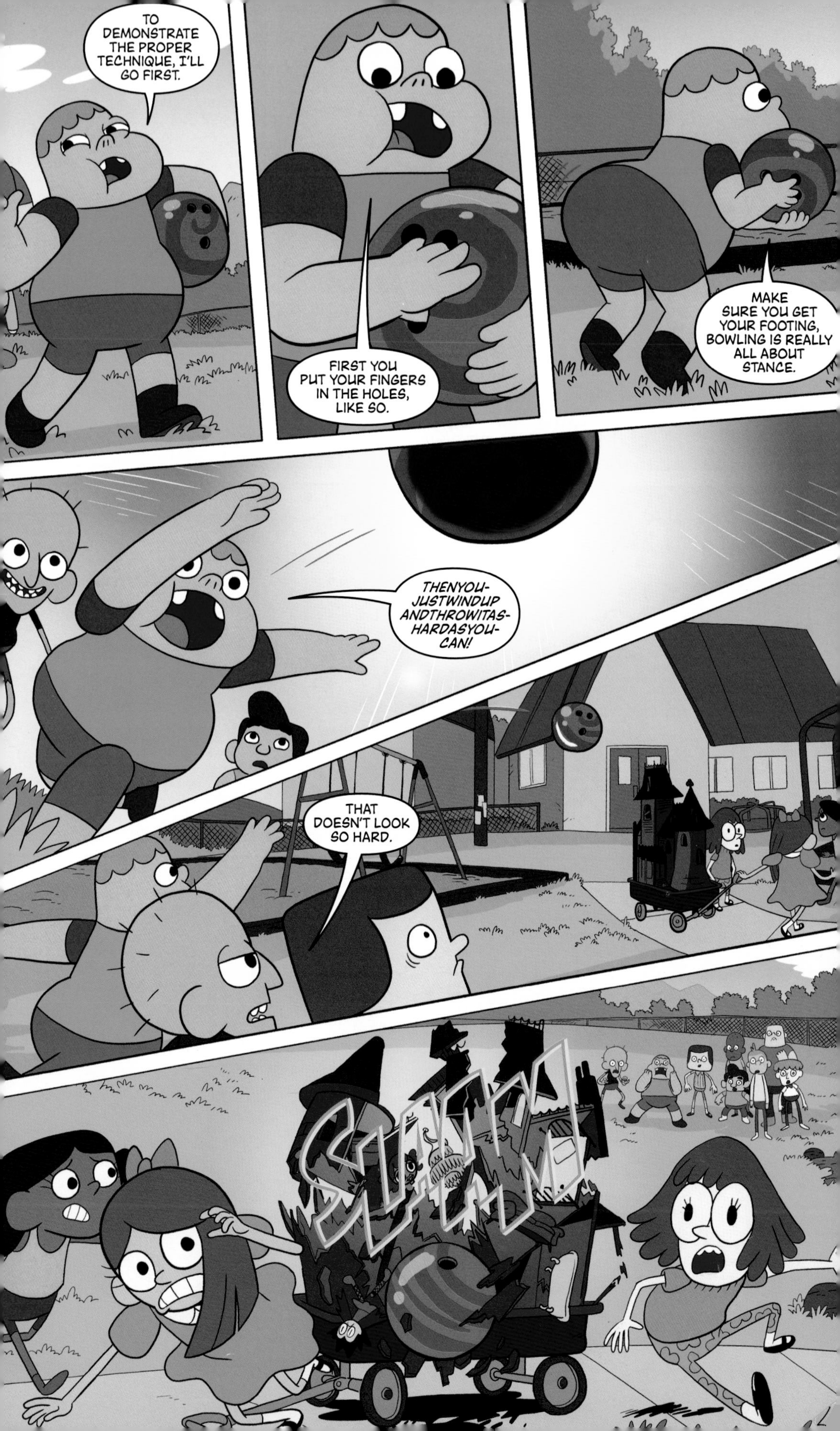
TO DEMONSTRATE THE PROPER TECHNIQUE, I'LL GO FIRST.
FIRST YOU PUT YOUR FINGERS IN THE HOLES, LIKE SO.
MAKE SURE YOU GET YOUR FOOTING, BOWLING IS REALLY ALL ABOUT STANCE.
THENYOU-JUSTWINDUP ANDTHROWITAS-HARDASYOU-CAN!
THAT DOESN'T LOOK SO HARD.
SLAM

OH MY GOSH, KIMBY! ARE YOU GUYS OK?!

WE'RE *FINE*, I THINK. BUT THE DOLLHOUSE IS *DESTROYED*.

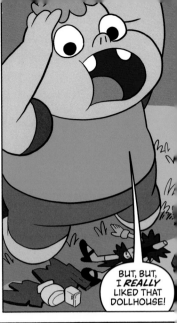

BUT, BUT, I *REALLY* LIKED THAT DOLLHOUSE!

NOooooOOOO.

KIMBY, I AM *SO SORRY*. I GUESS I'M SUPER STRONG AND I DIDN'T EVEN KNOW IT!

I PROMISE THAT I WILL MAKE IT UP TO YOU, AND IN THE FUTURE I'LL ON USE MY INCREDIBL PHYSICAL PROWESS *PROTECT*, NOT DESTROY!

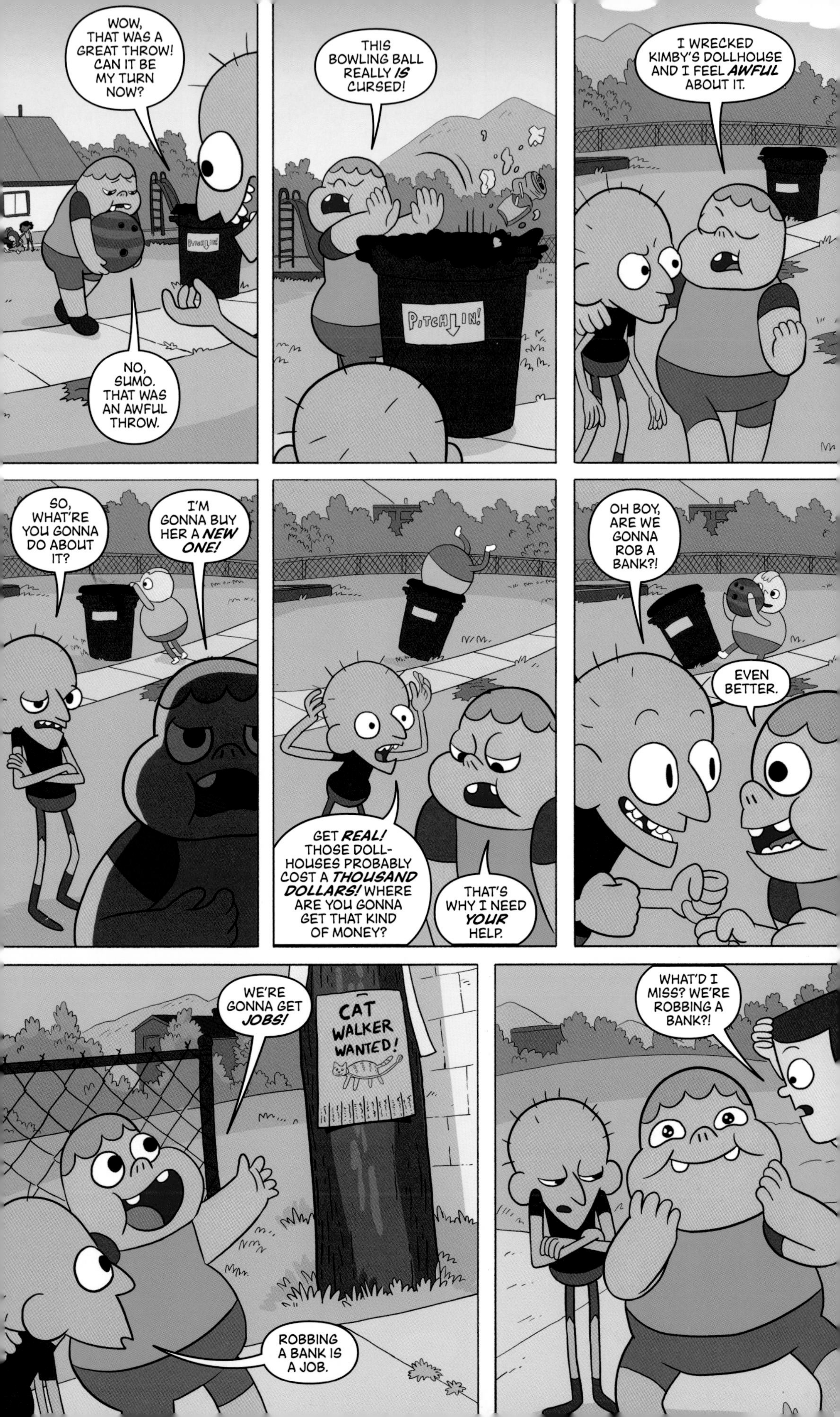
WOW, THAT WAS A GREAT THROW! CAN IT BE MY TURN NOW?
NO, SUMO. THAT WAS AN AWFUL THROW.
PITCH IN!
THIS BOWLING BALL REALLY IS CURSED!
PITCH IN!
I WRECKED KIMBY'S DOLLHOUSE AND I FEEL AWFUL ABOUT IT.
SO, WHAT'RE YOU GONNA DO ABOUT IT?
I'M GONNA BUY HER A NEW ONE!
GET REAL! THOSE DOLL-HOUSES PROBABLY COST A THOUSAND DOLLARS! WHERE ARE YOU GONNA GET THAT KIND OF MONEY?
THAT'S WHY I NEED YOUR HELP.
OH BOY, ARE WE GONNA ROB A BANK?!
EVEN BETTER.
WE'RE GONNA GET JOBS!
CAT WALKER WANTED!
ROBBING A BANK IS A JOB.
WHAT'D I MISS? WE'RE ROBBING A BANK?!

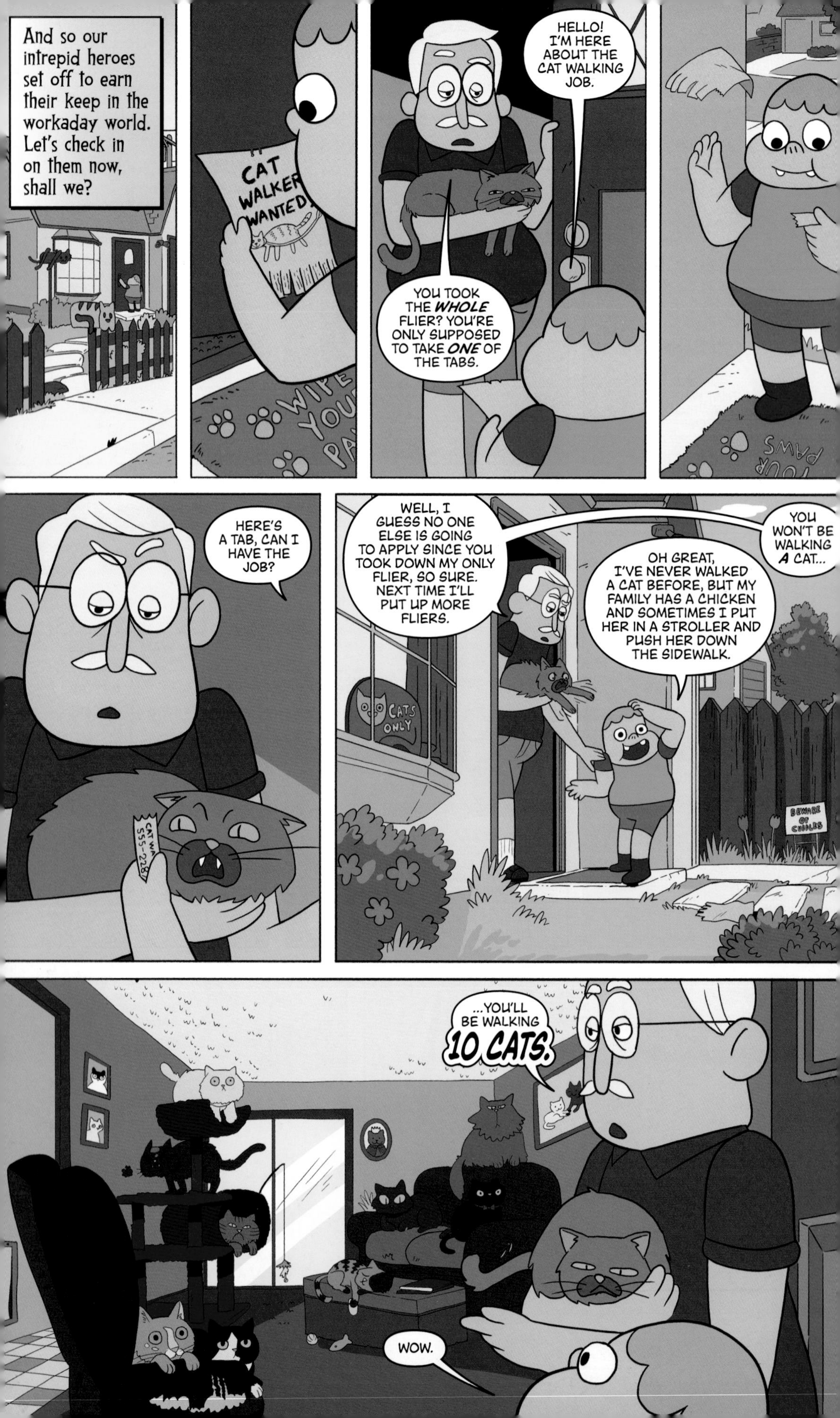

And so our intrepid heroes set off to earn their keep in the workaday world. Let's check in on them now, shall we?
CAT WALKER WANTED!
HELLO! I'M HERE ABOUT THE CAT WALKING JOB.
YOU TOOK THE WHOLE FLIER? YOU'RE ONLY SUPPOSED TO TAKE ONE OF THE TABS.
HERE'S A TAB, CAN I HAVE THE JOB?
WELL, I GUESS NO ONE ELSE IS GOING TO APPLY SINCE YOU TOOK DOWN MY ONLY FLIER, SO SURE. NEXT TIME I'LL PUT UP MORE FLIERS.
OH GREAT, I'VE NEVER WALKED A CAT BEFORE, BUT MY FAMILY HAS A CHICKEN AND SOMETIMES I PUT HER IN A STROLLER AND PUSH HER DOWN THE SIDEWALK.
YOU WON'T BE WALKING A CAT...
CATS ONLY
...YOU'LL BE WALKING 10 CATS.
WOW.

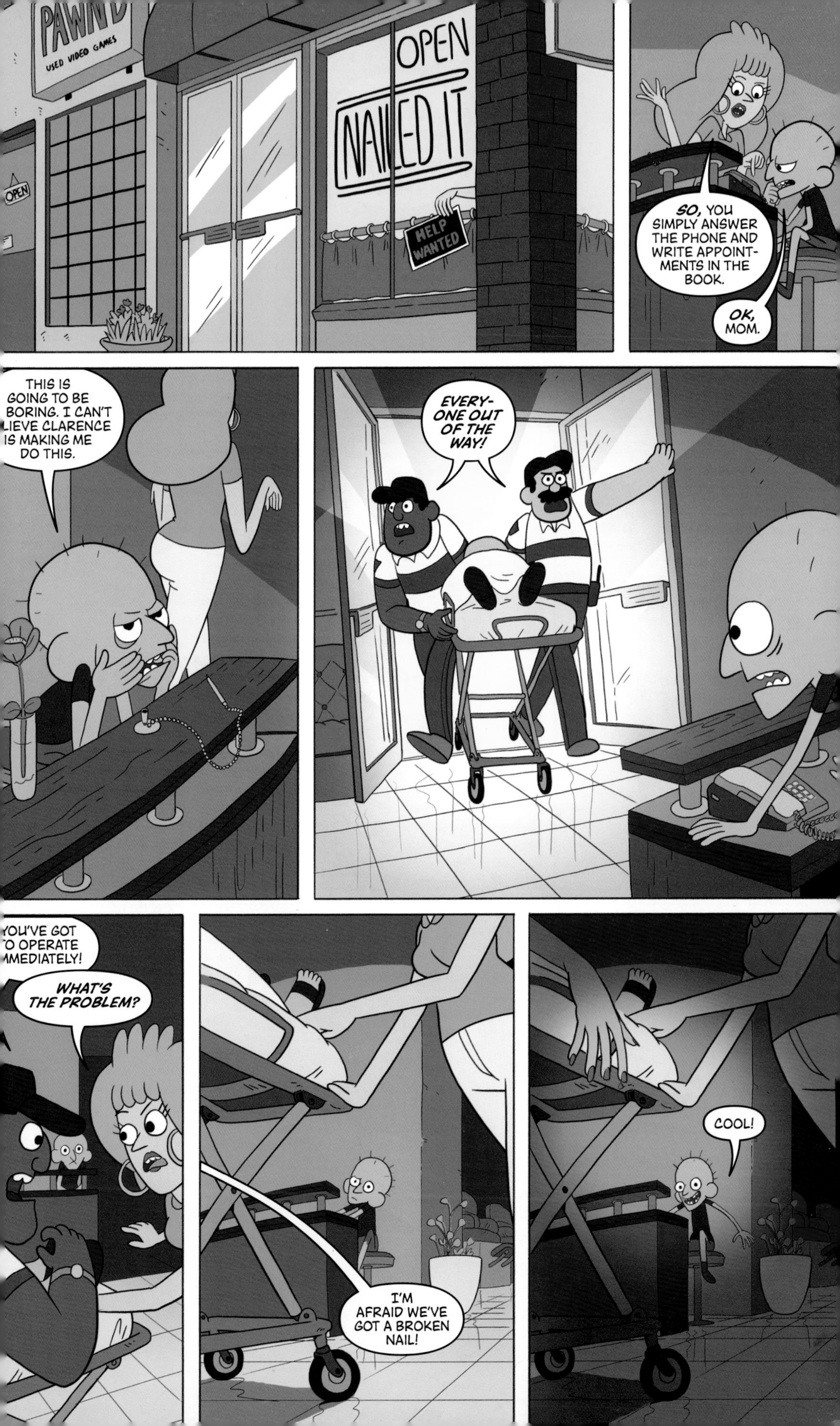
PAWN'D
USED VIDEO GAMES
OPEN
OPEN
NAILED IT
HELP WANTED
SO, YOU SIMPLY ANSWER THE PHONE AND WRITE APPOINT-MENTS IN THE BOOK.
OK, MOM.
THIS IS GOING TO BE BORING. I CAN'T LIEVE CLARENCE IS MAKING ME DO THIS.
EVERY-ONE OUT OF THE WAY!
YOU'VE GOT TO OPERATE MMEDIATELY!
WHAT'S THE PROBLEM?
I'M AFRAID WE'VE GOT A BROKEN NAIL!
COOL!

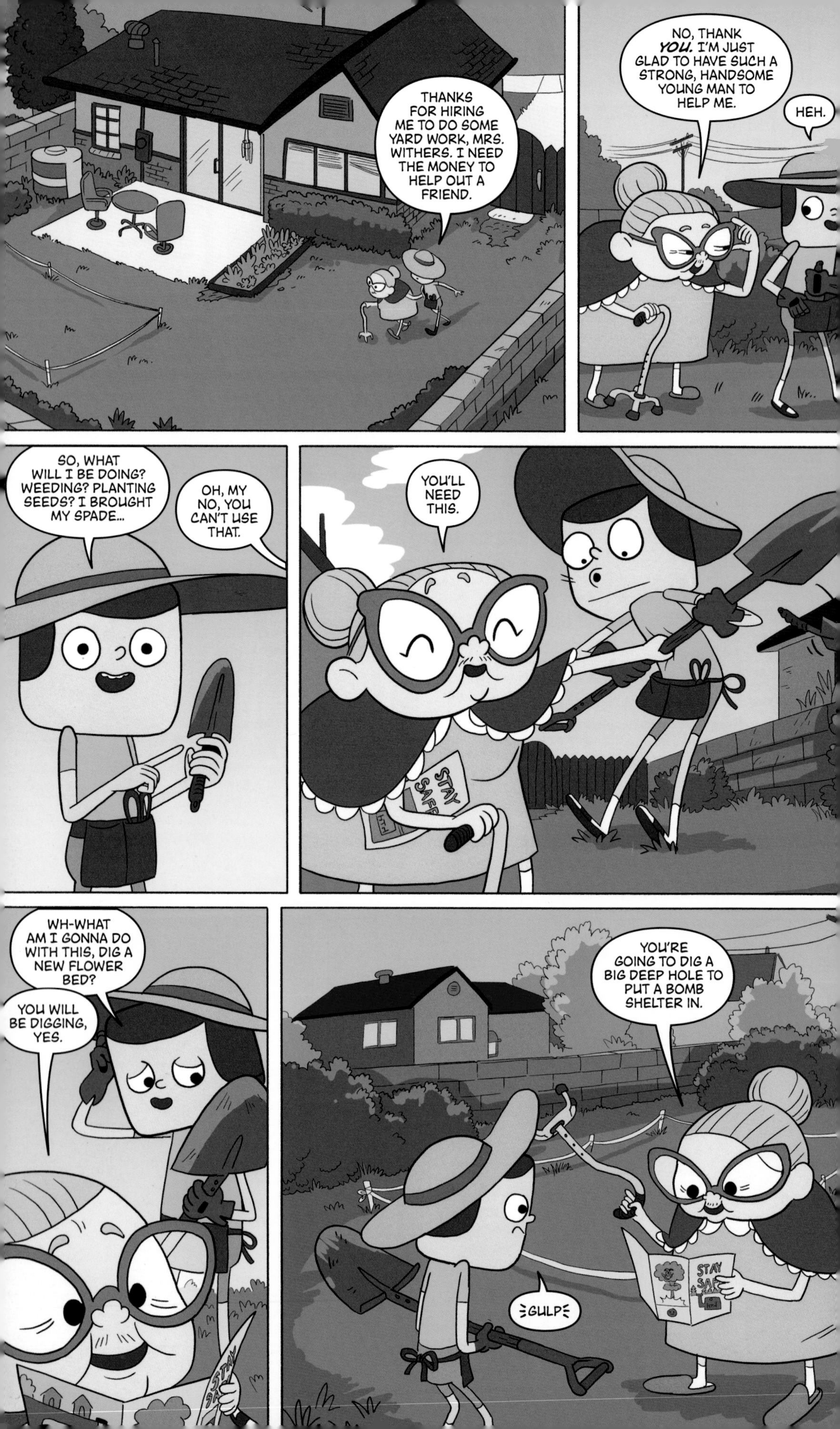
THANKS FOR HIRING ME TO DO SOME YARD WORK, MRS. WITHERS. I NEED THE MONEY TO HELP OUT A FRIEND.
NO, THANK *YOU.* I'M JUST GLAD TO HAVE SUCH A STRONG, HANDSOME YOUNG MAN TO HELP ME.
HEH.
SO, WHAT WILL I BE DOING? WEEDING? PLANTING SEEDS? I BROUGHT MY SPADE...
OH, MY NO, YOU CAN'T USE THAT.
YOU'LL NEED THIS.
STAY SAFE
WH-WHAT AM I GONNA DO WITH THIS, DIG A NEW FLOWER BED?
YOU WILL BE DIGGING, YES.
YOU'RE GOING TO DIG A BIG DEEP HOLE TO PUT A BOMB SHELTER IN.
GULP
STAY SAFE

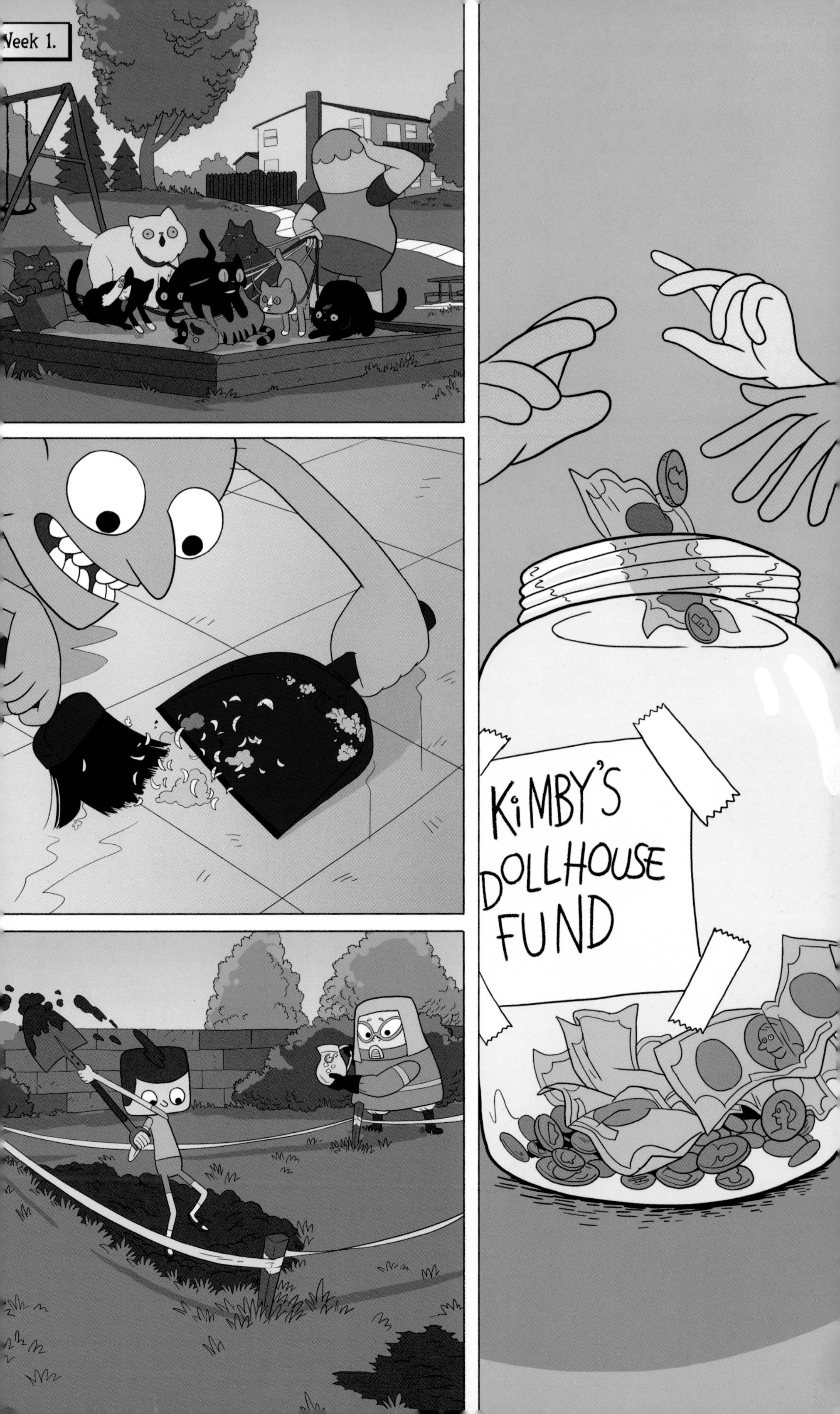
Week 1.
KiMBY'S DOLLHOUSE FUND

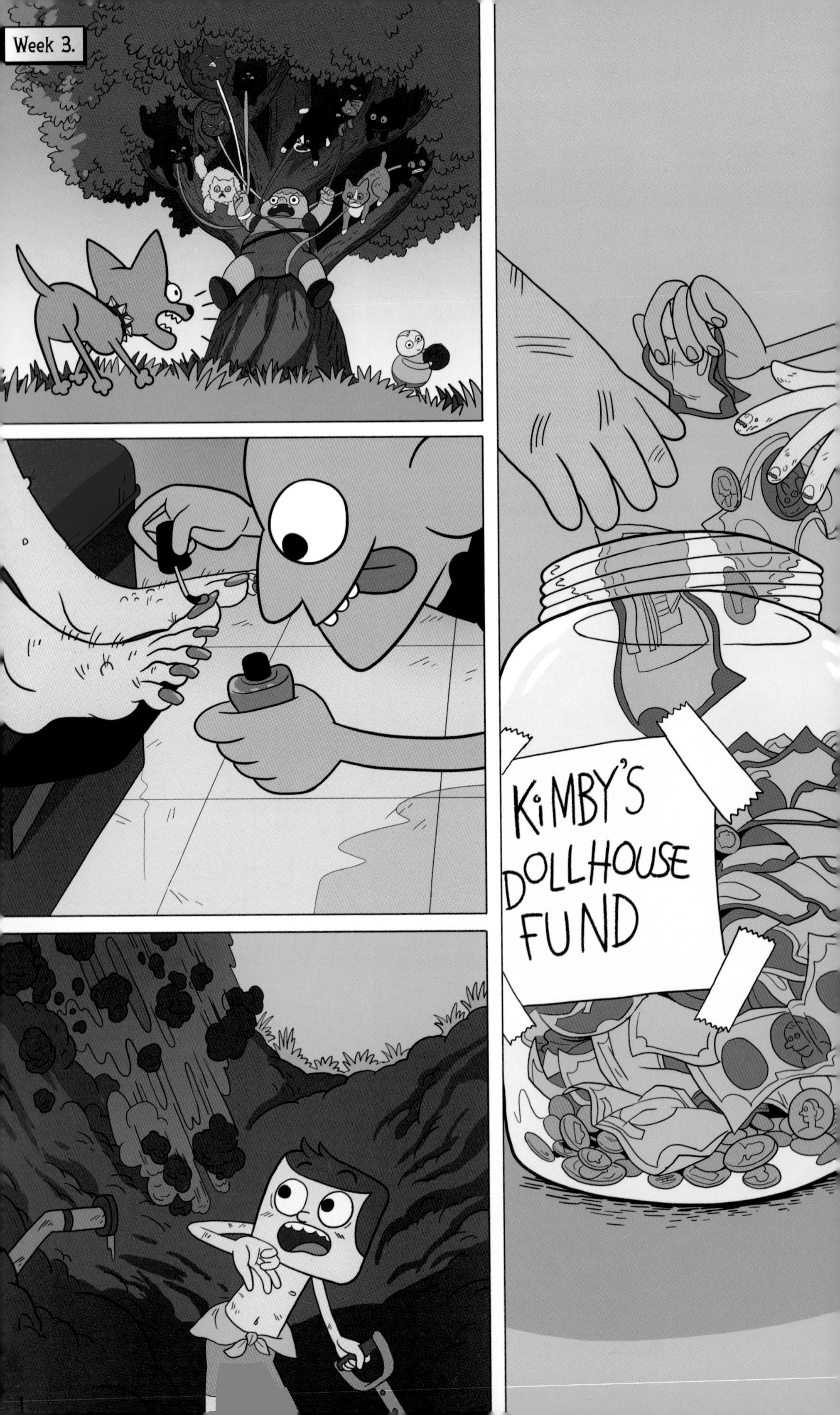
Week 3.
KiMBY'S
DOLLHOUSE
FUND

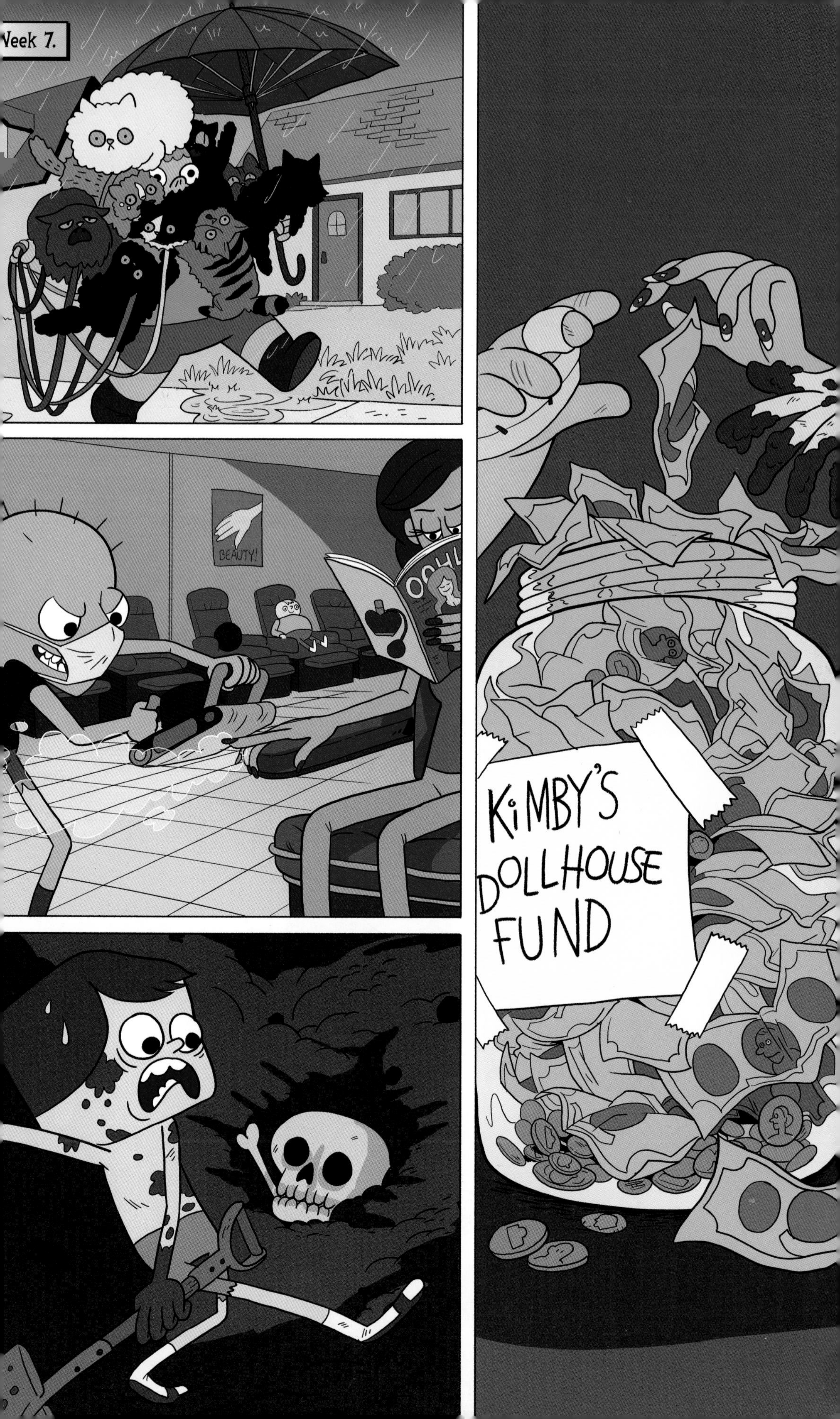
Week 7.
BEAUTY!
OOHL
KiMBY'S
DOLLHOUSE
FUND

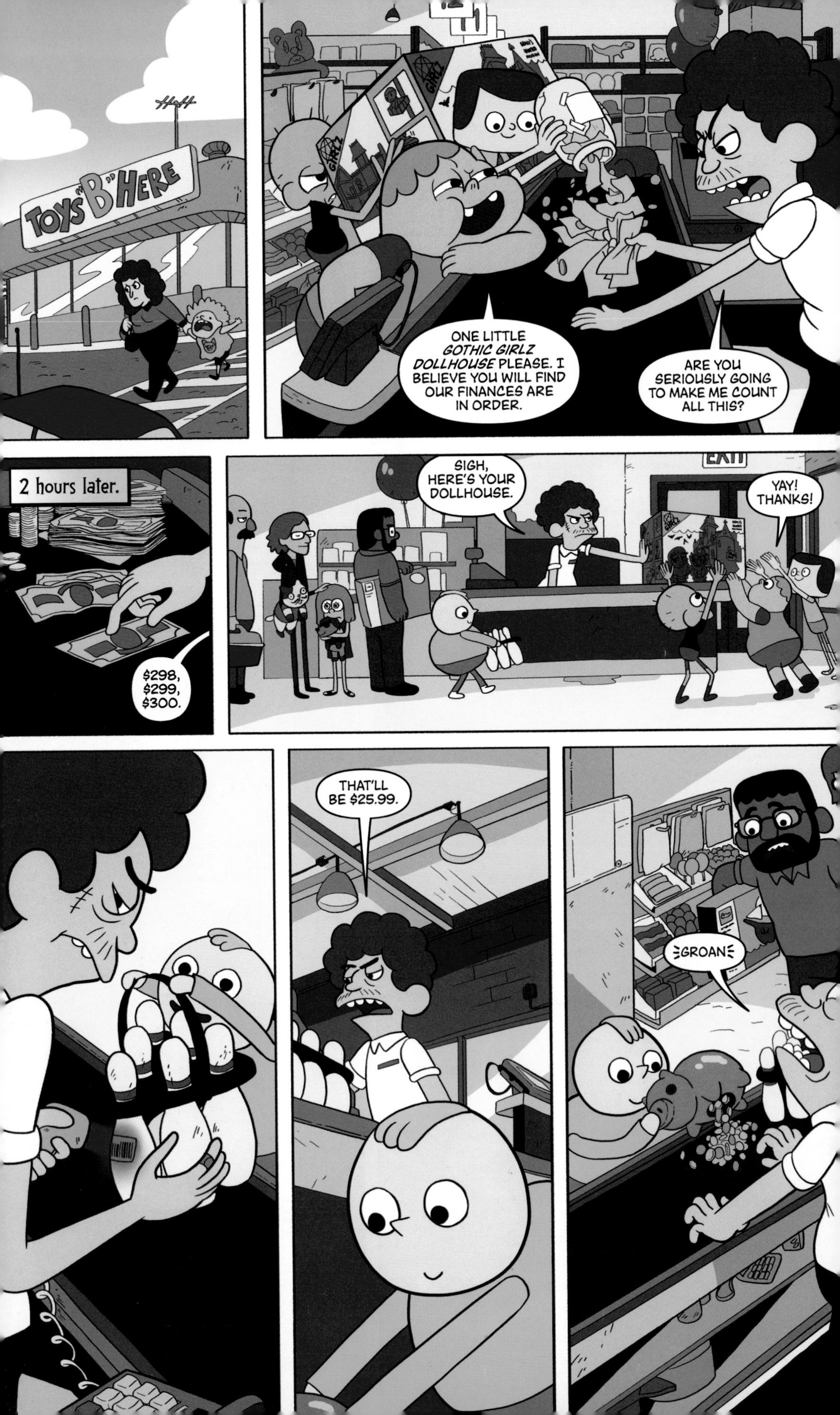
TOYS "B" HERE
ONE LITTLE *GOTHIC GIRLZ DOLLHOUSE* PLEASE. I BELIEVE YOU WILL FIND OUR FINANCES ARE IN ORDER.
ARE YOU SERIOUSLY GOING TO MAKE ME COUNT ALL THIS?
2 hours later.
$298, $299, $300.
SIGH, HERE'S YOUR DOLLHOUSE.
YAY! THANKS!
EXIT
THAT'LL BE $25.99.
GROAN

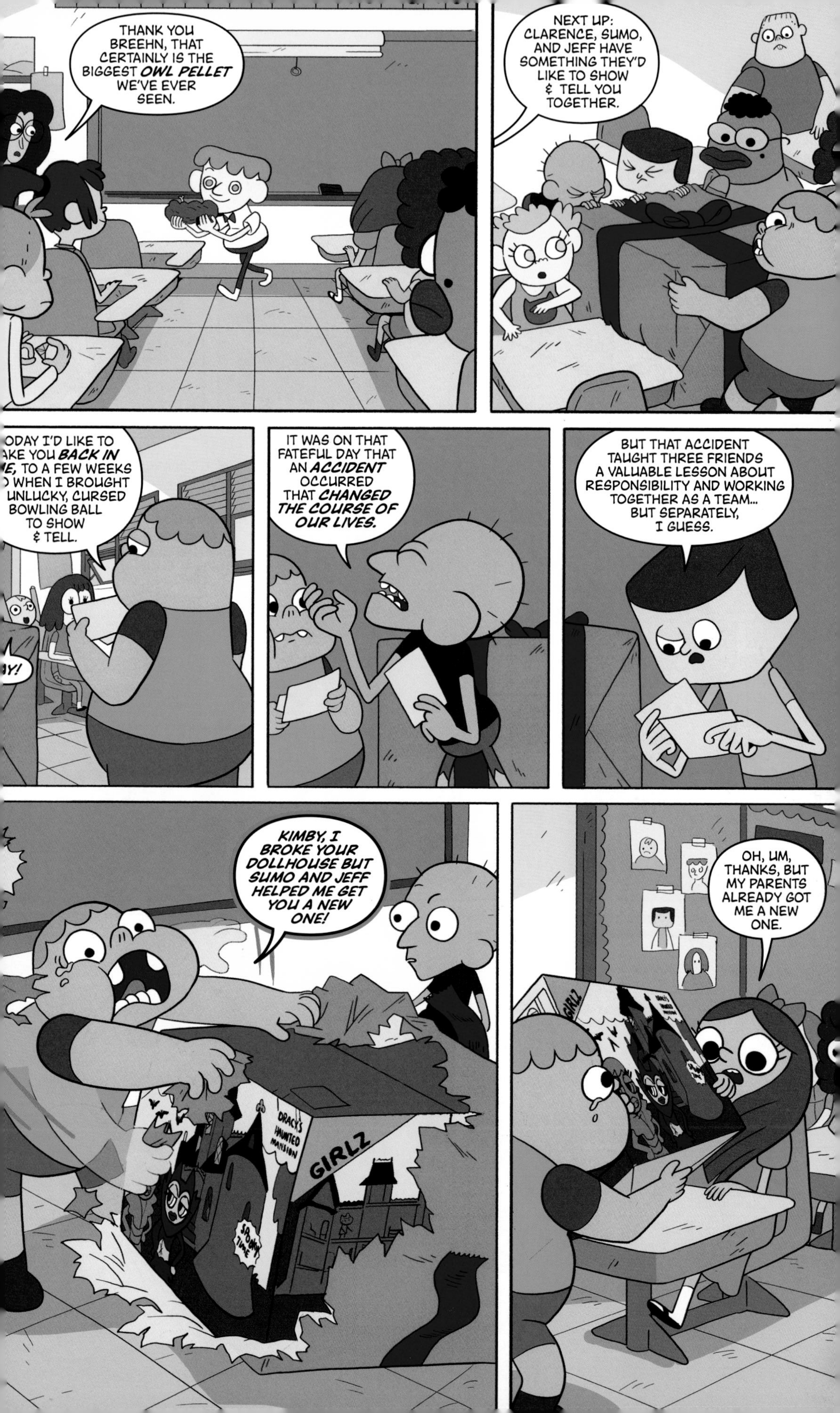
THANK YOU BREEHN, THAT CERTAINLY IS THE BIGGEST OWL PELLET WE'VE EVER SEEN.
NEXT UP: CLARENCE, SUMO, AND JEFF HAVE SOMETHING THEY'D LIKE TO SHOW & TELL YOU TOGETHER.
ODAY I'D LIKE TO AKE YOU BACK IN E, TO A FEW WEEKS WHEN I BROUGHT UNLUCKY, CURSED BOWLING BALL TO SHOW & TELL.
AY!
IT WAS ON THAT FATEFUL DAY THAT AN ACCIDENT OCCURRED THAT CHANGED THE COURSE OF OUR LIVES.
BUT THAT ACCIDENT TAUGHT THREE FRIENDS A VALUABLE LESSON ABOUT RESPONSIBILITY AND WORKING TOGETHER AS A TEAM... BUT SEPARATELY, I GUESS.
KIMBY, I BROKE YOUR DOLLHOUSE BUT SUMO AND JEFF HELPED ME GET YOU A NEW ONE!
DRACY'S HAUNTED MANSION
GIRLZ
OH, UM, THANKS, BUT MY PARENTS ALREADY GOT ME A NEW ONE.

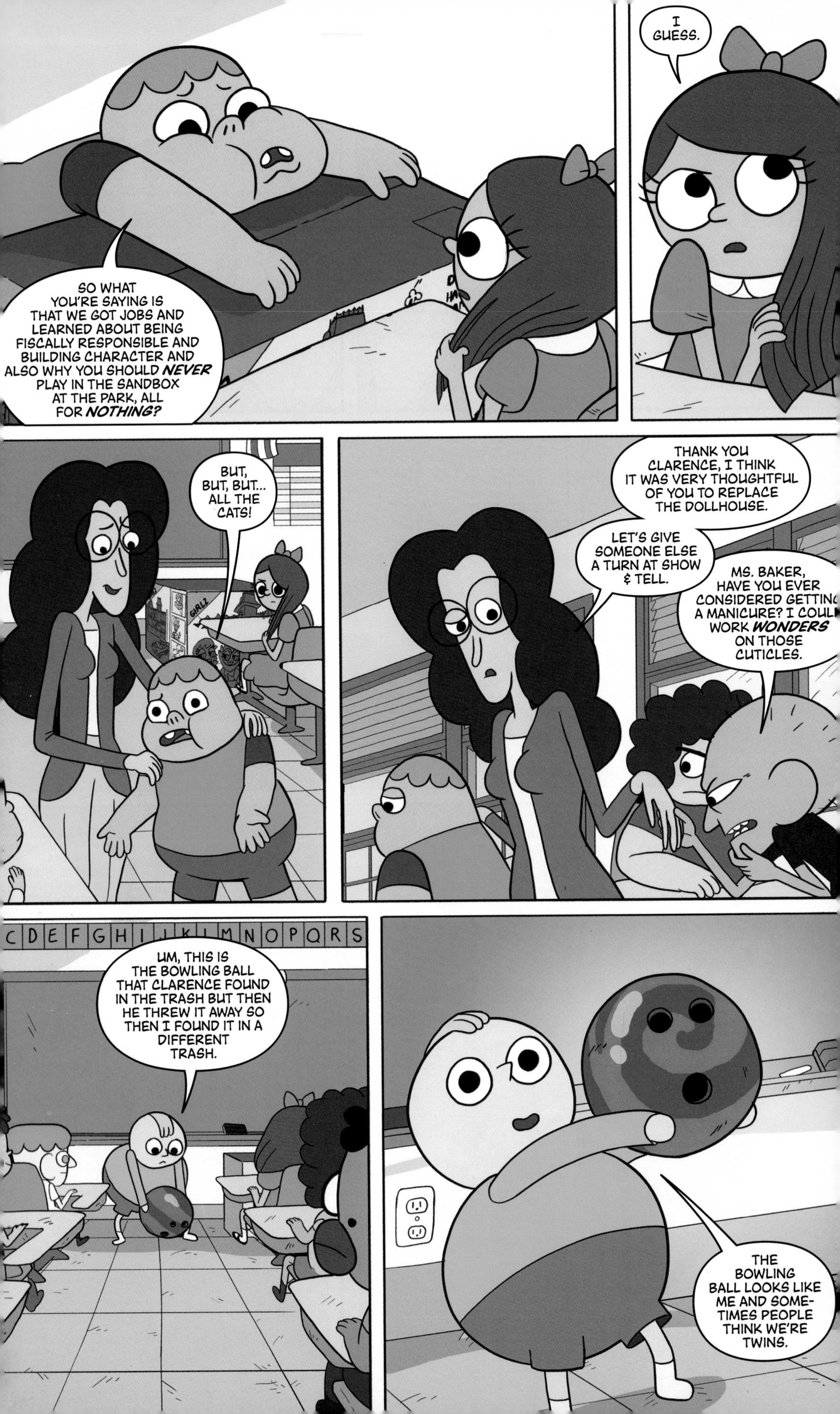
SO WHAT YOU'RE SAYING IS THAT WE GOT JOBS AND LEARNED ABOUT BEING FISCALLY RESPONSIBLE AND BUILDING CHARACTER AND ALSO WHY YOU SHOULD *NEVER* PLAY IN THE SANDBOX AT THE PARK, ALL FOR *NOTHING?*
I GUESS.
BUT, BUT, BUT... ALL THE CATS!
THANK YOU CLARENCE, I THINK IT WAS VERY THOUGHTFUL OF YOU TO REPLACE THE DOLLHOUSE.
LET'S GIVE SOMEONE ELSE A TURN AT SHOW & TELL.
MS. BAKER, HAVE YOU EVER CONSIDERED GETTING A MANICURE? I COULD WORK *WONDERS* ON THOSE CUTICLES.
UM, THIS IS THE BOWLING BALL THAT CLARENCE FOUND IN THE TRASH BUT THEN HE THREW IT AWAY SO THEN I FOUND IT IN A DIFFERENT TRASH.
THE BOWLING BALL LOOKS LIKE ME AND SOME-TIMES PEOPLE THINK WE'RE TWINS.

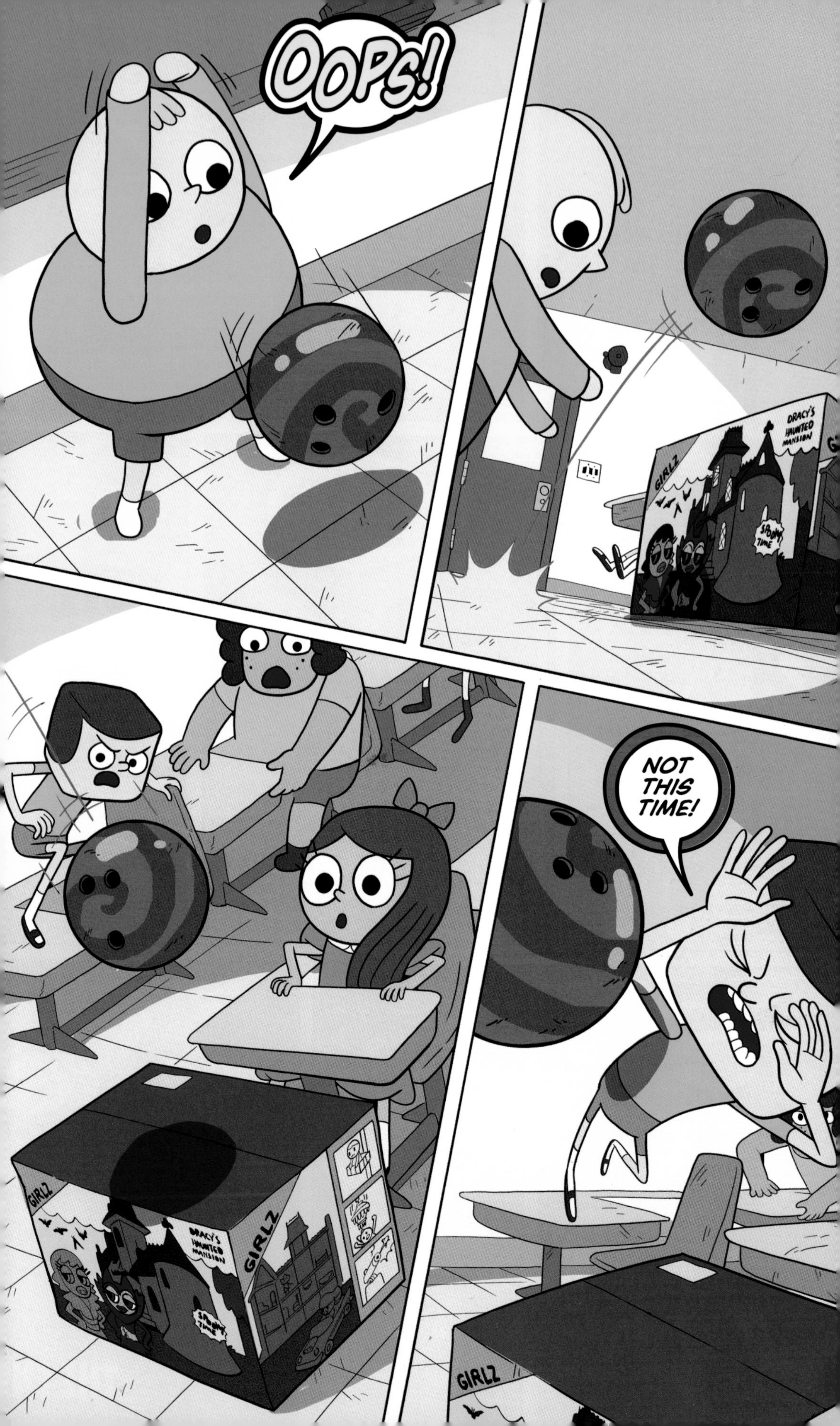
OOPS!
DRACY'S HAUNTED MANSION
GIRLZ
SPOOKY TIME
NOT THIS TIME!

I KNEW THIS HOUSE IS *PERFECT* FOR LOBSTERS.

HOW ARE YOU FEELING, JEFF? THAT WAS REALLY HEROIC, HOW YOU SAVED THE DOLLHOUSE LIKE THAT.

HEH, WELL, BROKE MY ARM, BUT IT WAS BETTER THAN HAVING ALL MY HARD WORK WITH MRS. WITHERS GO TO WASTE.

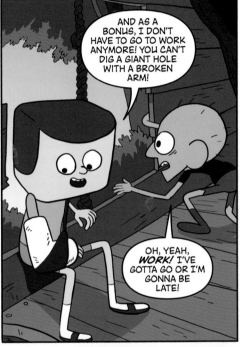

AND AS A BONUS, I DON'T HAVE TO GO TO WORK ANYMORE! YOU CAN'T DIG A GIANT HOLE WITH A BROKEN ARM!

OH, YEAH, *WORK!* I'VE GOTTA GO OR I'M GONNA BE LATE!

BUT YOU CAN QUIT YOUR JOB NOW, WE DON'T NEED MONEY ANYMORE. STAY AND PLAY WITH *US!*

QUIT THE NAIL SALON? NO WAY! I GET TO SEE THE *GROSSEST* THINGS THERE!

WELL, I GUESS IT'S JUST YOU AND ME, THEN.

YOU QUIT YOUR JOB?

YEP. I HOPE I NEVER SEE ANOTHER CAT AS LONG AS I LIVE.

MEOW.

MEOW.

OH, YOU! HAHA.

THE EN

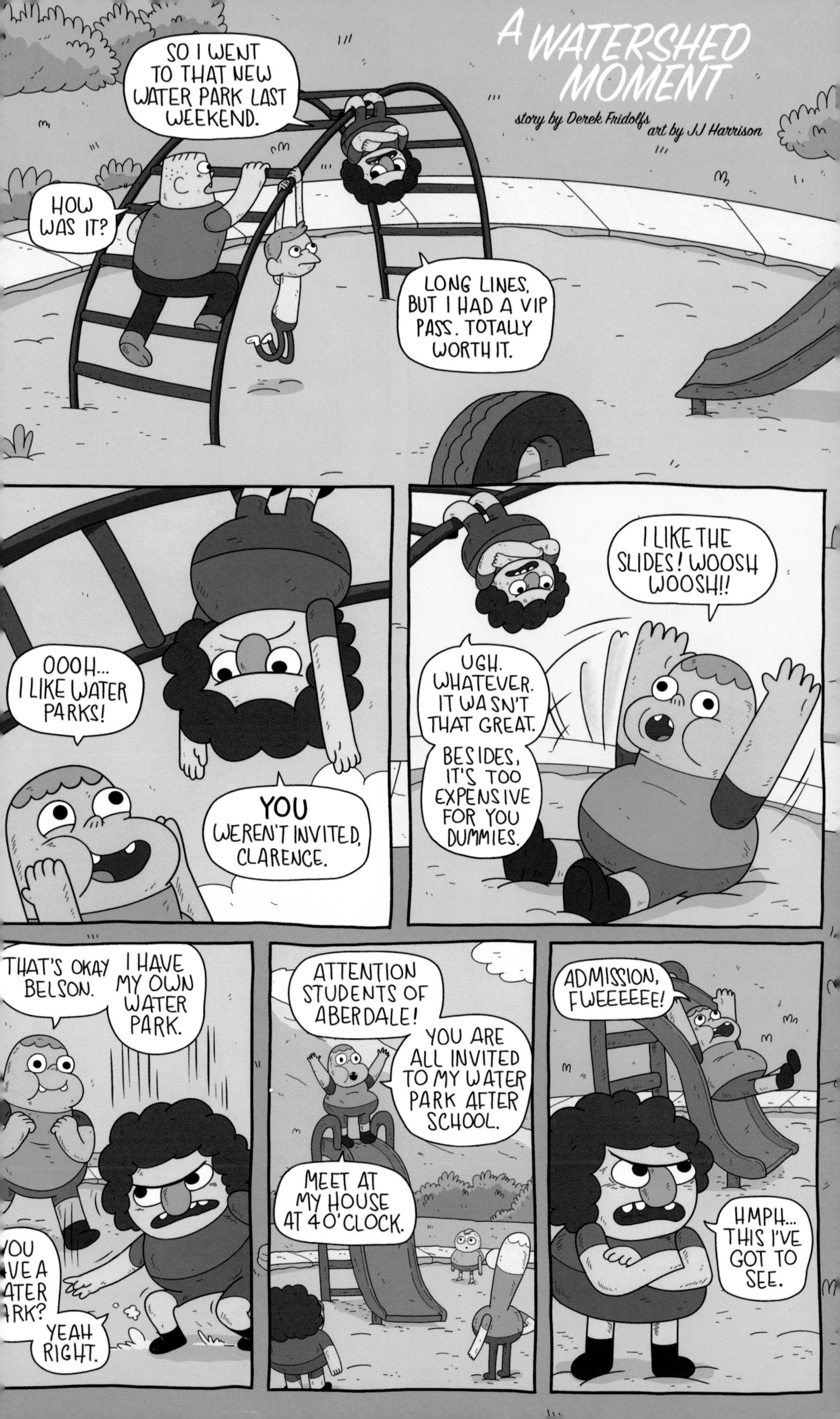
A WATERSHED MOMENT
story by Derek Fridolfs art by JJ Harrison
SO I WENT TO THAT NEW WATER PARK LAST WEEKEND.
HOW WAS IT?
LONG LINES, BUT I HAD A VIP PASS. TOTALLY WORTH IT.
OOOH... I LIKE WATER PARKS!
YOU WEREN'T INVITED, CLARENCE.
I LIKE THE SLIDES! WOOSH WOOSH!!
UGH. WHATEVER. IT WASN'T THAT GREAT.
BESIDES, IT'S TOO EXPENSIVE FOR YOU DUMMIES.
THAT'S OKAY BELSON.
I HAVE MY OWN WATER PARK.
YEAH RIGHT.
ATTENTION STUDENTS OF ABERDALE!
YOU ARE ALL INVITED TO MY WATER PARK AFTER SCHOOL.
MEET AT MY HOUSE AT 4 O'CLOCK.
ADMISSION, FWEEEEEE!
HMPH... THIS I'VE GOT TO SEE.

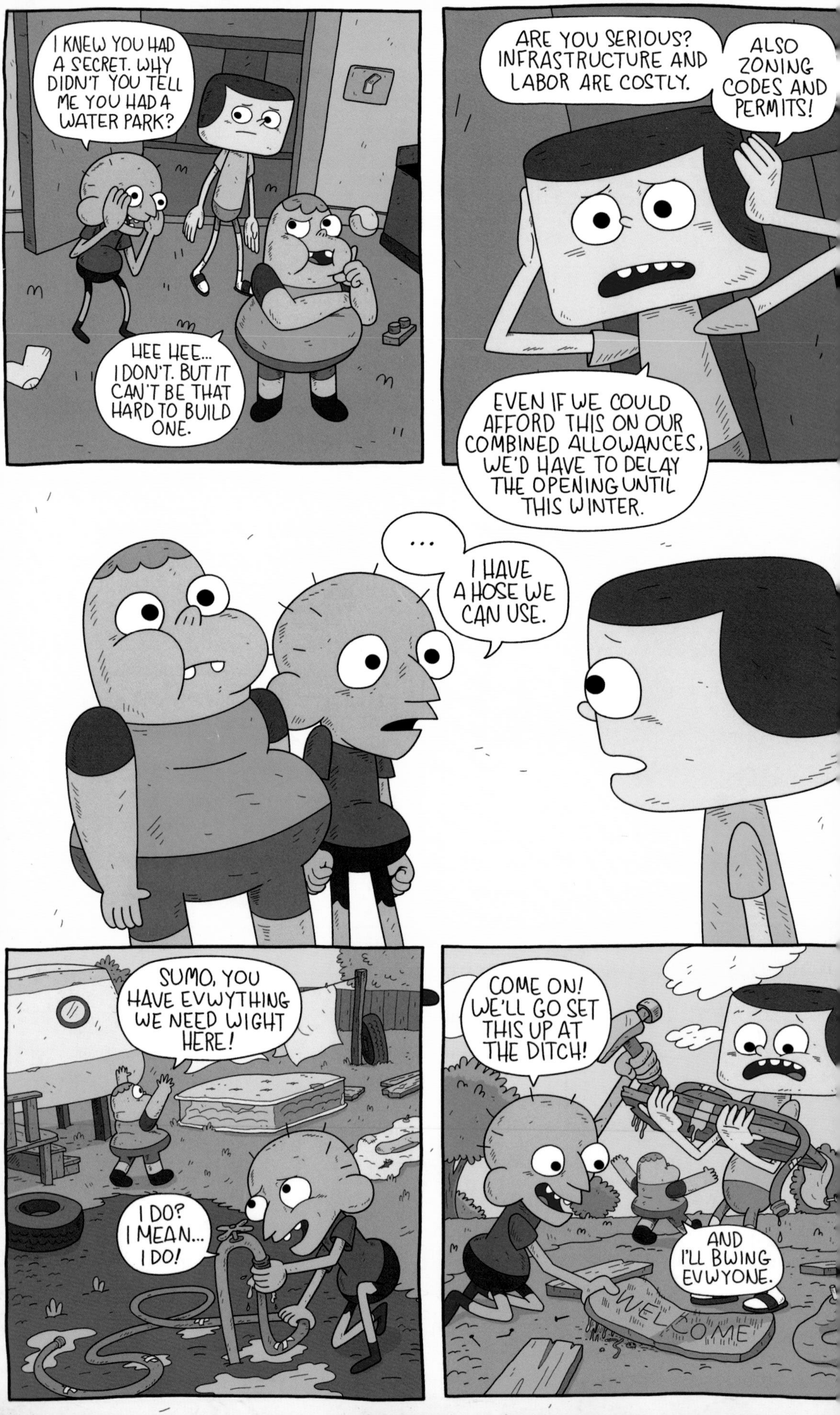
I KNEW YOU HAD A SECRET. WHY DIDN'T YOU TELL ME YOU HAD A WATER PARK?
HEE HEE... I DON'T. BUT IT CAN'T BE THAT HARD TO BUILD ONE.
ARE YOU SERIOUS? INFRASTRUCTURE AND LABOR ARE COSTLY.
ALSO ZONING CODES AND PERMITS!
EVEN IF WE COULD AFFORD THIS ON OUR COMBINED ALLOWANCES, WE'D HAVE TO DELAY THE OPENING UNTIL THIS WINTER.
...
I HAVE A HOSE WE CAN USE.
SUMO, YOU HAVE EVWYTHING WE NEED WIGHT HERE!
I DO? I MEAN... I DO!
COME ON! WE'LL GO SET THIS UP AT THE DITCH!
AND I'LL BWING EVWYONE.
WELCOME

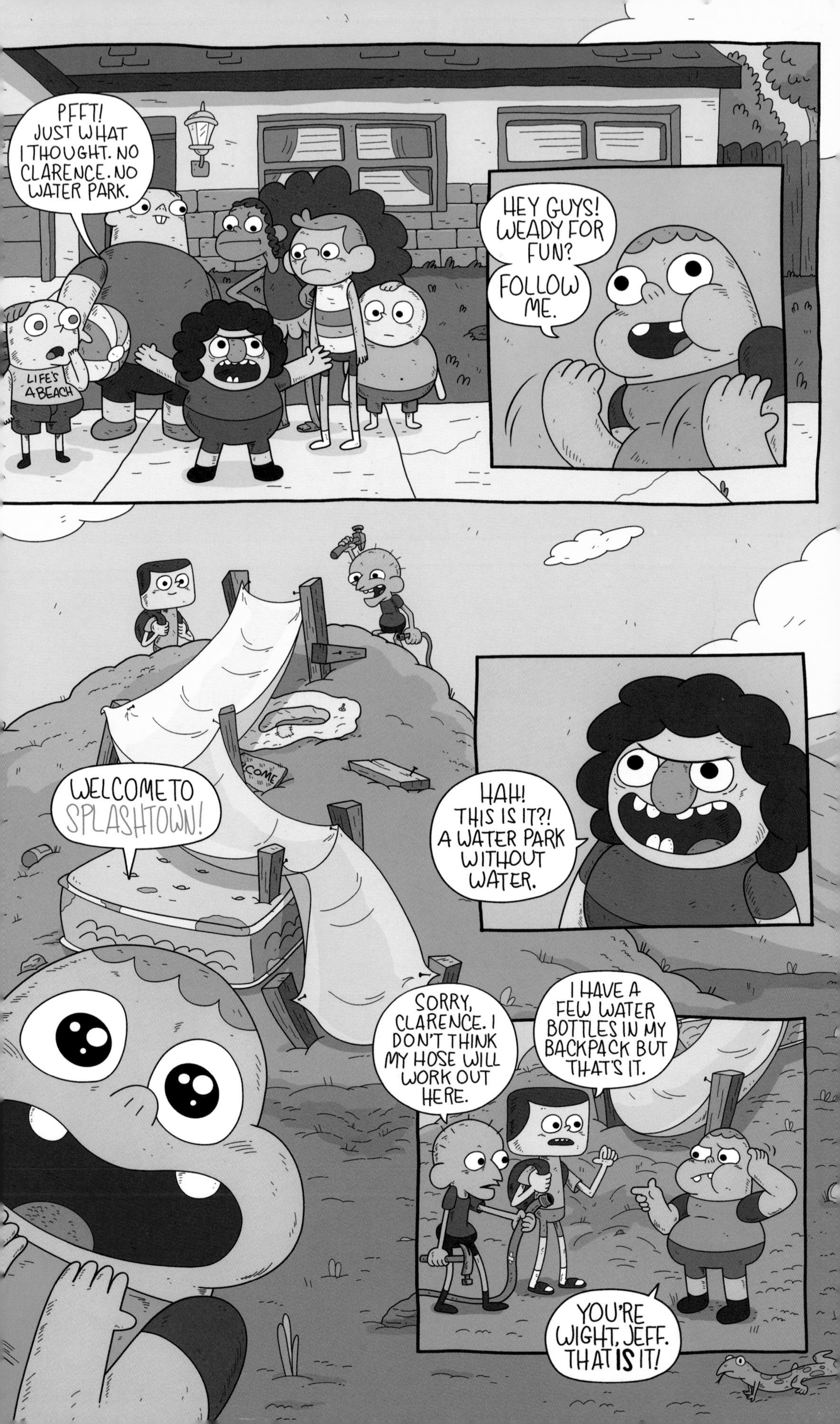
PFFT! JUST WHAT I THOUGHT. NO CLARENCE. NO WATER PARK.
LIFE'S A BEACH
HEY GUYS! WEADY FOR FUN?
FOLLOW ME.
WELCOME TO SPLASHTOWN!
HAH! THIS IS IT?! A WATER PARK WITHOUT WATER.
SORRY, CLARENCE. I DON'T THINK MY HOSE WILL WORK OUT HERE.
I HAVE A FEW WATER BOTTLES IN MY BACKPACK BUT THAT'S IT.
YOU'RE WIGHT, JEFF. THAT **IS** IT!

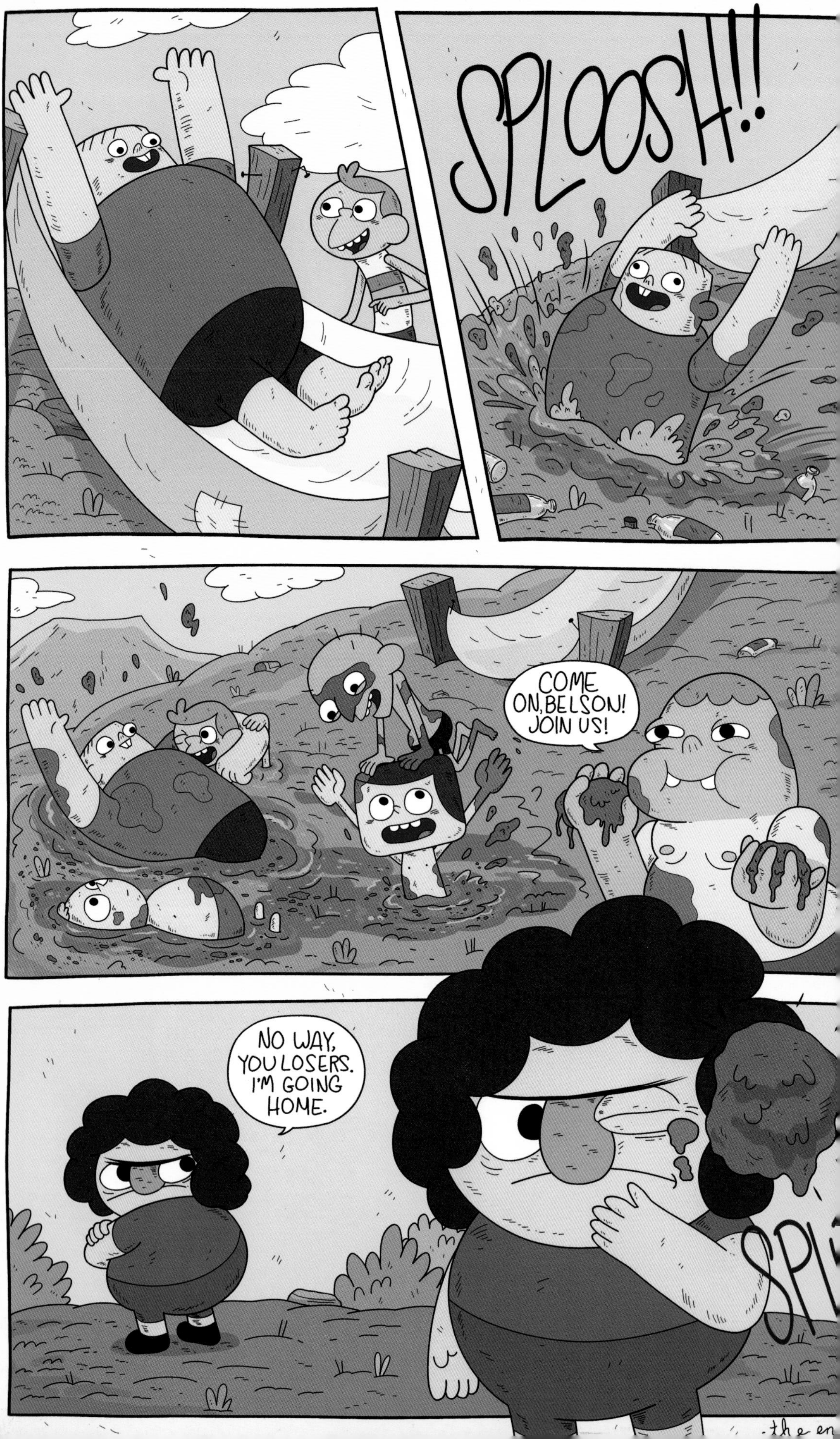
SPLOOSH!!
COME ON, BELSON! JOIN US!
NO WAY, YOU LOSERS. I'M GOING HOME.

Chapter Four

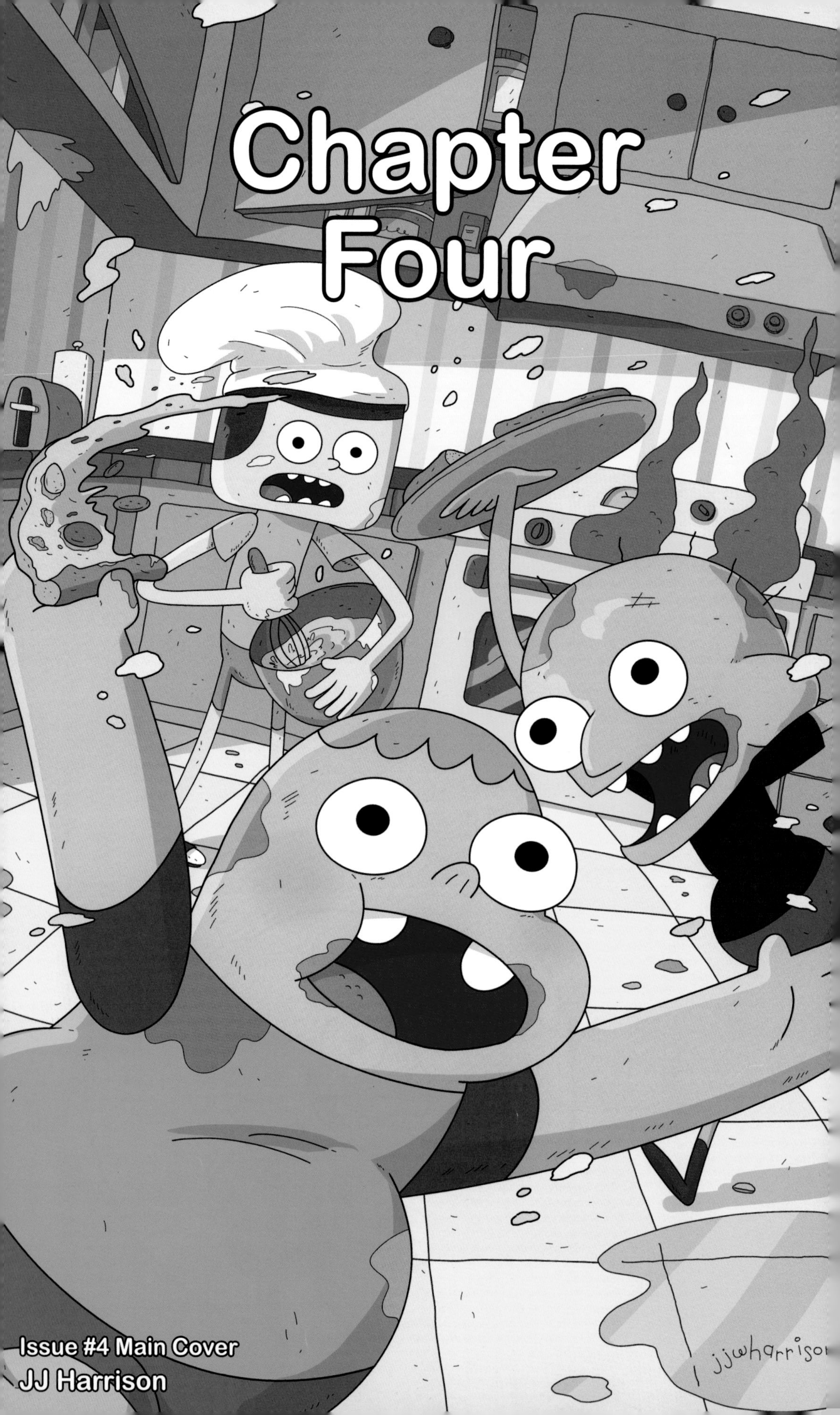
jjwharrison

Issue #4 Main Cover
JJ Harrison

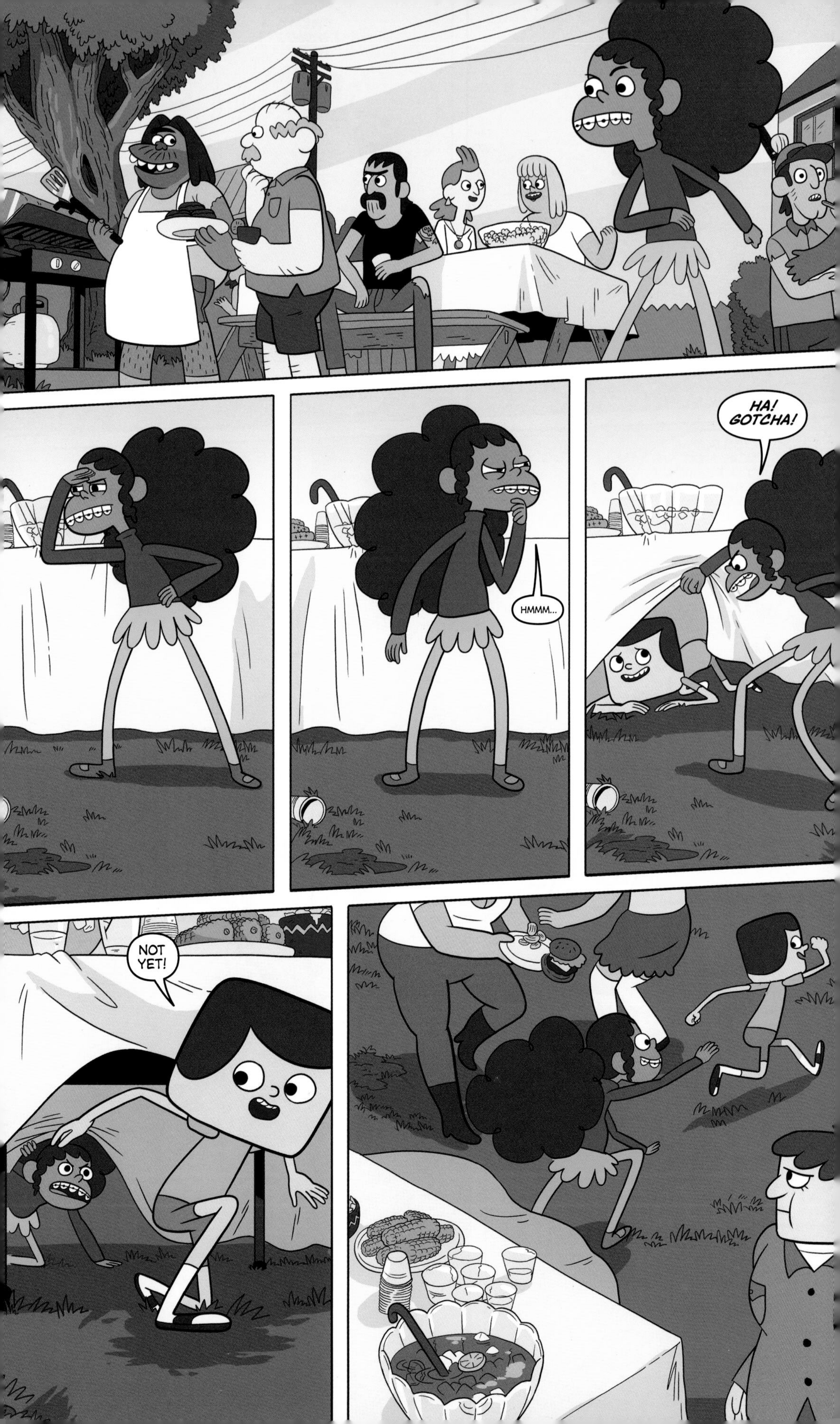
HMMM...
HA! GOTCHA!
NOT YET!

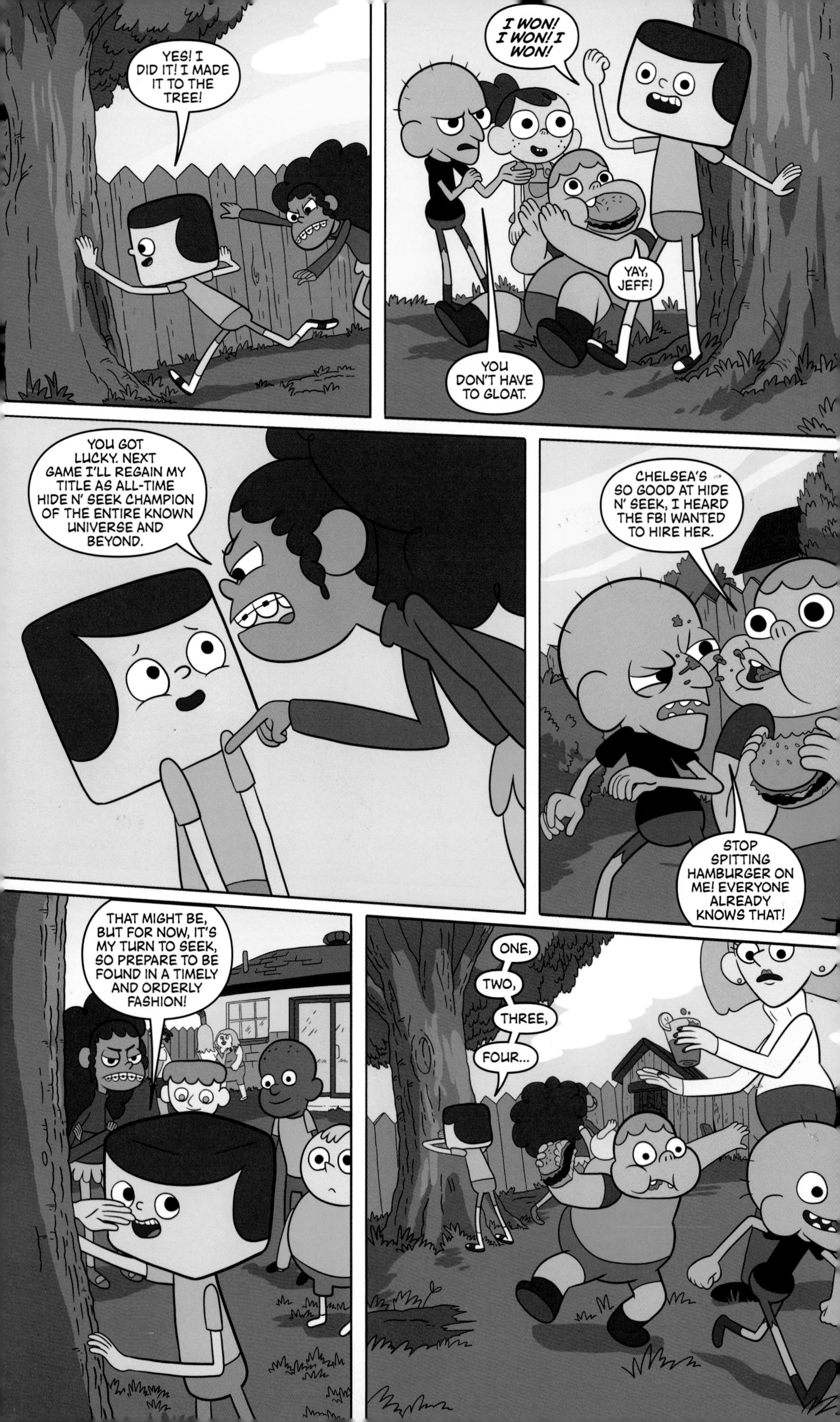
YES! I DID IT! I MADE IT TO THE TREE!
I WON! I WON! I WON!
YAY, JEFF!
YOU DON'T HAVE TO GLOAT.
YOU GOT LUCKY. NEXT GAME I'LL REGAIN MY TITLE AS ALL-TIME HIDE N' SEEK CHAMPION OF THE ENTIRE KNOWN UNIVERSE AND BEYOND.
CHELSEA'S SO GOOD AT HIDE N' SEEK, I HEARD THE FBI WANTED TO HIRE HER.
STOP SPITTING HAMBURGER ON ME! EVERYONE ALREADY KNOWS THAT!
THAT MIGHT BE, BUT FOR NOW, IT'S MY TURN TO SEEK, SO PREPARE TO BE FOUND IN A TIMELY AND ORDERLY FASHION!
ONE,
TWO,
THREE,
FOUR...

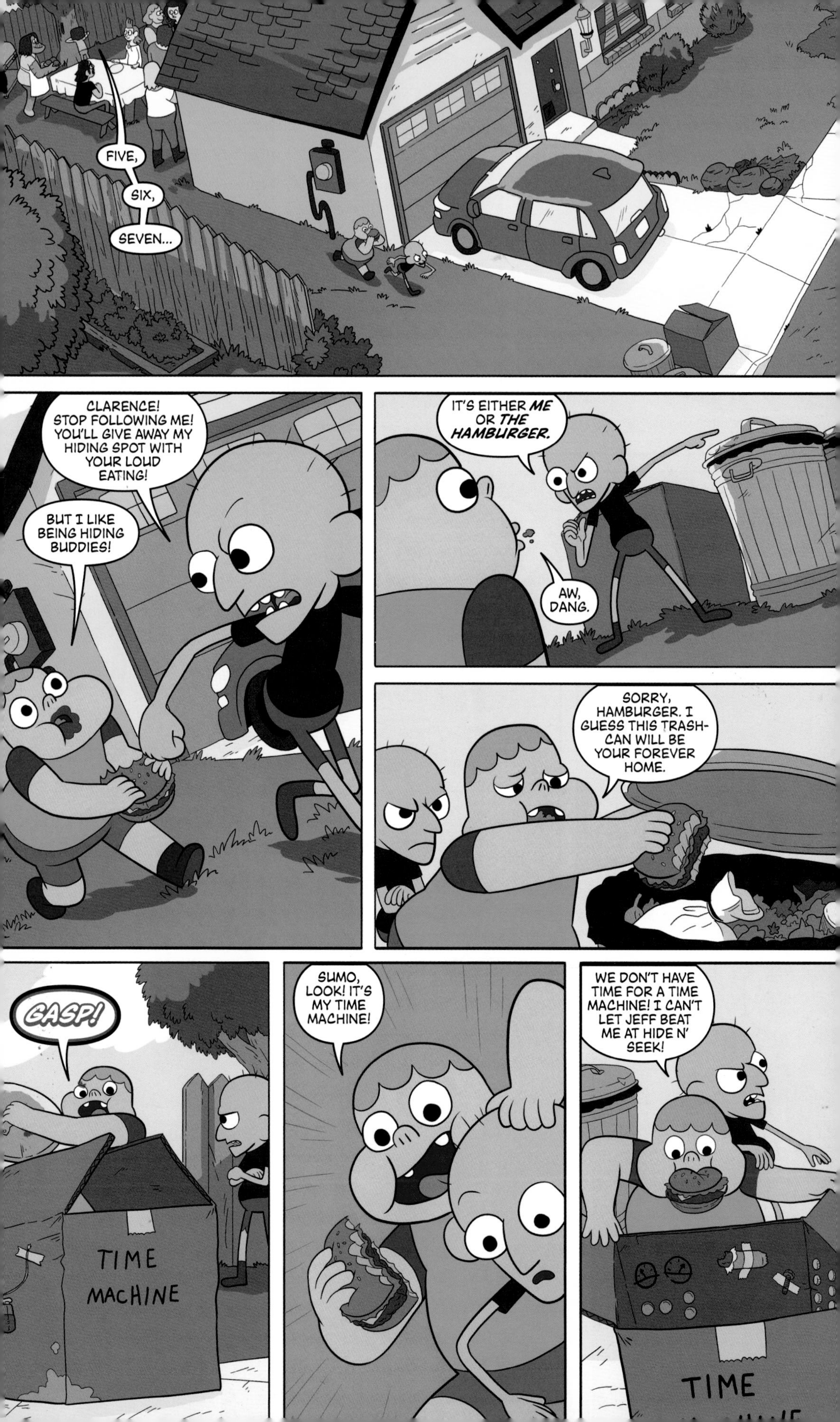
FIVE,
SIX,
SEVEN...
CLARENCE! STOP FOLLOWING ME! YOU'LL GIVE AWAY MY HIDING SPOT WITH YOUR LOUD EATING!
BUT I LIKE BEING HIDING BUDDIES!
IT'S EITHER *ME* OR *THE HAMBURGER.*
AW, DANG.
SORRY, HAMBURGER. I GUESS THIS TRASH-CAN WILL BE YOUR FOREVER HOME.
GASP!
TIME MACHINE
SUMO, LOOK! IT'S MY TIME MACHINE!
WE DON'T HAVE TIME FOR A TIME MACHINE! I CAN'T LET JEFF BEAT ME AT HIDE N' SEEK!
TIME

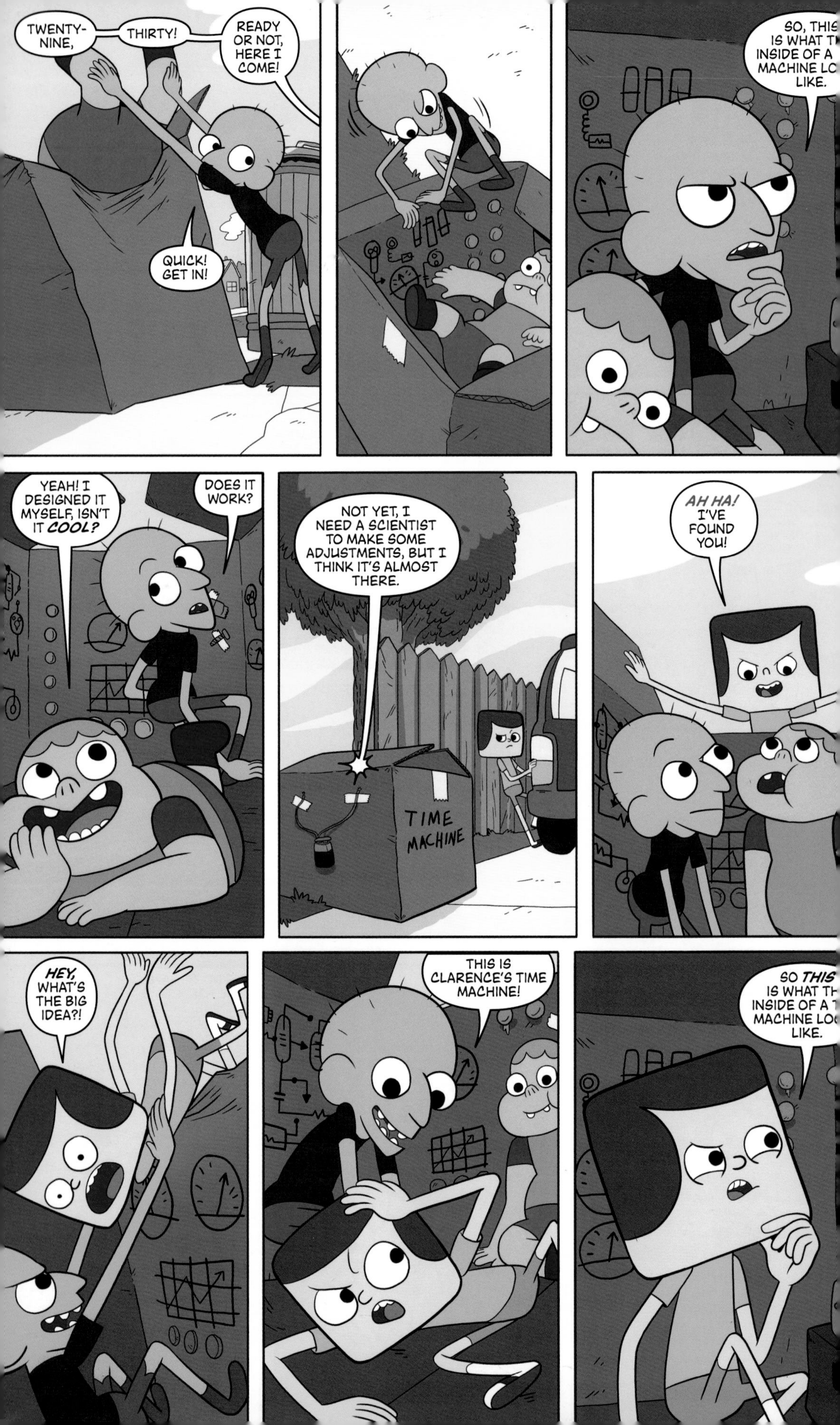
TWENTY-NINE,
THIRTY!
READY OR NOT, HERE I COME!
QUICK! GET IN!
SO, THIS IS WHAT T INSIDE OF A MACHINE LO LIKE.
YEAH! I DESIGNED IT MYSELF, ISN'T IT COOL?
DOES IT WORK?
NOT YET, I NEED A SCIENTIST TO MAKE SOME ADJUSTMENTS, BUT I THINK IT'S ALMOST THERE.
TIME MACHINE
AH HA! I'VE FOUND YOU!
HEY, WHAT'S THE BIG IDEA?!
THIS IS CLARENCE'S TIME MACHINE!
SO THIS IS WHAT TH INSIDE OF A T MACHINE LO LIKE.

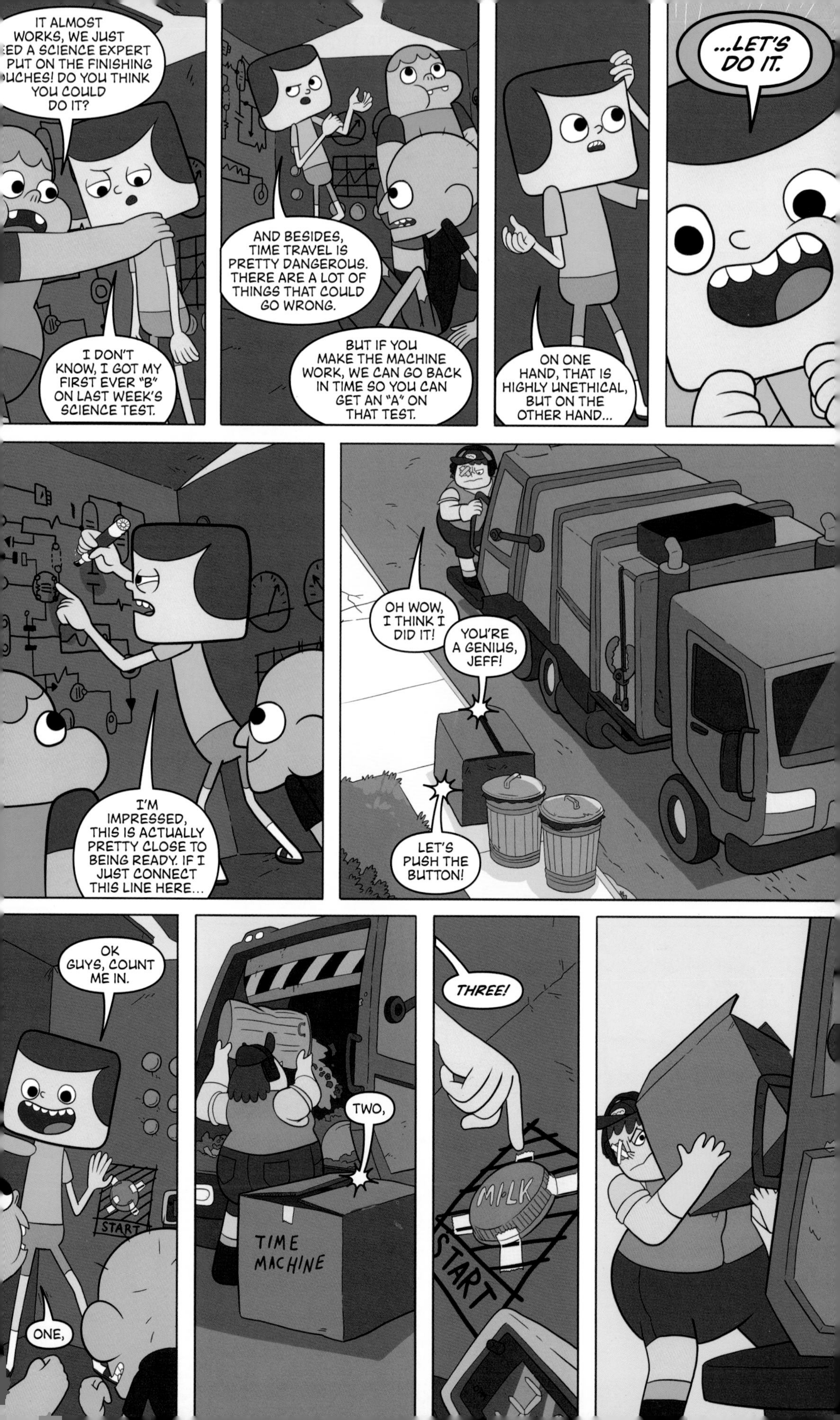
IT ALMOST WORKS, WE JUST EED A SCIENCE EXPERT PUT ON THE FINISHING UCHES! DO YOU THINK YOU COULD DO IT?
I DON'T KNOW, I GOT MY FIRST EVER "B" ON LAST WEEK'S SCIENCE TEST.
AND BESIDES, TIME TRAVEL IS PRETTY DANGEROUS. THERE ARE A LOT OF THINGS THAT COULD GO WRONG.
BUT IF YOU MAKE THE MACHINE WORK, WE CAN GO BACK IN TIME SO YOU CAN GET AN "A" ON THAT TEST.
ON ONE HAND, THAT IS HIGHLY UNETHICAL, BUT ON THE OTHER HAND...
...LET'S DO IT.
I'M IMPRESSED, THIS IS ACTUALLY PRETTY CLOSE TO BEING READY. IF I JUST CONNECT THIS LINE HERE...
OH WOW, I THINK I DID IT!
YOU'RE A GENIUS, JEFF!
LET'S PUSH THE BUTTON!
OK GUYS, COUNT ME IN.
START
ONE,
TWO,
TIME MACHINE
THREE!
MILK
START

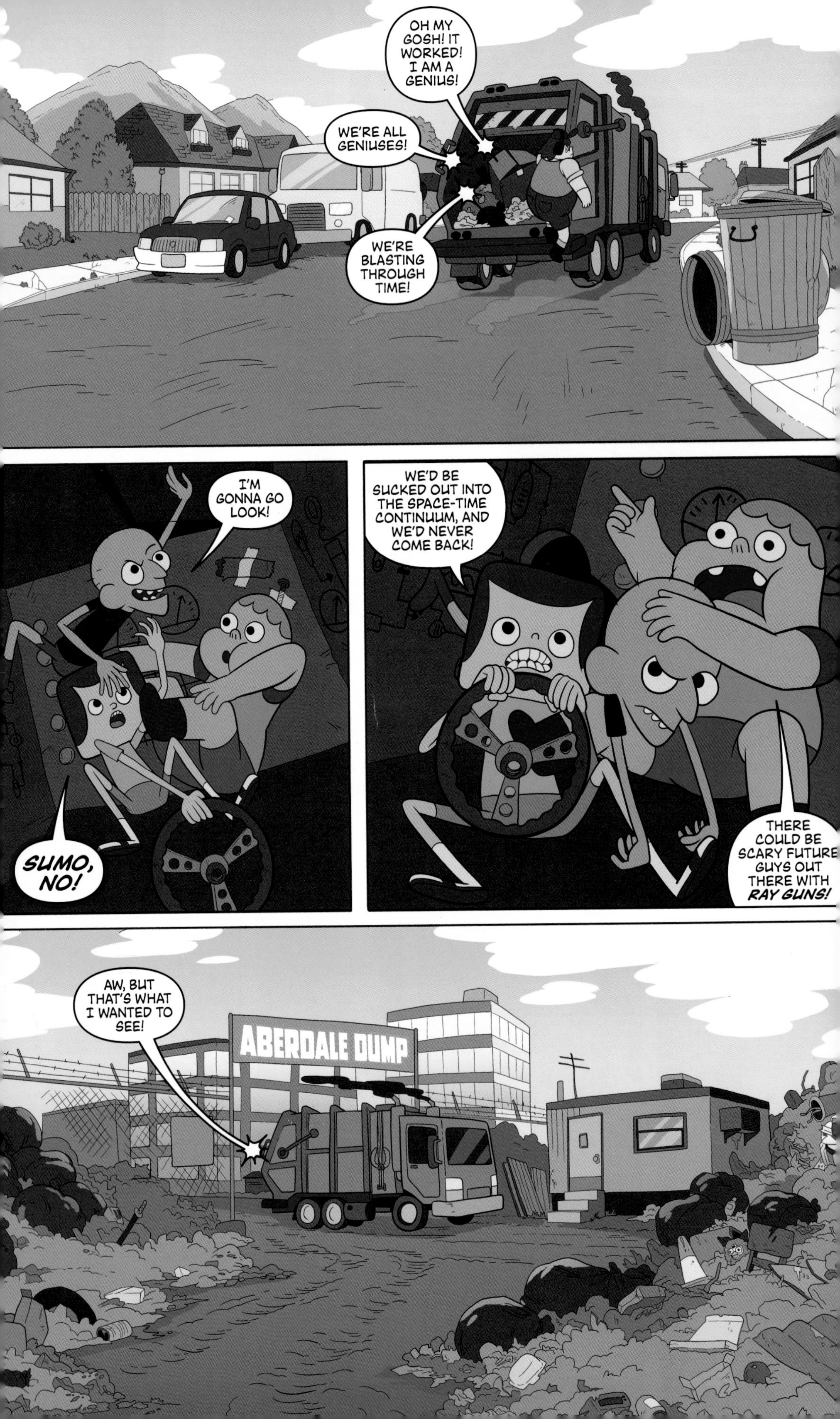
OH MY GOSH! IT WORKED! I AM A GENIUS!
WE'RE ALL GENIUSES!
WE'RE BLASTING THROUGH TIME!
I'M GONNA GO LOOK!
SUMO, NO!
WE'D BE SUCKED OUT INTO THE SPACE-TIME CONTINUUM, AND WE'D NEVER COME BACK!
THERE COULD BE SCARY FUTURE GUYS OUT THERE WITH RAY GUNS!
ABERDALE DUMP
AW, BUT THAT'S WHAT I WANTED TO SEE!

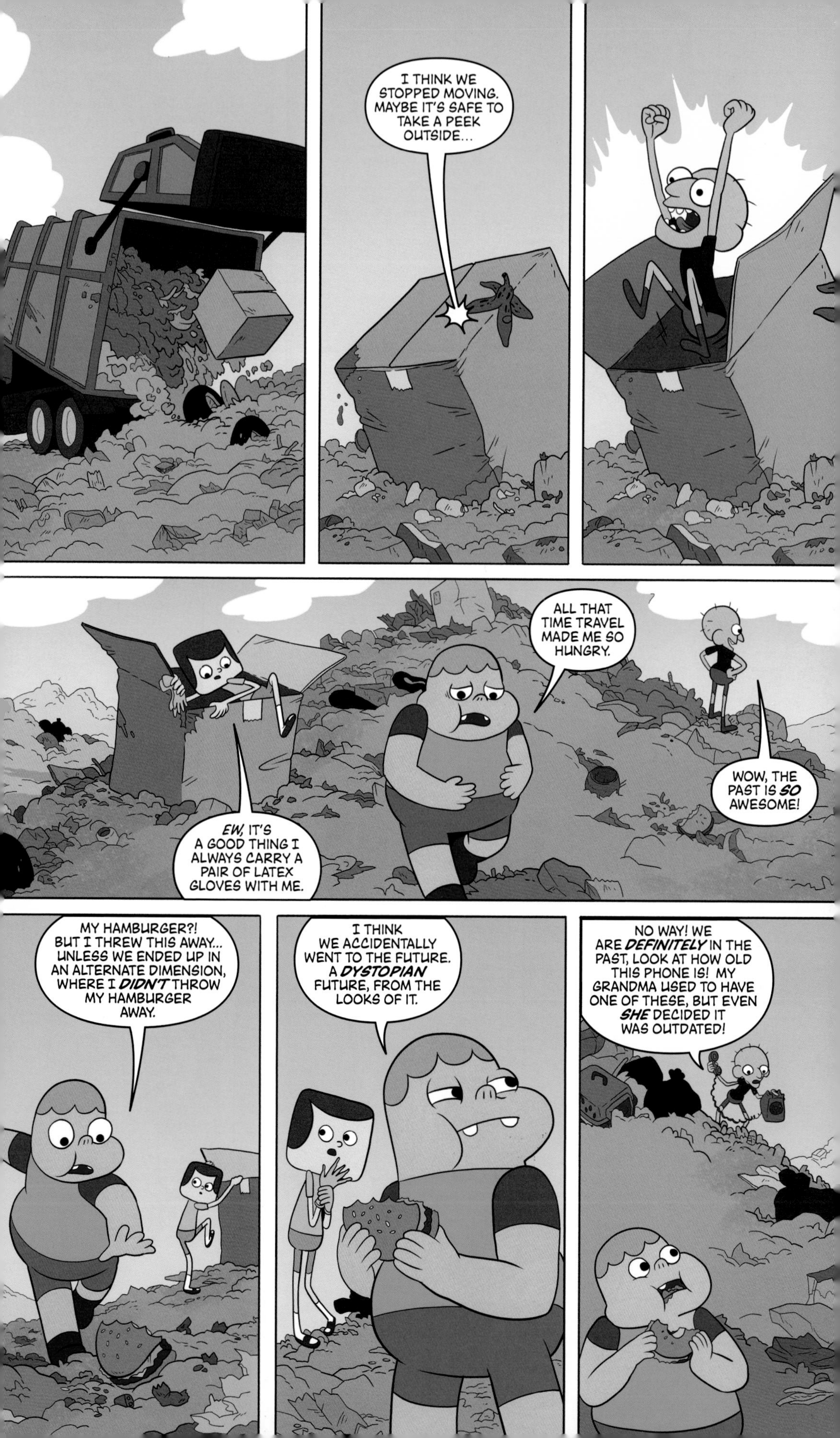
I THINK WE STOPPED MOVING. MAYBE IT'S SAFE TO TAKE A PEEK OUTSIDE...
ALL THAT TIME TRAVEL MADE ME SO HUNGRY.
WOW, THE PAST IS *SO* AWESOME!
EW, IT'S A GOOD THING I ALWAYS CARRY A PAIR OF LATEX GLOVES WITH ME.
MY HAMBURGER?! BUT I THREW THIS AWAY... UNLESS WE ENDED UP IN AN ALTERNATE DIMENSION, WHERE I *DIDN'T* THROW MY HAMBURGER AWAY.
I THINK WE ACCIDENTALLY WENT TO THE FUTURE. A *DYSTOPIAN* FUTURE, FROM THE LOOKS OF IT.
NO WAY! WE ARE *DEFINITELY* IN THE PAST, LOOK AT HOW OLD THIS PHONE IS! MY GRANDMA USED TO HAVE ONE OF THESE, BUT EVEN *SHE* DECIDED IT WAS OUTDATED!

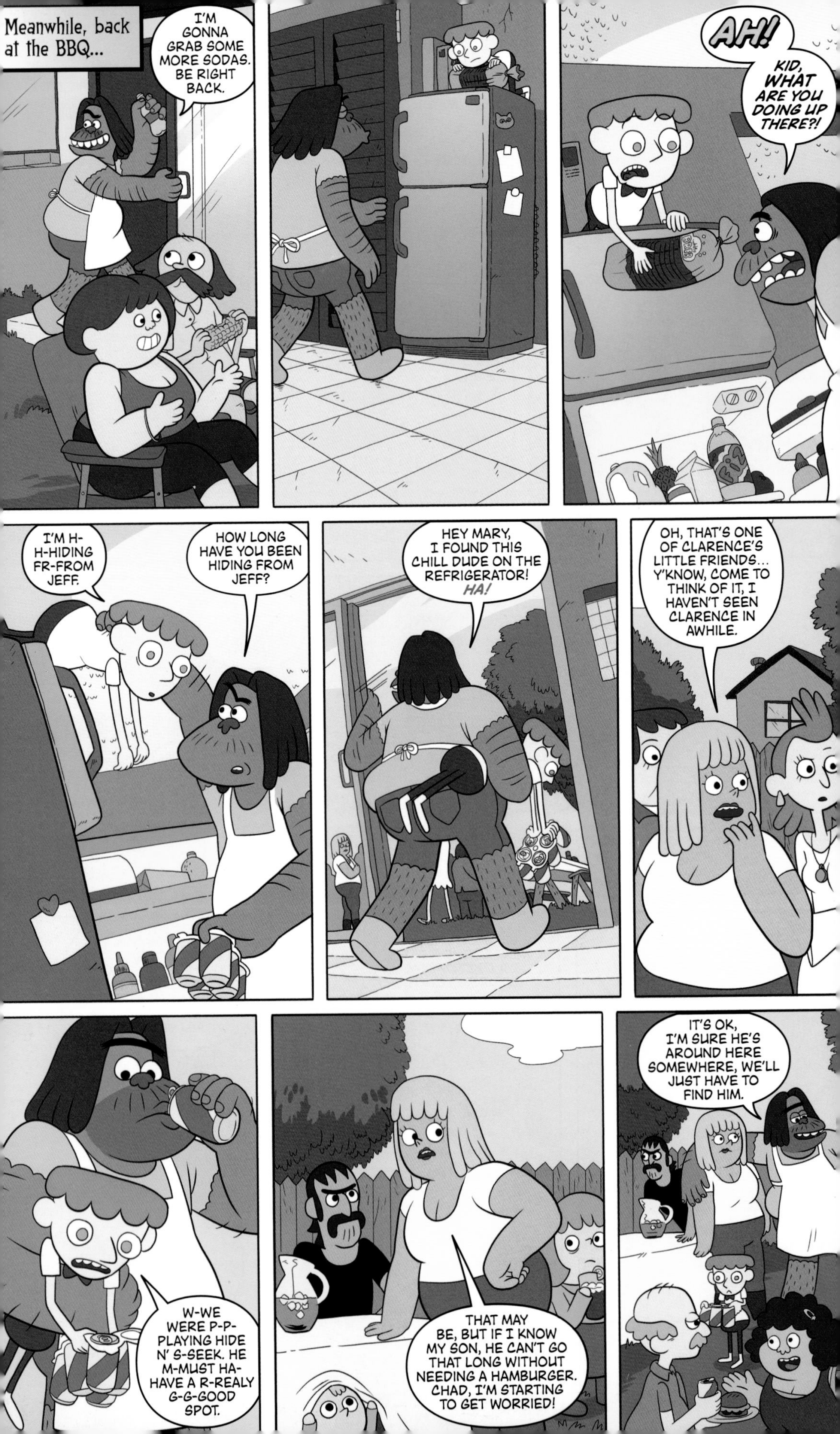
Meanwhile, back at the BBQ...
I'M GONNA GRAB SOME MORE SODAS. BE RIGHT BACK.
AH!
KID, WHAT ARE YOU DOING UP THERE?!
I'M H-H-HIDING FR-FROM JEFF.
HOW LONG HAVE YOU BEEN HIDING FROM JEFF?
HEY MARY, I FOUND THIS CHILL DUDE ON THE REFRIGERATOR! HA!
OH, THAT'S ONE OF CLARENCE'S LITTLE FRIENDS... Y'KNOW, COME TO THINK OF IT, I HAVEN'T SEEN CLARENCE IN AWHILE.
W-WE WERE P-P-PLAYING HIDE N' S-SEEK. HE M-MUST HA-HAVE A R-REALY G-G-GOOD SPOT.
THAT MAY BE, BUT IF I KNOW MY SON, HE CAN'T GO THAT LONG WITHOUT NEEDING A HAMBURGER. CHAD, I'M STARTING TO GET WORRIED!
IT'S OK, I'M SURE HE'S AROUND HERE SOMEWHERE, WE'LL JUST HAVE TO FIND HIM.

I THINK IT'S PRETTY OBVIOUS THAT *WHEN*EVER WE ARE--

PAST!

I RESPECTFULLY DISAGREE, BUT AS I WAS SAYING, WHENEVER WE ARE, IT'S NOT WHERE WE MEANT TO BE, SO I THINK WE SHOULD FOCUS ON GETTING BACK TO OUR OWN TIME.

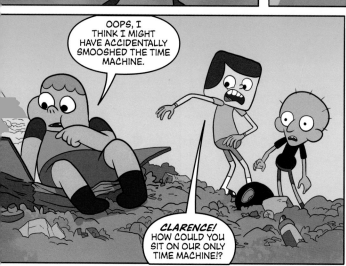

OOPS, I THINK I MIGHT HAVE ACCIDENTALLY SMOOSHED THE TIME MACHINE.

CLARENCE! HOW COULD YOU SIT ON OUR ONLY TIME MACHINE!?

I JUST LIKE SITTING ON BOXES.

JEFF, RELAX. YOU'RE SUCH A BRAINIAC, I'M SURE YOU CAN MAKE A NEW ONE OUT OF ALL THIS OLD JUNK.

I MEAN, IF ANYONE CAN DO IT, YOU CAN.

YEAH JEFF, YOU'RE THE SMARTEST KID IN THE WHOLE SCHOOL! REMEMBER WHEN YOU TOLD US WHY WE SHOULDN'T DARE EACH OTHER TO DRINK THE JANITOR'S MOP WATER AND THEN EMILIO DIDN'T LISTEN AND THEN HE BARFED AND THE JANITOR HAD TO CLEAN IT UP?

HEH, SHUCKS, WELL IF YOU GUYS REALLY THINK I CAN, I'LL GIVE IT A SHOT.

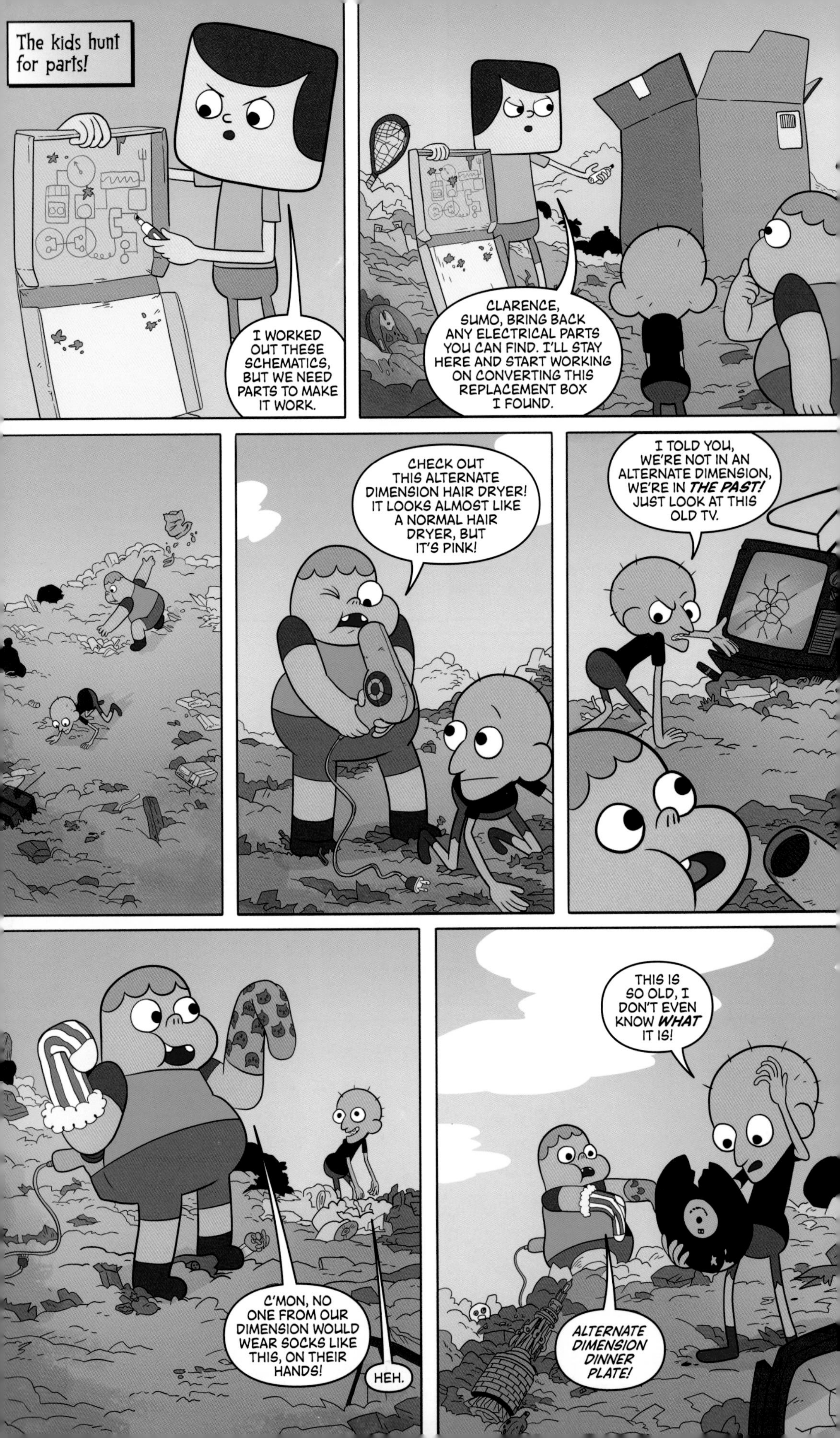
The kids hunt for parts!
I WORKED OUT THESE SCHEMATICS, BUT WE NEED PARTS TO MAKE IT WORK.
CLARENCE, SUMO, BRING BACK ANY ELECTRICAL PARTS YOU CAN FIND. I'LL STAY HERE AND START WORKING ON CONVERTING THIS REPLACEMENT BOX I FOUND.
CHECK OUT THIS ALTERNATE DIMENSION HAIR DRYER! IT LOOKS ALMOST LIKE A NORMAL HAIR DRYER, BUT IT'S PINK!
I TOLD YOU, WE'RE NOT IN AN ALTERNATE DIMENSION, WE'RE IN *THE PAST!* JUST LOOK AT THIS OLD TV.
C'MON, NO ONE FROM OUR DIMENSION WOULD WEAR SOCKS LIKE THIS, ON THEIR HANDS!
HEH.
THIS IS SO OLD, I DON'T EVEN KNOW *WHAT* IT IS!
ALTERNATE DIMENSION DINNER PLATE!

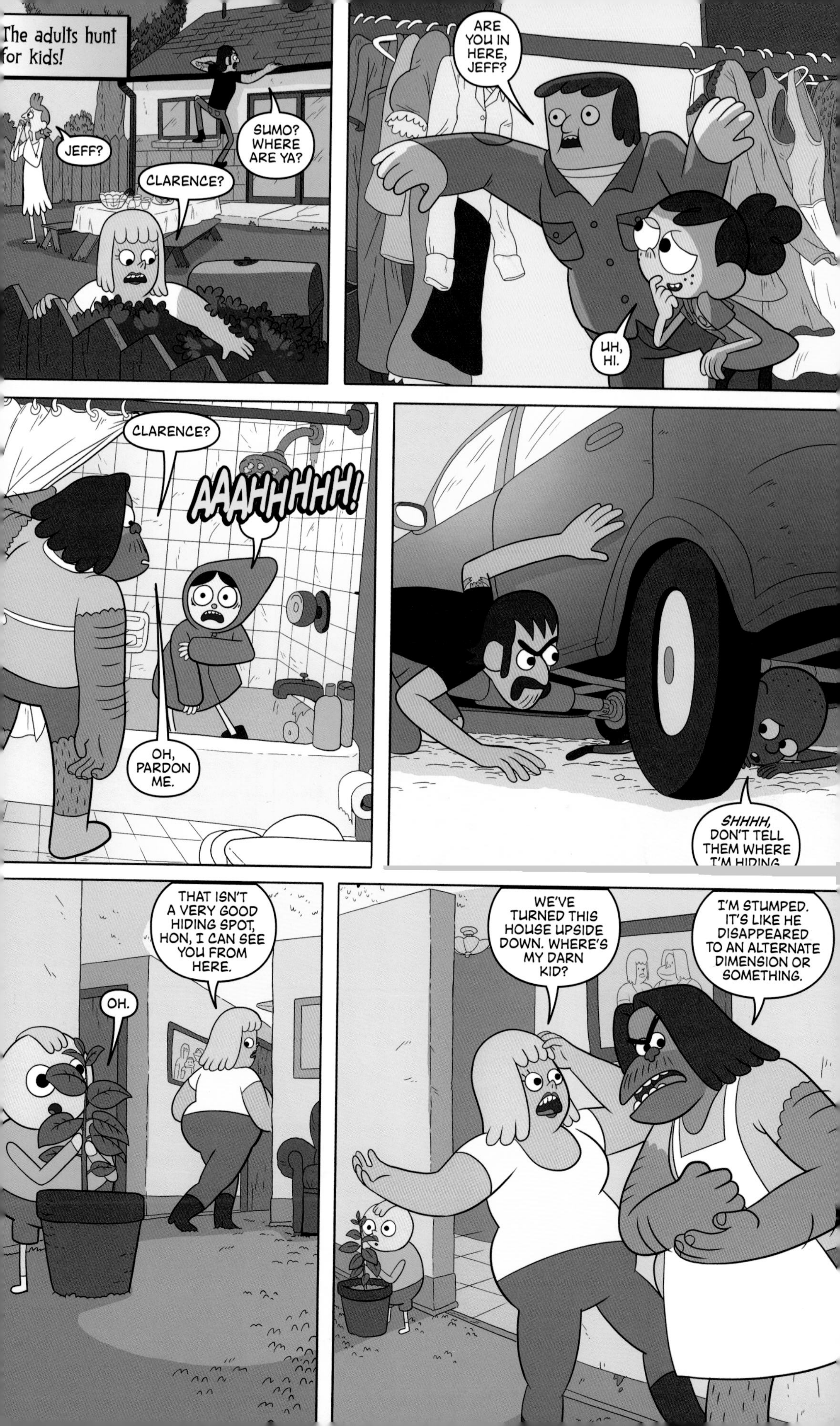

The adults hunt for kids!
JEFF?
SUMO? WHERE ARE YA?
CLARENCE?
ARE YOU IN HERE, JEFF?
UH, HI.
CLARENCE?
AAAHHHHH!
OH, PARDON ME.
SHHHH, DON'T TELL THEM WHERE
THAT ISN'T A VERY GOOD HIDING SPOT, HON, I CAN SEE YOU FROM HERE.
OH.
WE'VE TURNED THIS HOUSE UPSIDE DOWN. WHERE'S MY DARN KID?
I'M STUMPED. IT'S LIKE HE DISAPPEARED TO AN ALTERNATE DIMENSION OR SOMETHING.

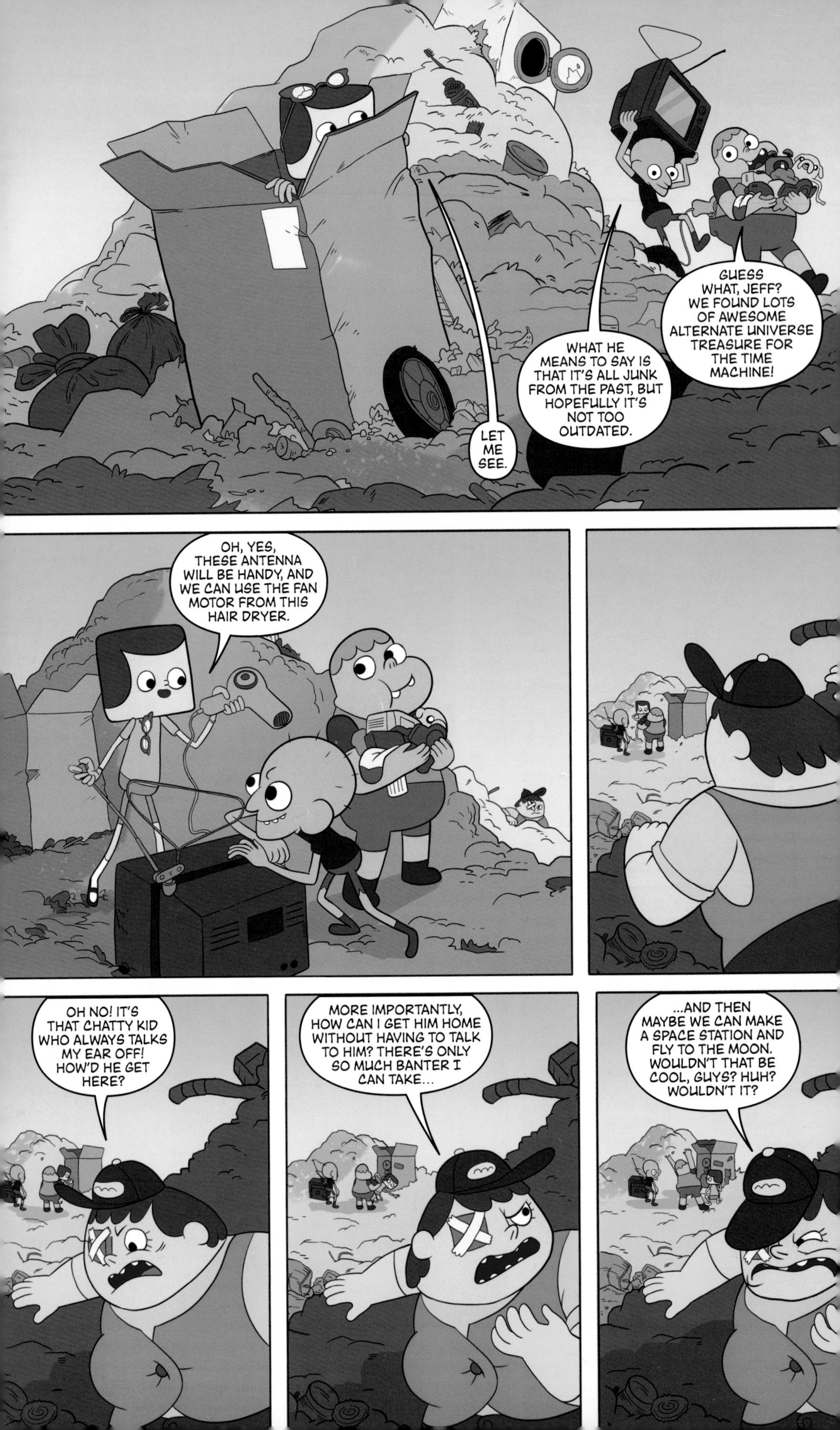

GUESS WHAT, JEFF? WE FOUND LOTS OF AWESOME ALTERNATE UNIVERSE TREASURE FOR THE TIME MACHINE!
WHAT HE MEANS TO SAY IS THAT IT'S ALL JUNK FROM THE PAST, BUT HOPEFULLY IT'S NOT TOO OUTDATED.
LET ME SEE.
OH, YES, THESE ANTENNA WILL BE HANDY, AND WE CAN USE THE FAN MOTOR FROM THIS HAIR DRYER.
OH NO! IT'S THAT CHATTY KID WHO ALWAYS TALKS MY EAR OFF! HOW'D HE GET HERE?
MORE IMPORTANTLY, HOW CAN I GET HIM HOME WITHOUT HAVING TO TALK TO HIM? THERE'S ONLY SO MUCH BANTER I CAN TAKE...
...AND THEN MAYBE WE CAN MAKE A SPACE STATION AND FLY TO THE MOON. WOULDN'T THAT BE COOL, GUYS? HUH? WOULDN'T IT?

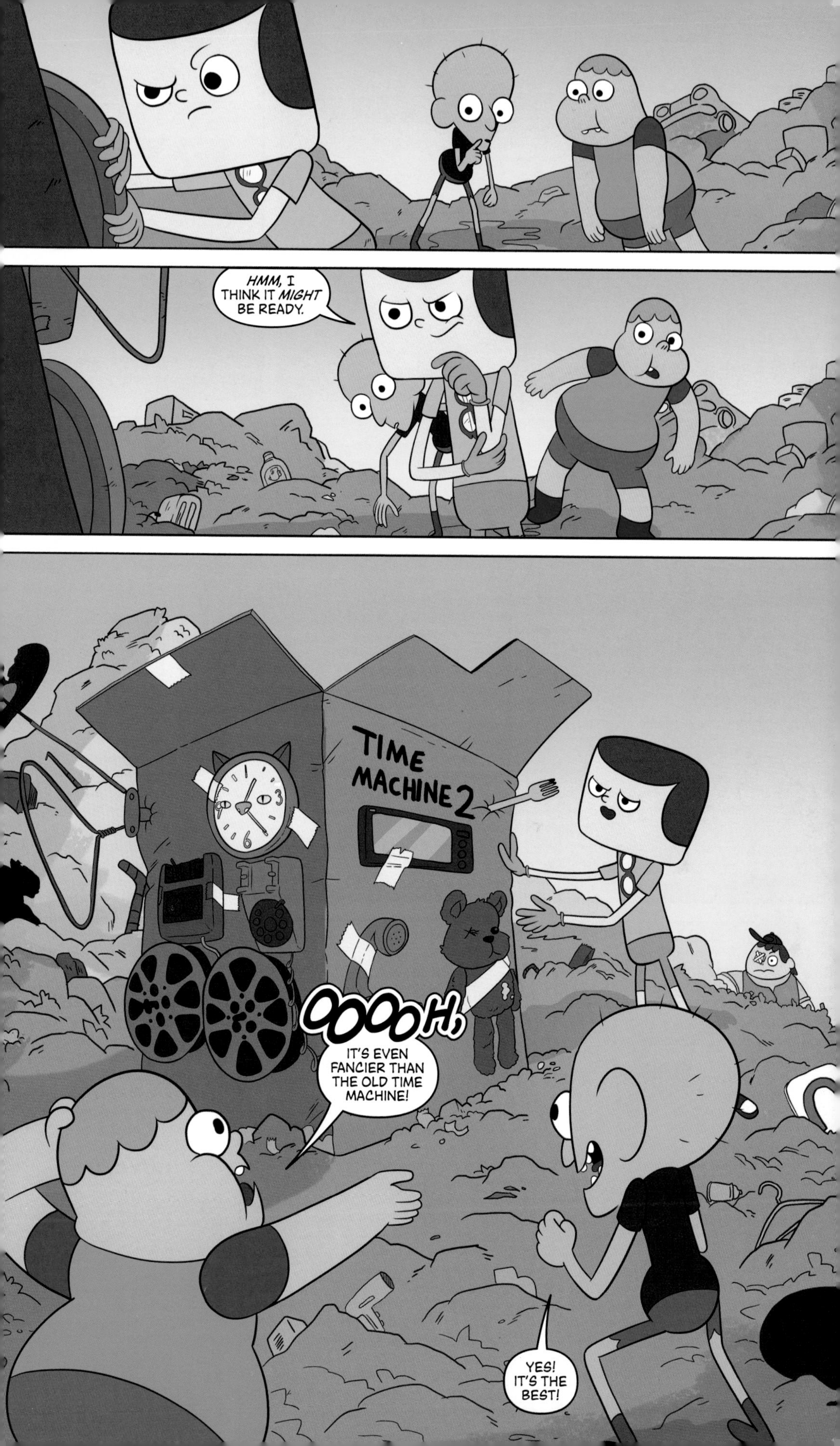
HMM, I THINK IT MIGHT BE READY.
TIME MACHINE 2
OOOOH,
IT'S EVEN FANCIER THAN THE OLD TIME MACHINE!
YES! IT'S THE BEST!

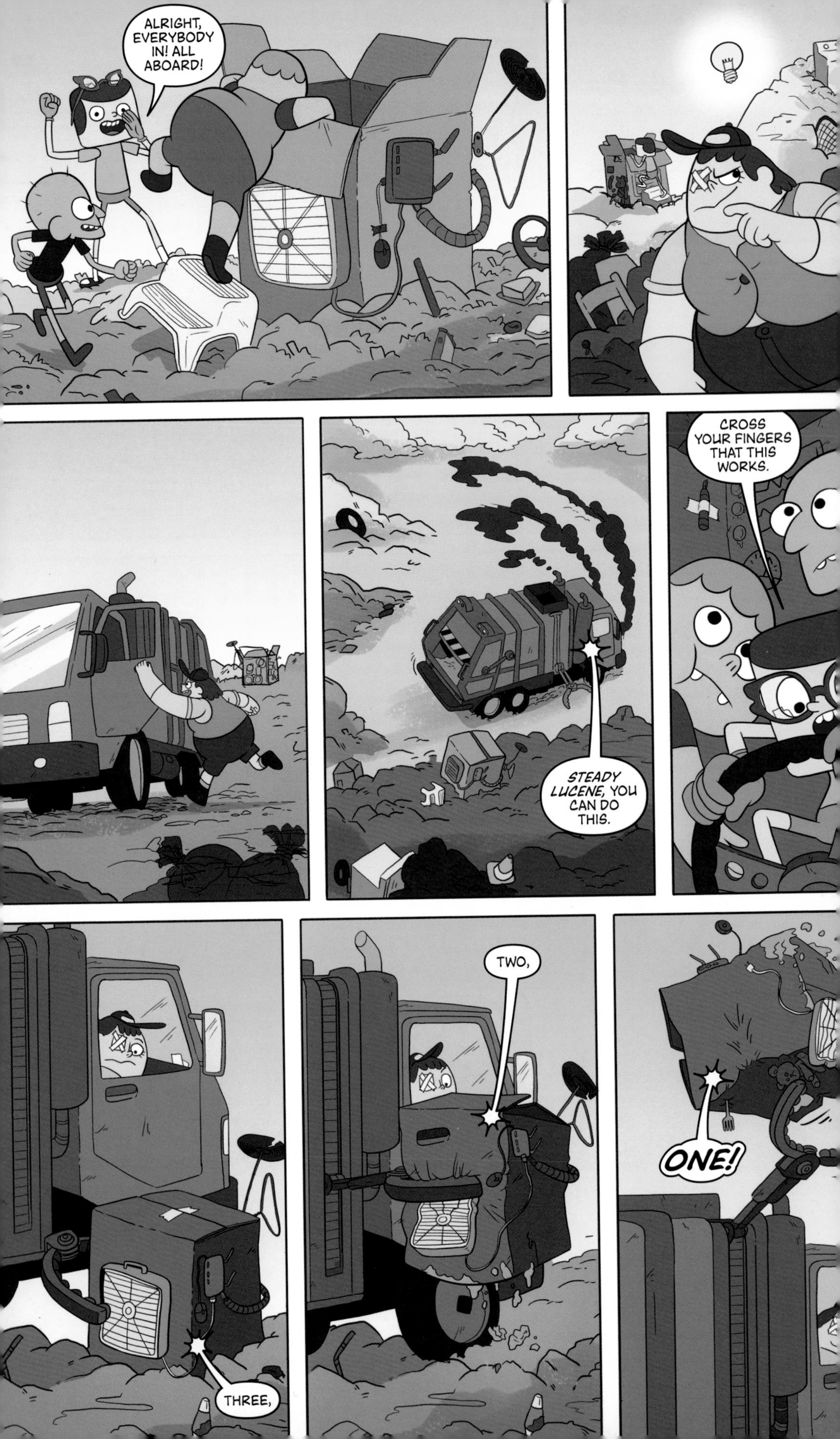
ALRIGHT, EVERYBODY IN! ALL ABOARD!
CROSS YOUR FINGERS THAT THIS WORKS.
STEADY LUCENE, YOU CAN DO THIS.
THREE,
TWO,
ONE!

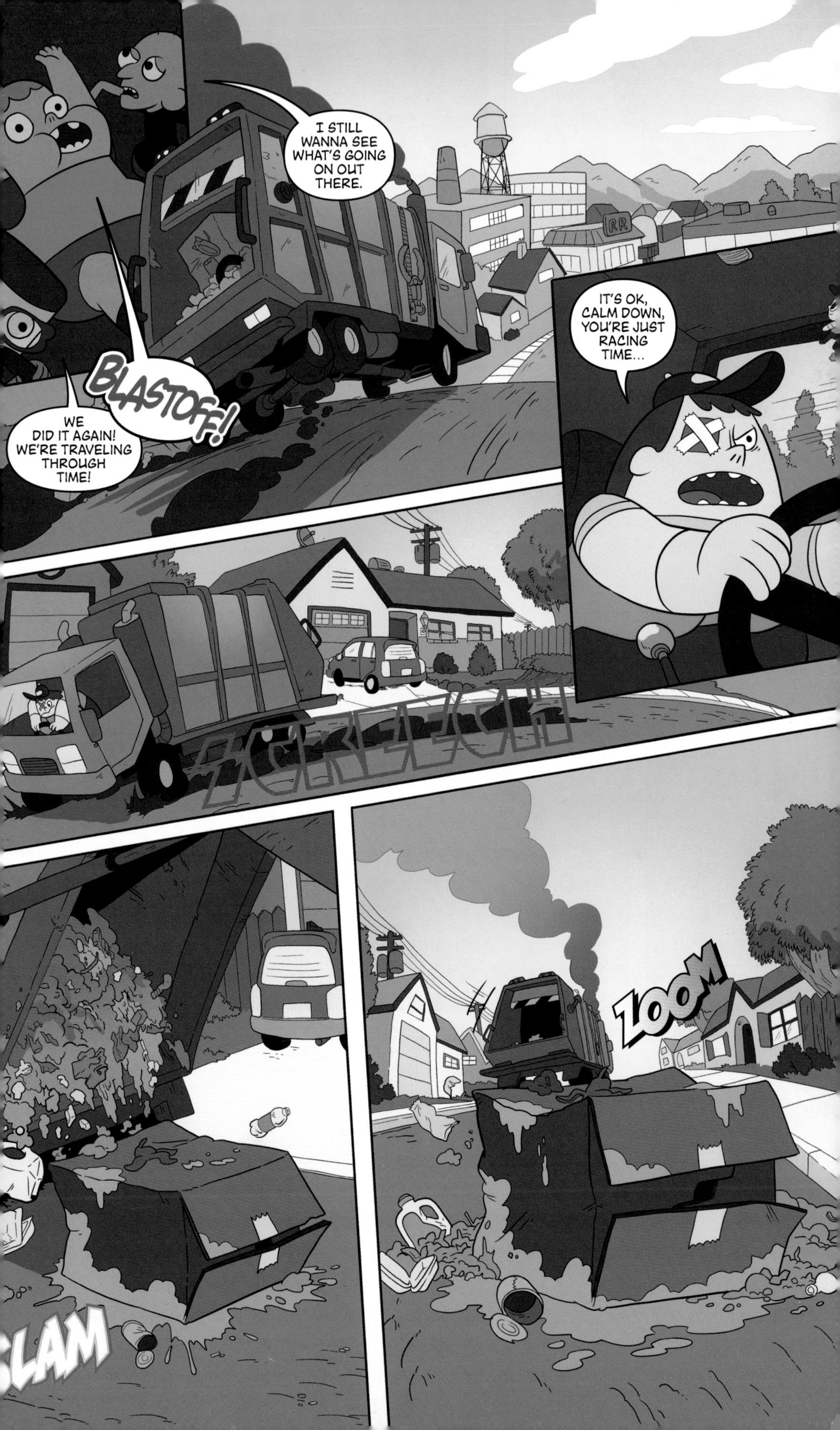
I STILL WANNA SEE WHAT'S GOING ON OUT THERE.
BLASTOFF!
WE DID IT AGAIN! WE'RE TRAVELING THROUGH TIME!
IT'S OK, CALM DOWN, YOU'RE JUST RACING TIME...
SCREECH
SLAM
ZOOM

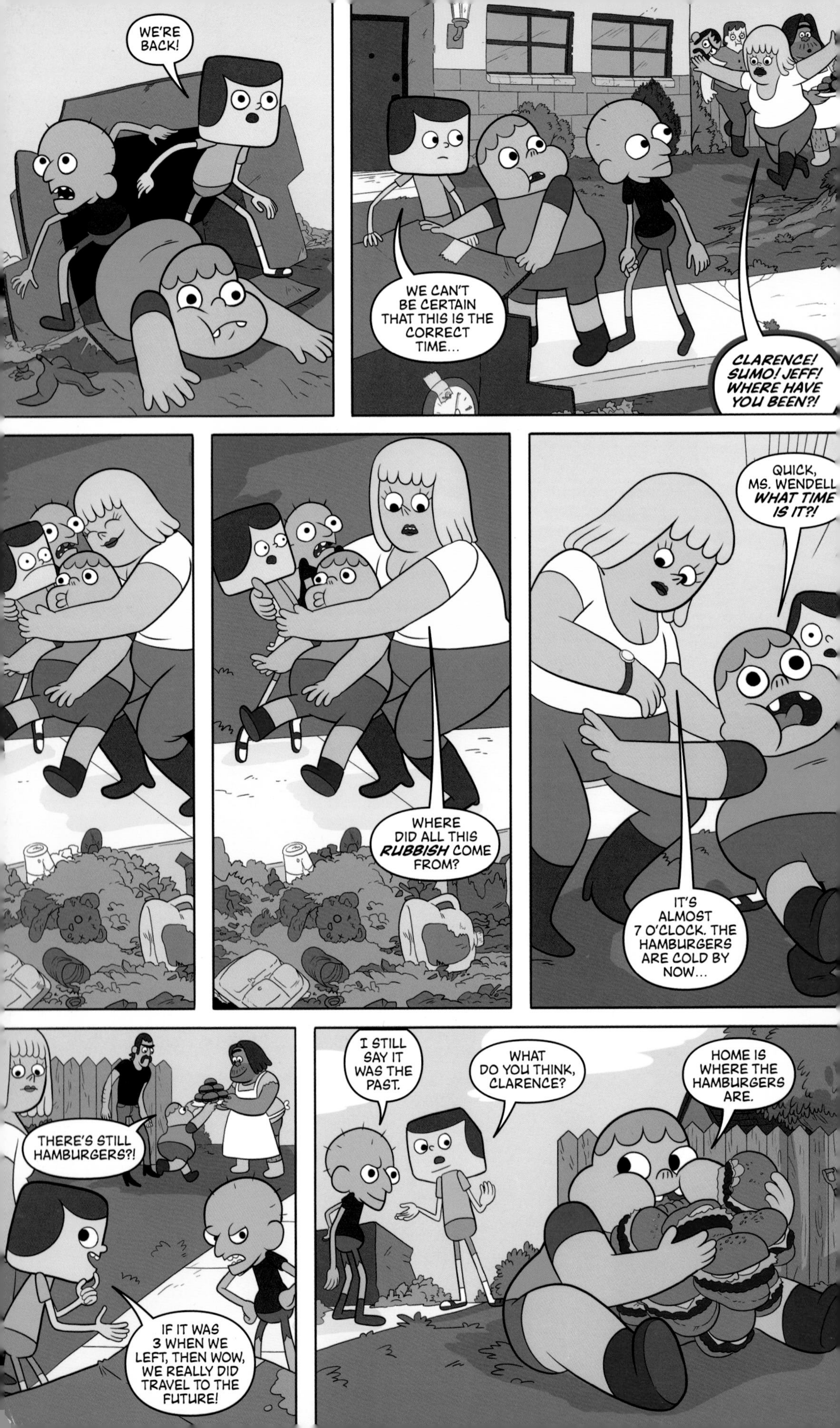
WE'RE BACK!
WE CAN'T BE CERTAIN THAT THIS IS THE CORRECT TIME...
CLARENCE! SUMO! JEFF! WHERE HAVE YOU BEEN?!
WHERE DID ALL THIS RUBBISH COME FROM?
QUICK, MS. WENDELL, WHAT TIME IS IT?!
IT'S ALMOST 7 O'CLOCK. THE HAMBURGERS ARE COLD BY NOW...
THERE'S STILL HAMBURGERS?!
IF IT WAS 3 WHEN WE LEFT, THEN WOW, WE REALLY DID TRAVEL TO THE FUTURE!
I STILL SAY IT WAS THE PAST.
WHAT DO YOU THINK, CLARENCE?
HOME IS WHERE THE HAMBURGERS ARE.

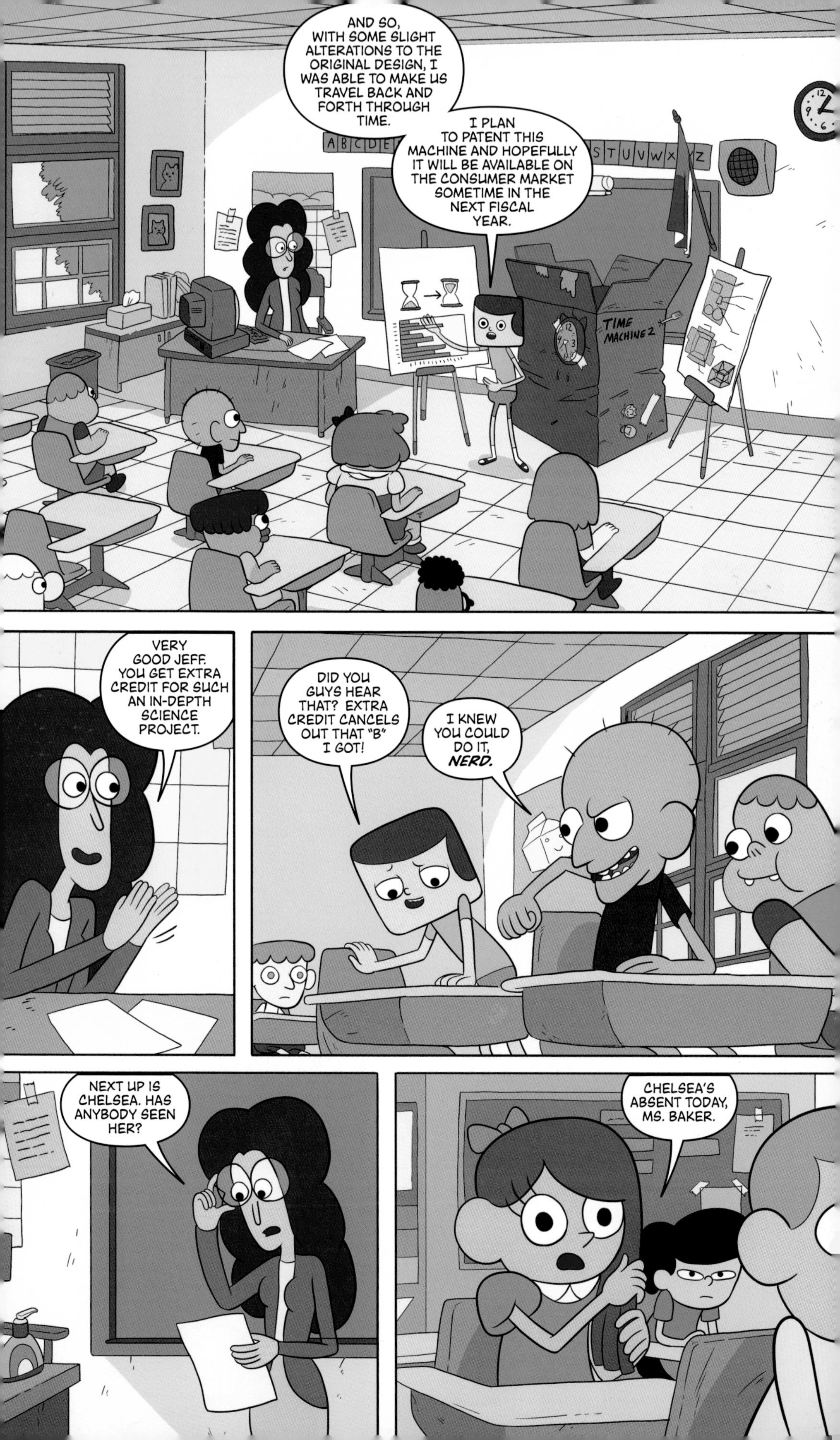
AND SO, WITH SOME SLIGHT ALTERATIONS TO THE ORIGINAL DESIGN, I WAS ABLE TO MAKE US TRAVEL BACK AND FORTH THROUGH TIME.
I PLAN TO PATENT THIS MACHINE AND HOPEFULLY IT WILL BE AVAILABLE ON THE CONSUMER MARKET SOMETIME IN THE NEXT FISCAL YEAR.
TIME MACHINE 2
VERY GOOD JEFF. YOU GET EXTRA CREDIT FOR SUCH AN IN-DEPTH SCIENCE PROJECT.
DID YOU GUYS HEAR THAT? EXTRA CREDIT CANCELS OUT THAT "B" I GOT!
I KNEW YOU COULD DO IT, ***NERD.***
NEXT UP IS CHELSEA. HAS ANYBODY SEEN HER?
CHELSEA'S ABSENT TODAY, MS. BAKER.

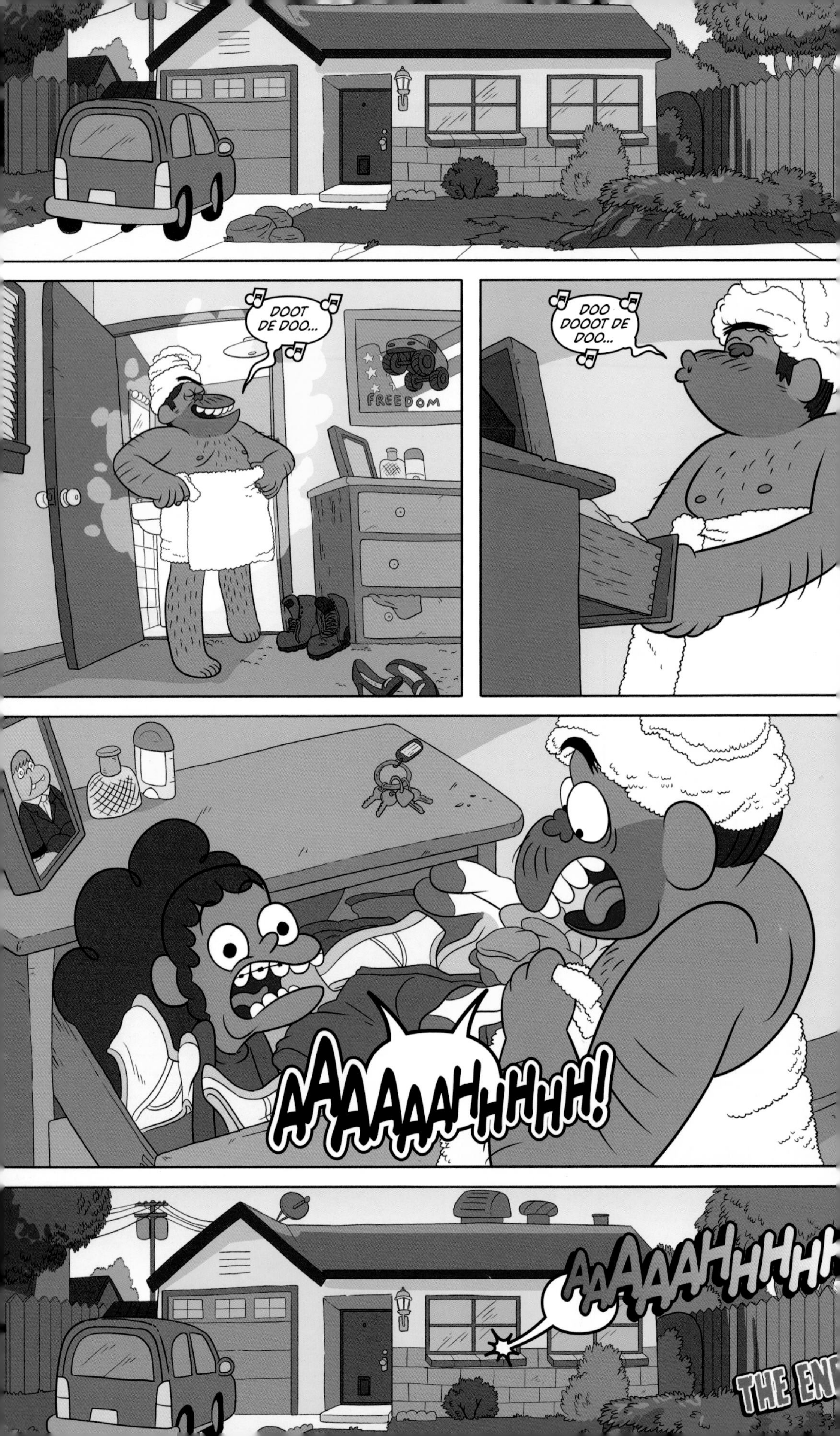
DOOT DE DOO...
FREEDOM
DOO DOOOT DE DOO...
AAAAAAHHHHH!
AAAAAHHHHH
THE END

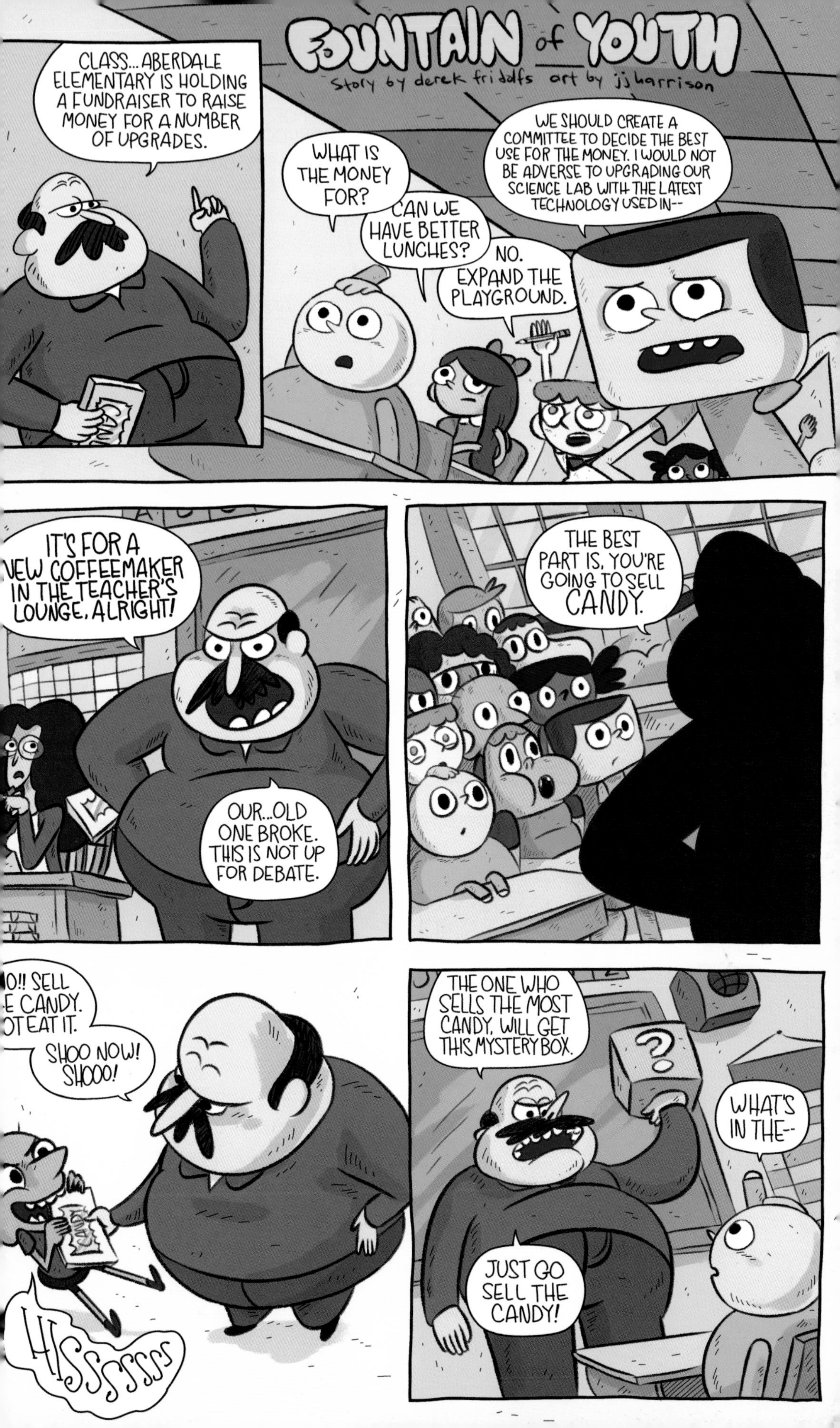
FOUNTAIN of YOUTH
story by derek fridolfs art by jj harrison
CLASS... ABERDALE ELEMENTARY IS HOLDING A FUNDRAISER TO RAISE MONEY FOR A NUMBER OF UPGRADES.
WHAT IS THE MONEY FOR?
CAN WE HAVE BETTER LUNCHES?
NO. EXPAND THE PLAYGROUND.
WE SHOULD CREATE A COMMITTEE TO DECIDE THE BEST USE FOR THE MONEY. I WOULD NOT BE ADVERSE TO UPGRADING OUR SCIENCE LAB WITH THE LATEST TECHNOLOGY USED IN--
IT'S FOR A NEW COFFEEMAKER IN THE TEACHER'S LOUNGE, ALRIGHT!
OUR...OLD ONE BROKE. THIS IS NOT UP FOR DEBATE.
THE BEST PART IS, YOU'RE GOING TO SELL CANDY.
SHOO NOW! SHOOO!
HISSSSSSS
THE ONE WHO SELLS THE MOST CANDY, WILL GET THIS MYSTERY BOX.
WHAT'S IN THE--
JUST GO SELL THE CANDY!

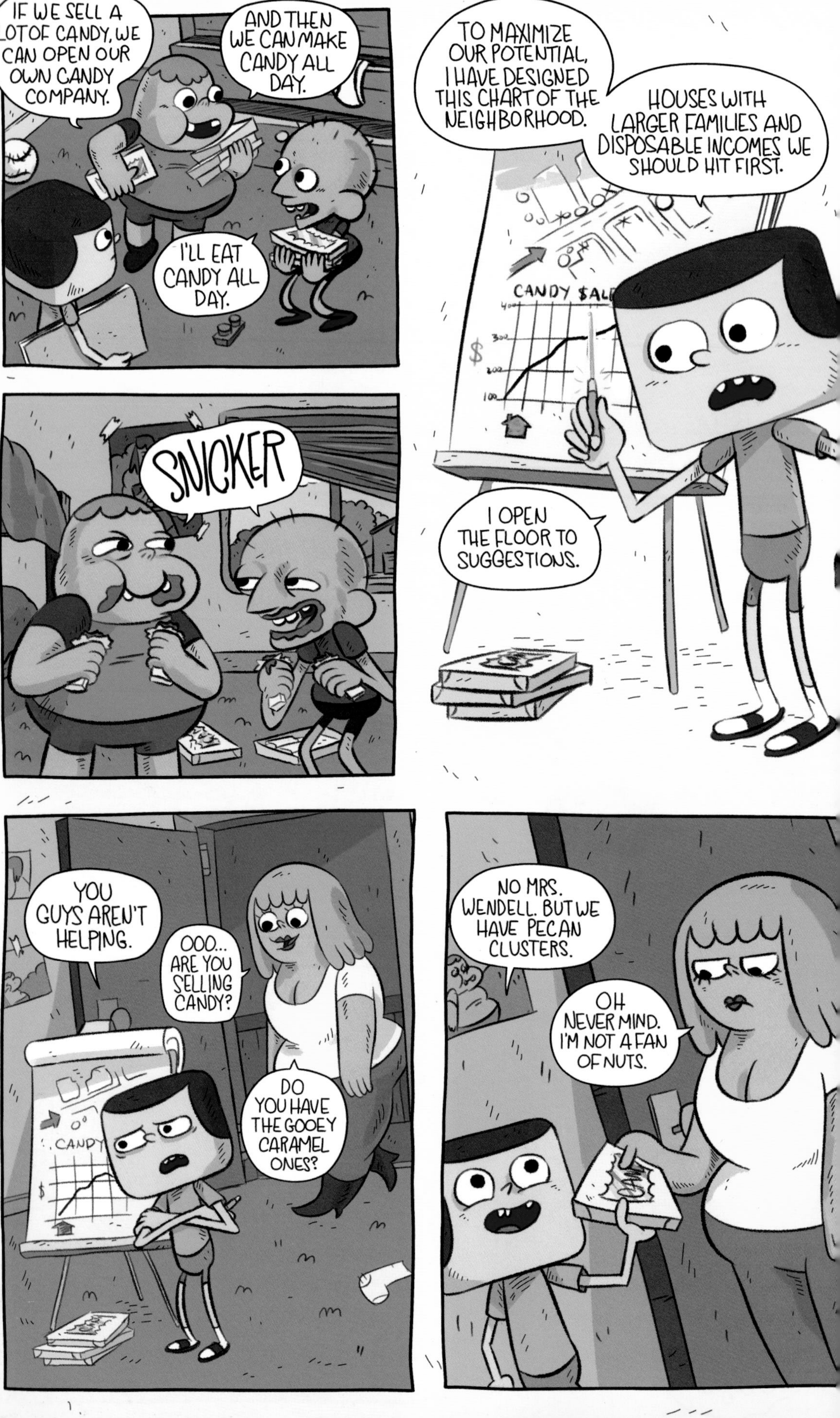
IF WE SELL A LOT OF CANDY, WE CAN OPEN OUR OWN CANDY COMPANY.
AND THEN WE CAN MAKE CANDY ALL DAY.
I'LL EAT CANDY ALL DAY.
TO MAXIMIZE OUR POTENTIAL, I HAVE DESIGNED THIS CHART OF THE NEIGHBORHOOD.
HOUSES WITH LARGER FAMILIES AND DISPOSABLE INCOMES WE SHOULD HIT FIRST.
CANDY $AL
SNICKER
I OPEN THE FLOOR TO SUGGESTIONS.
YOU GUYS AREN'T HELPING.
OOO... ARE YOU SELLING CANDY?
DO YOU HAVE THE GOOEY CARAMEL ONES?
CANDY
NO MRS. WENDELL. BUT WE HAVE PECAN CLUSTERS.
OH NEVER MIND. I'M NOT A FAN OF NUTS.

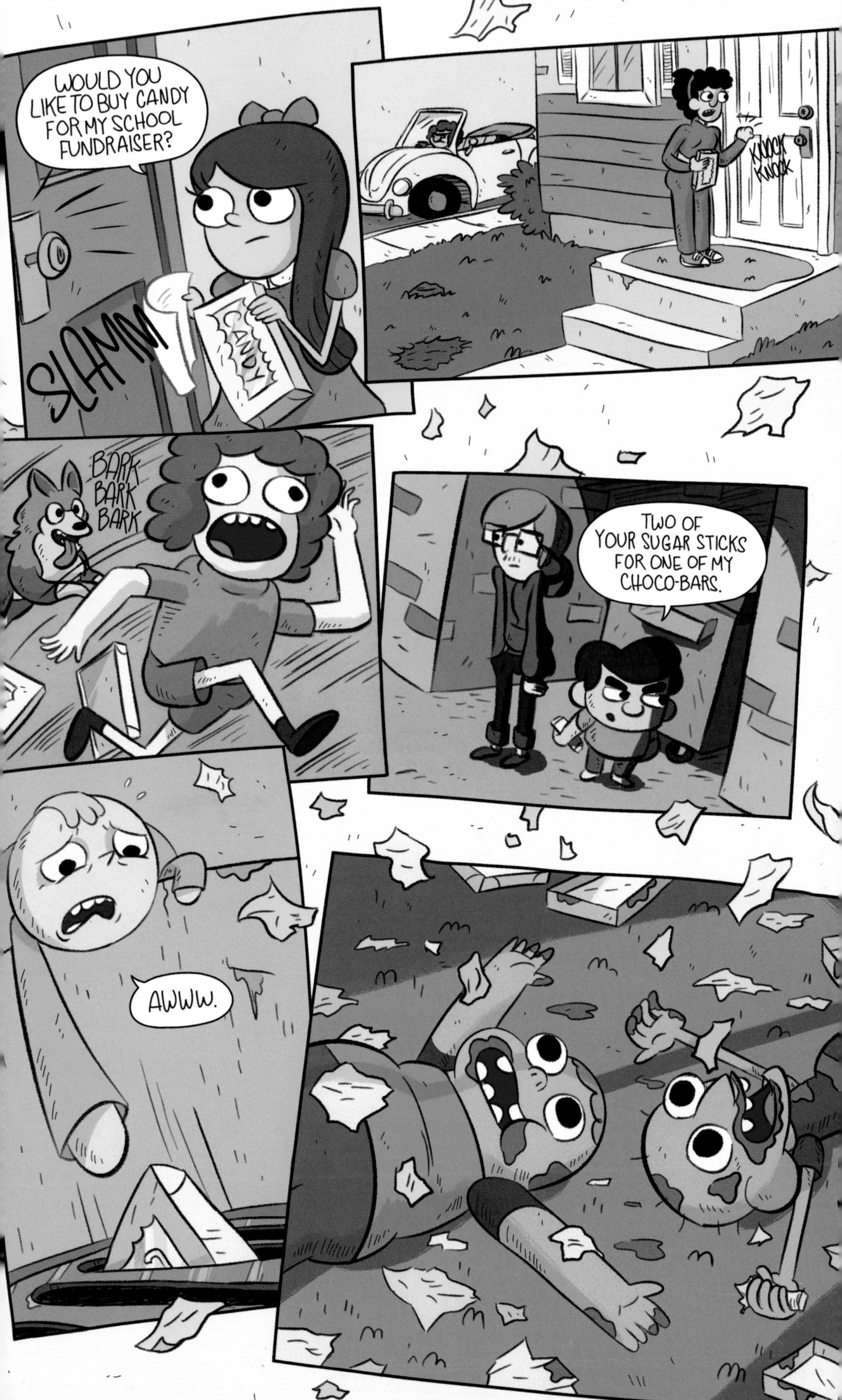
WOULD YOU LIKE TO BUY CANDY FOR MY SCHOOL FUNDRAISER?
SLAMM
CANDY
KNOCK KNOCK
BARK BARK BARK
TWO OF YOUR SUGAR STICKS FOR ONE OF MY CHOCO-BARS.
AWWW.

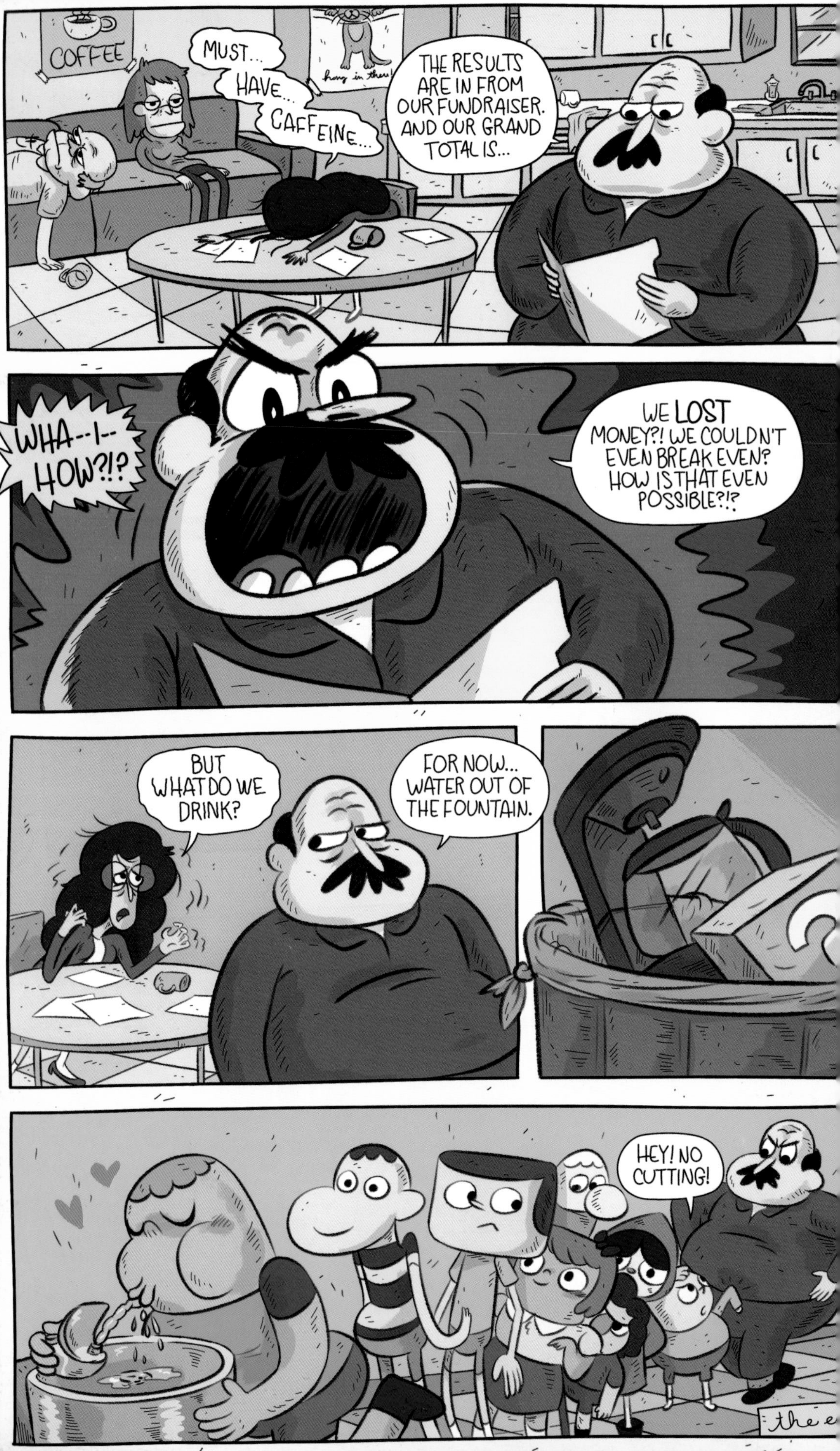
COFFEE
hang in there!
MUST...
HAVE...
CAFFEINE...
THE RESULTS ARE IN FROM OUR FUNDRAISER. AND OUR GRAND TOTAL IS...
WHA--I--HOW?!?
WE LOST MONEY?! WE COULDN'T EVEN BREAK EVEN? HOW IS THAT EVEN POSSIBLE?!?
BUT WHAT DO WE DRINK?
FOR NOW... WATER OUT OF THE FOUNTAIN.
HEY! NO CUTTING!

Cover Gallery

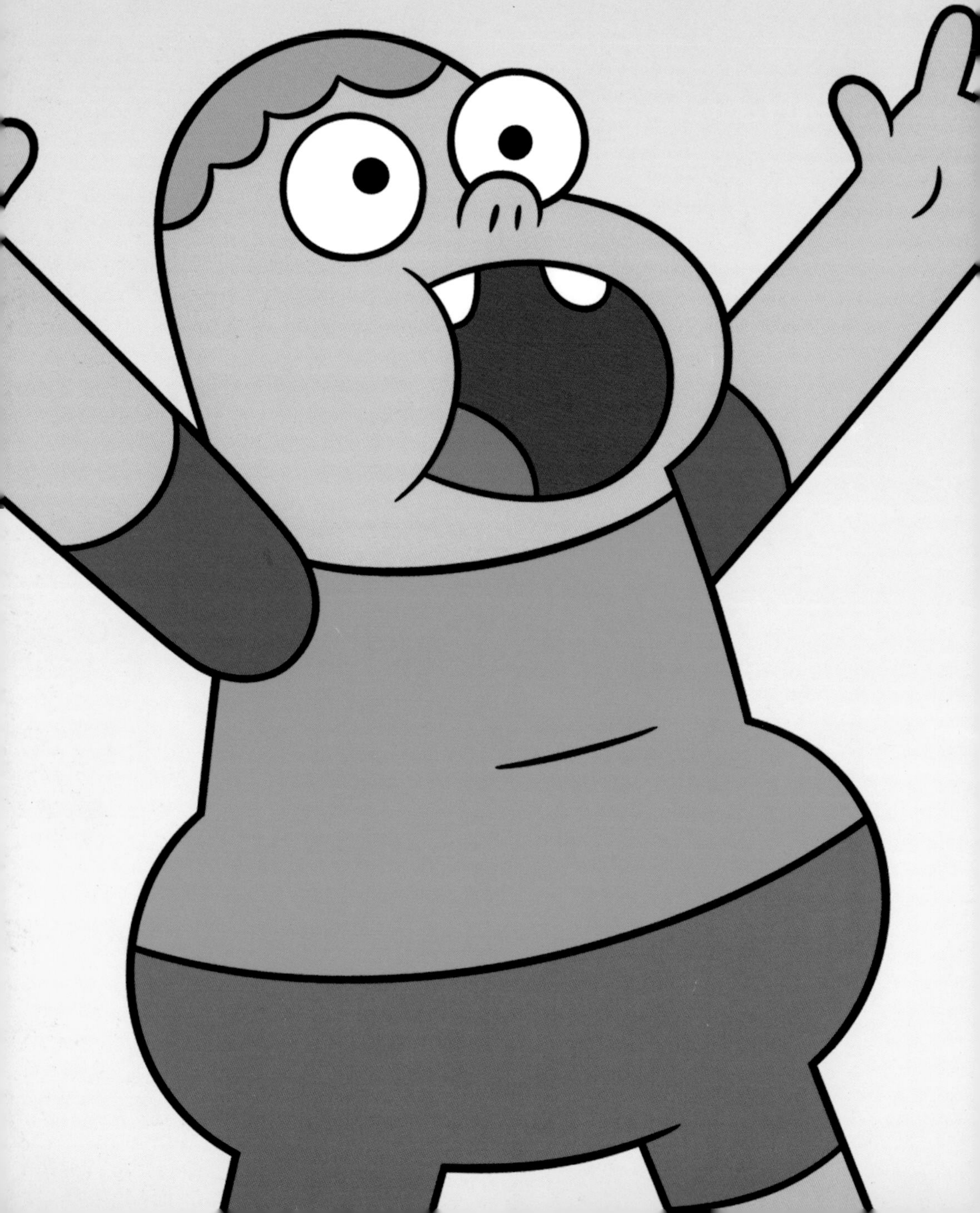

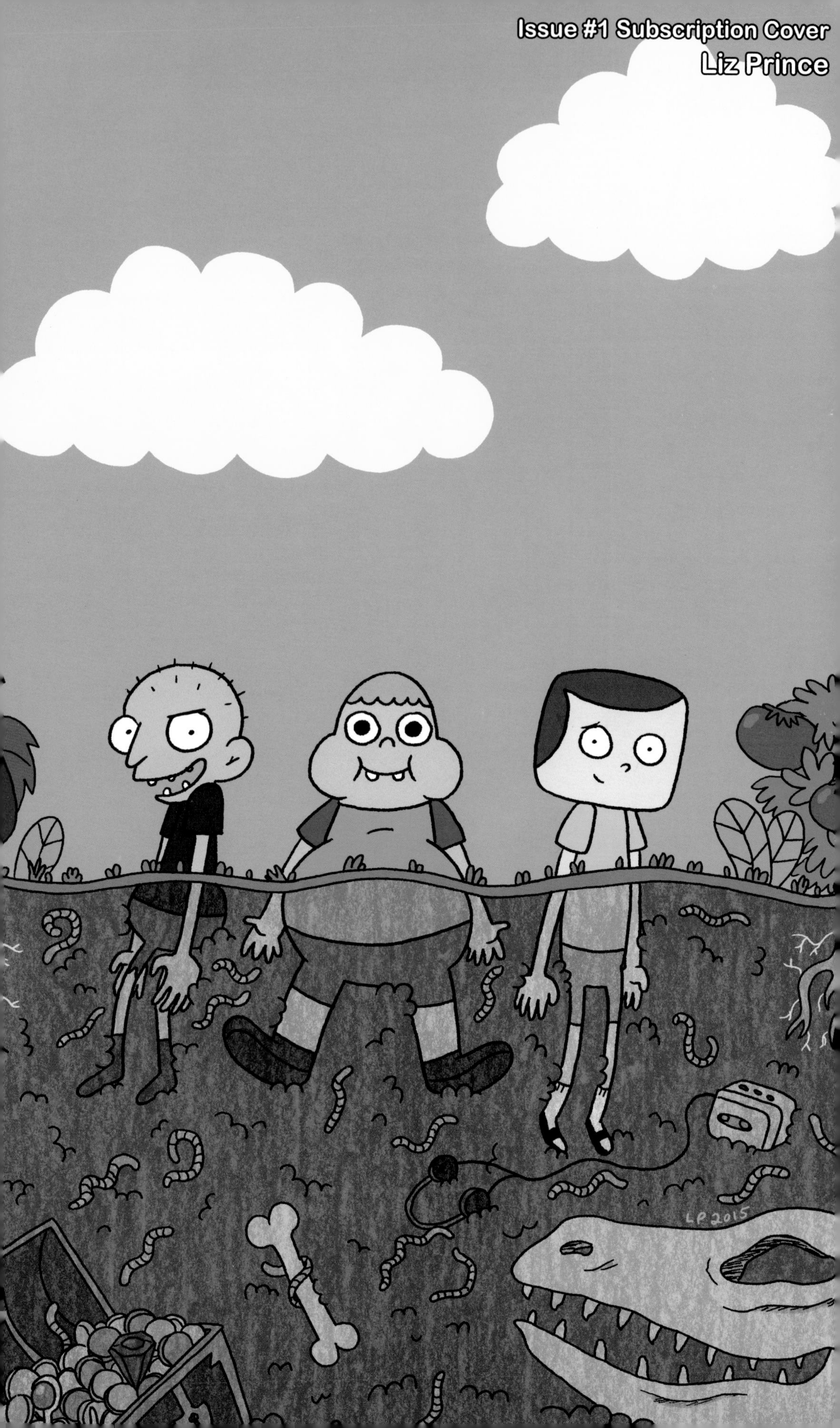
LP 2015

Issue #1 Subscription Cover
Liz Prince

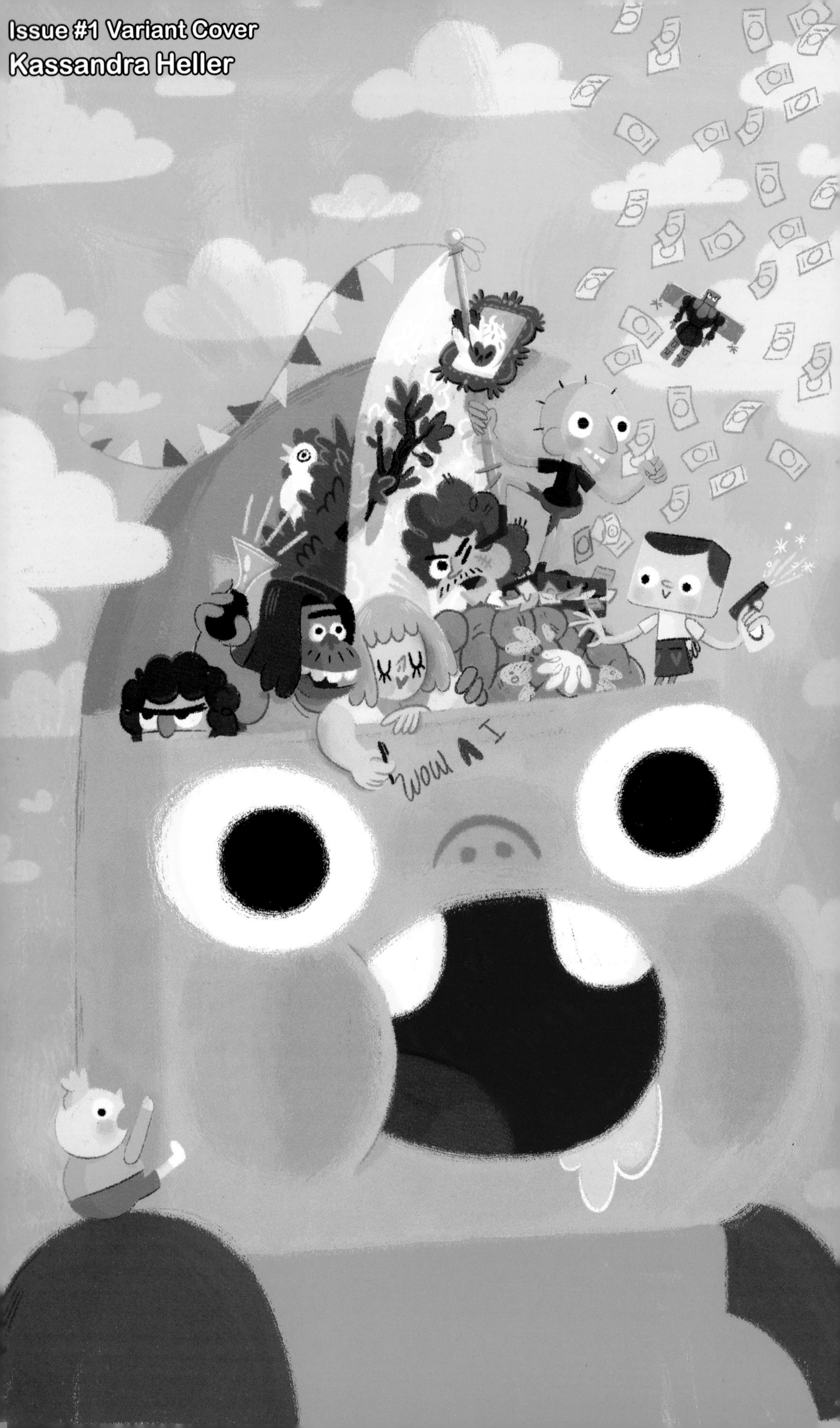

Issue #1 Variant Cover
Kassandra Heller

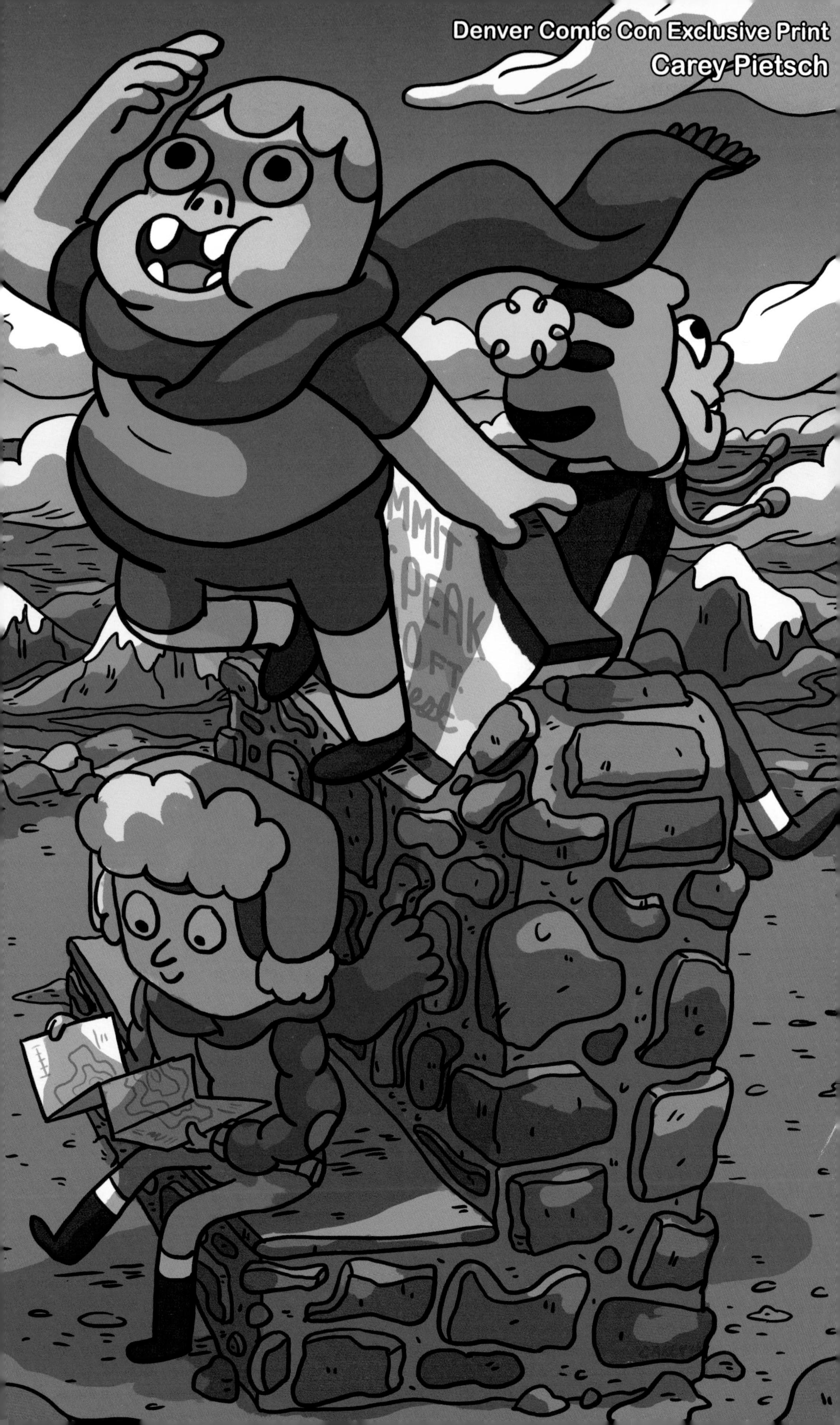

Denver Comic Con Exclusive Print
Carey Pietsch

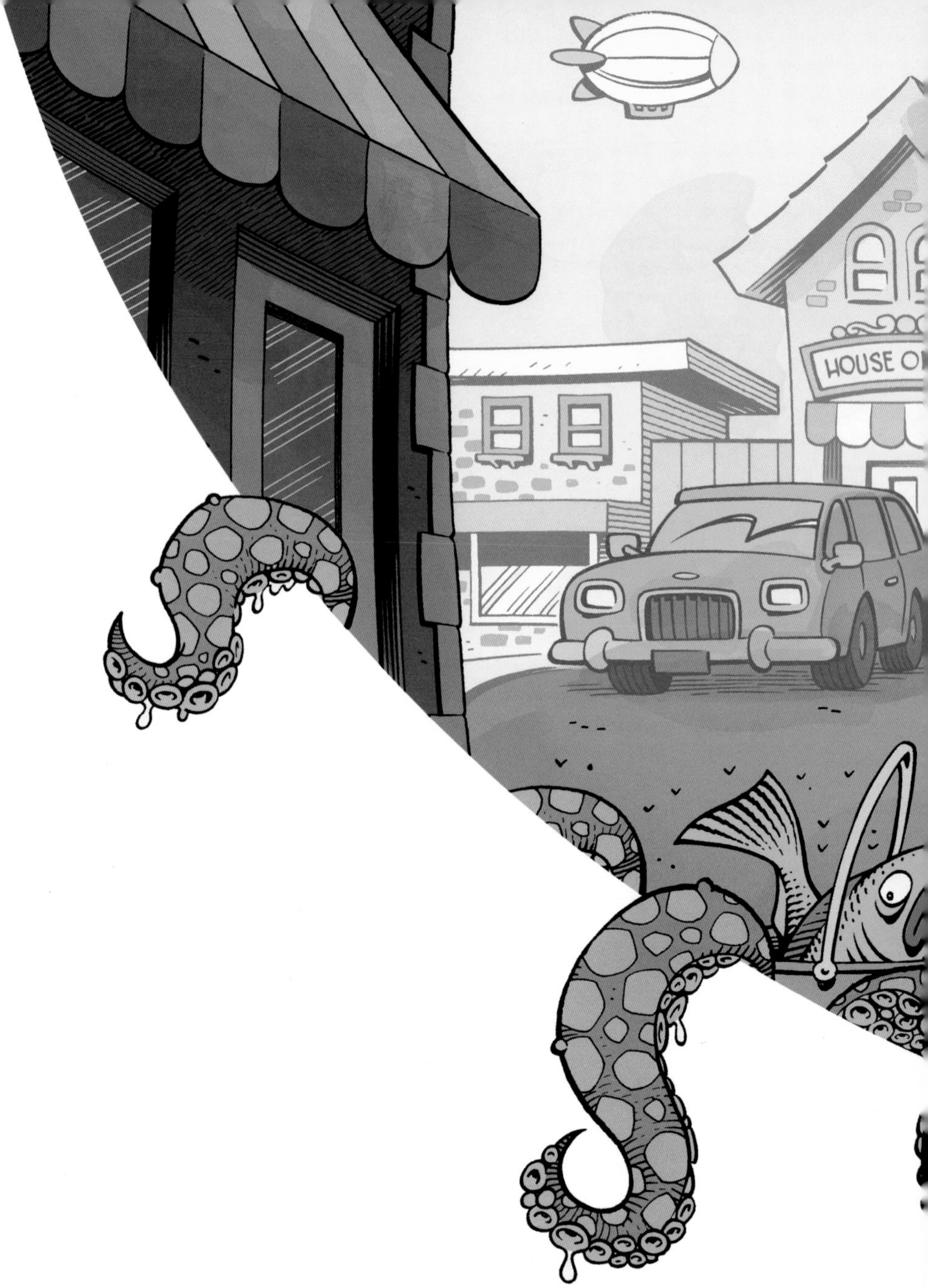

Issue #1 BOOM! Ten Years Variant Cover

Roger Langridge

with colors by **Whitney Cogar**

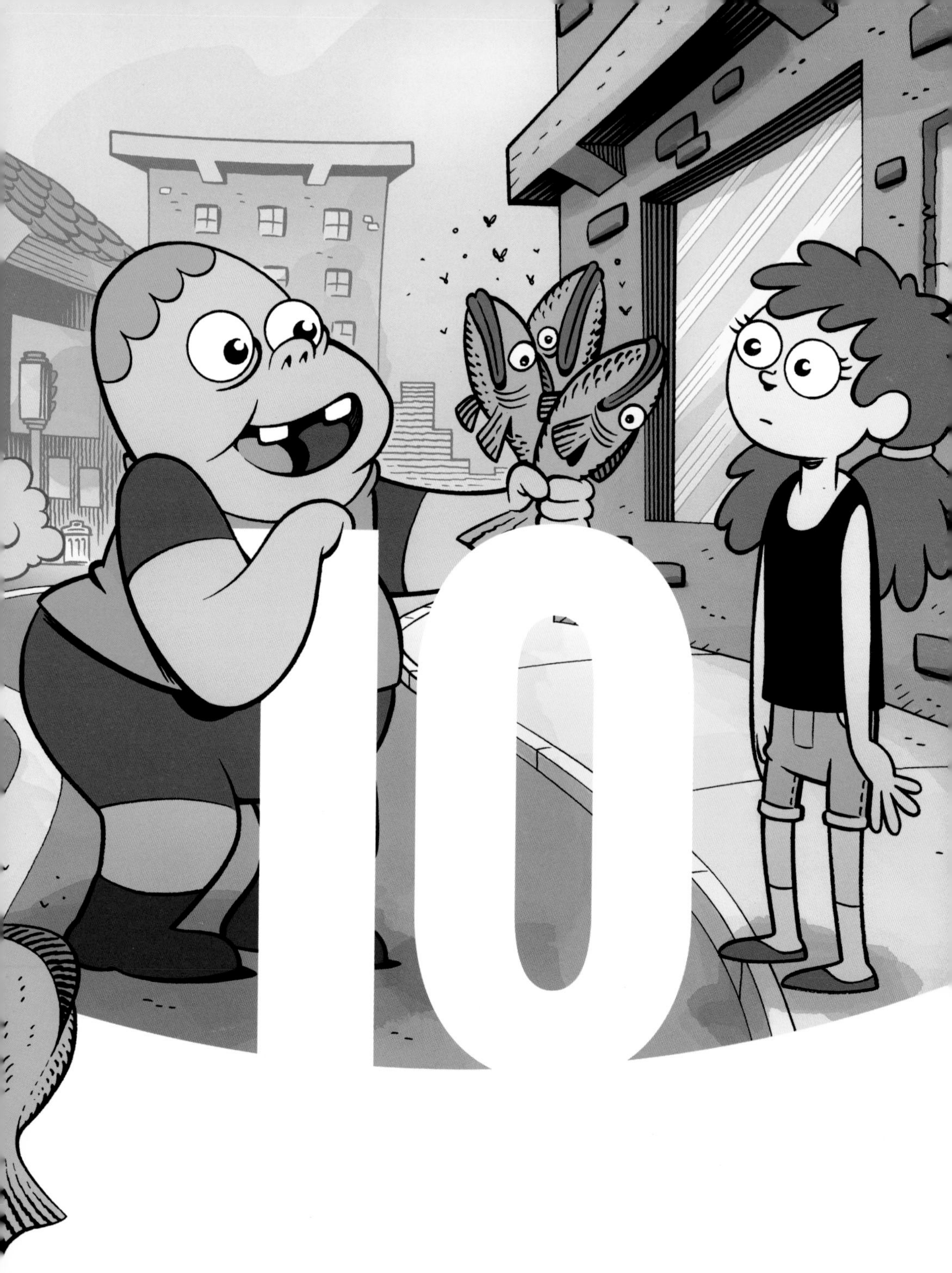

10

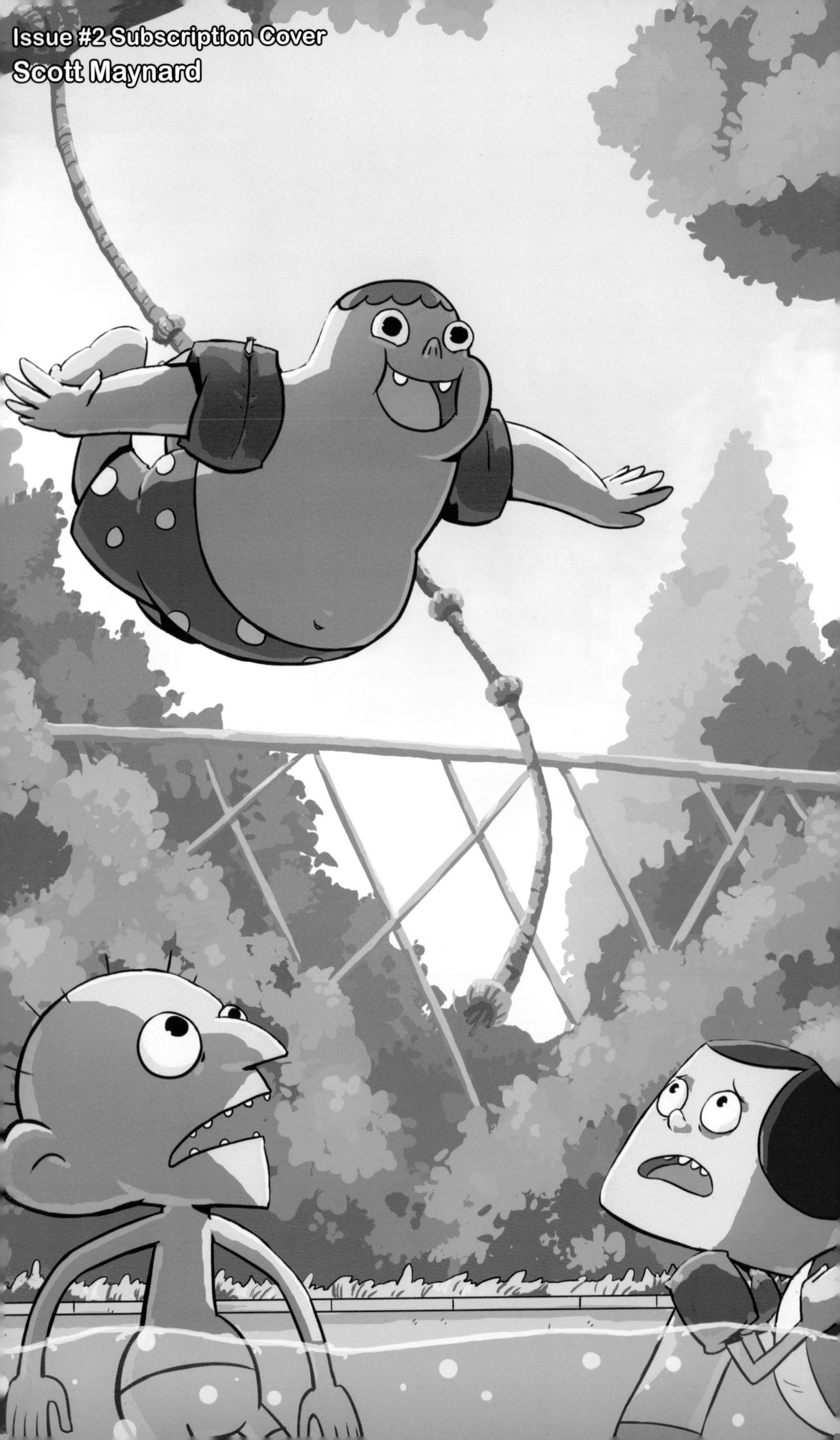

Issue #2 Subscription Cover
Scott Maynard

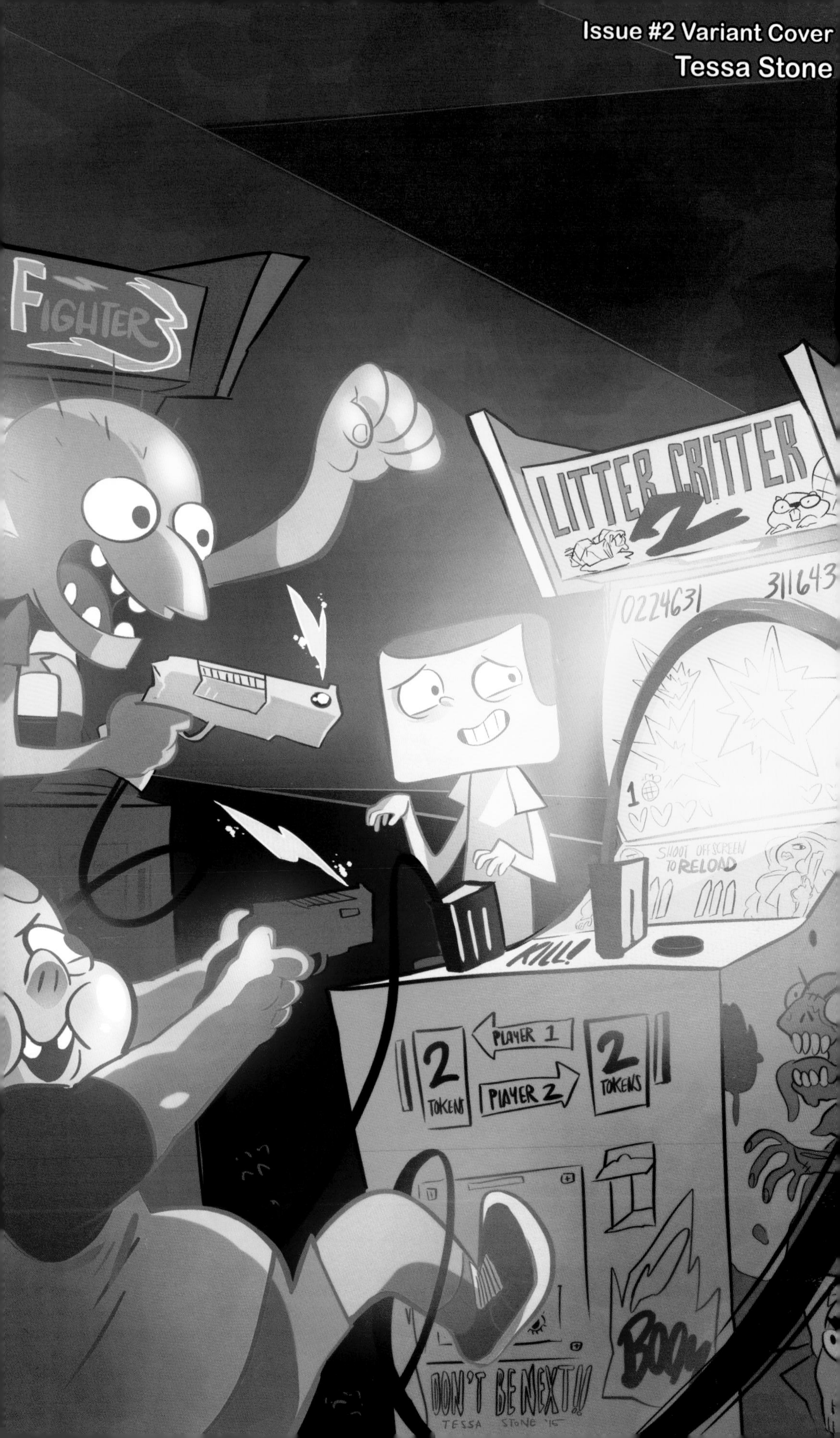
FIGHTER
LITTER CRITTER 2
0224631
311643
SHOOT OFFSCREEN TO RELOAD
KILL!
2 TOKENS
PLAYER 1
PLAYER 2
2 TOKENS
DON'T BE NEXT!!
TESSA STONE '15

Issue #2 Variant Cover
Tessa Stone

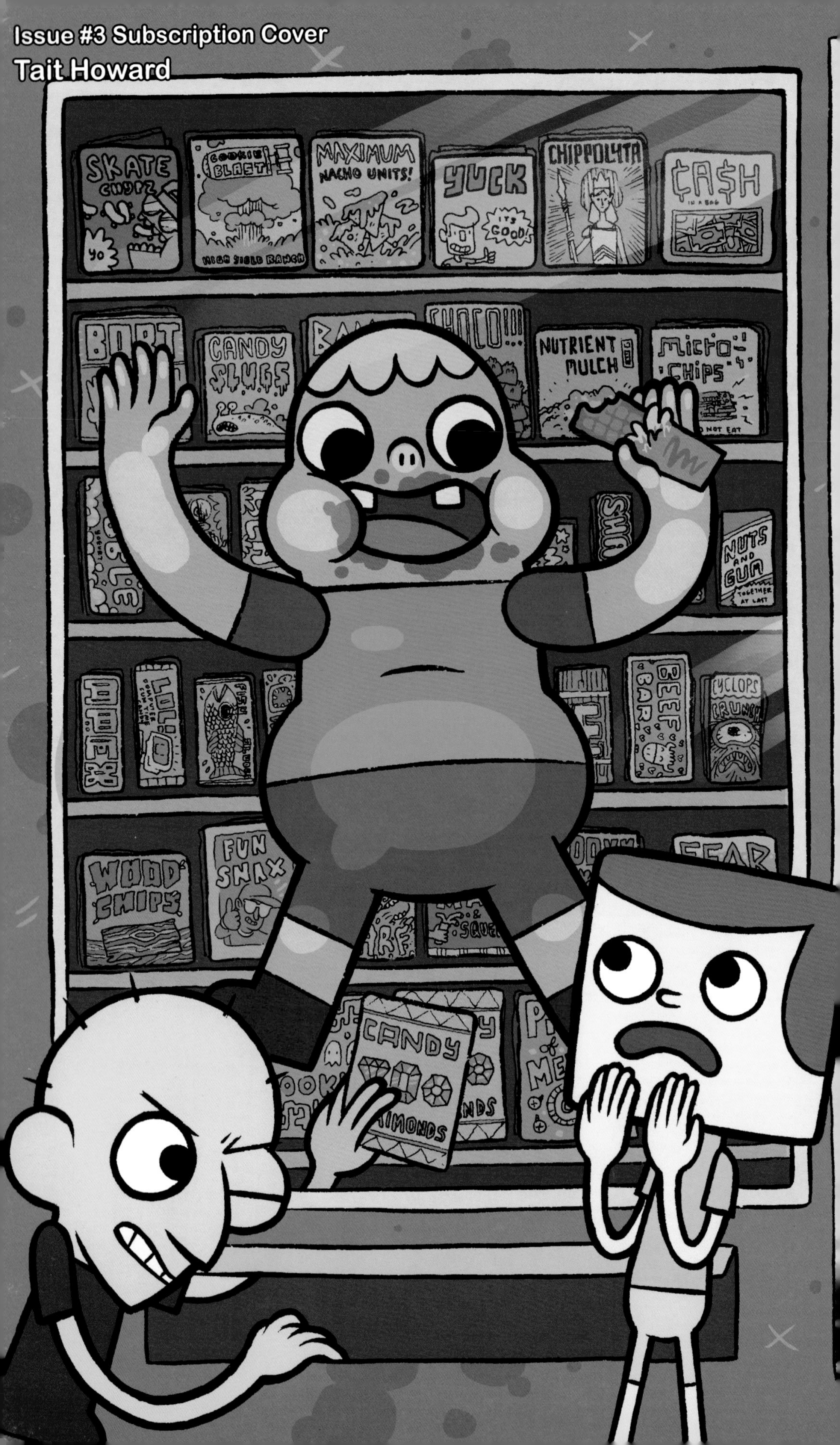

Issue #3 Subscription Cover
Tait Howard

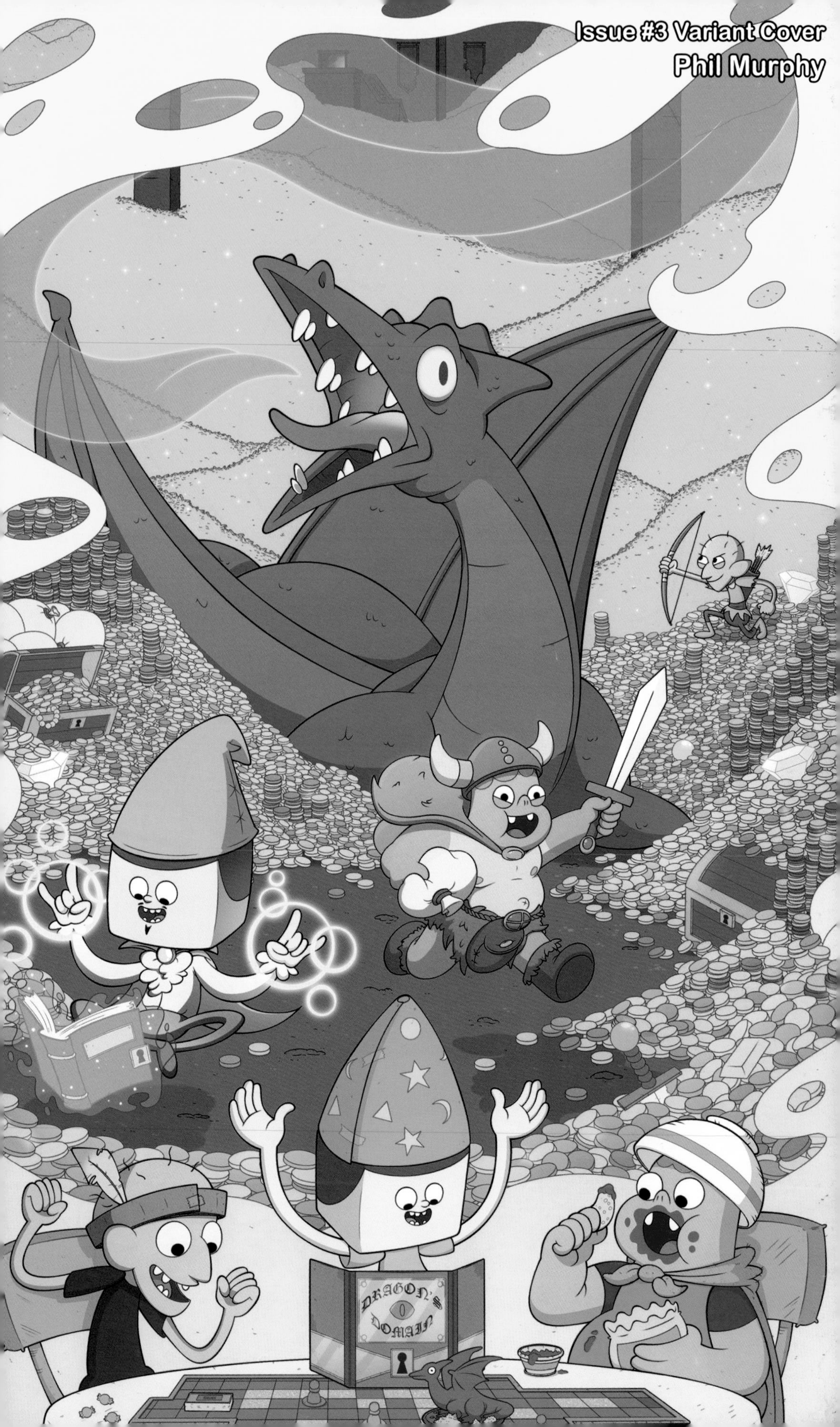
DRAGON'S
DOMAIN

Issue #3 Variant Cover
Phil Murphy

Issue #4 Subscription Cover
Steve Wells

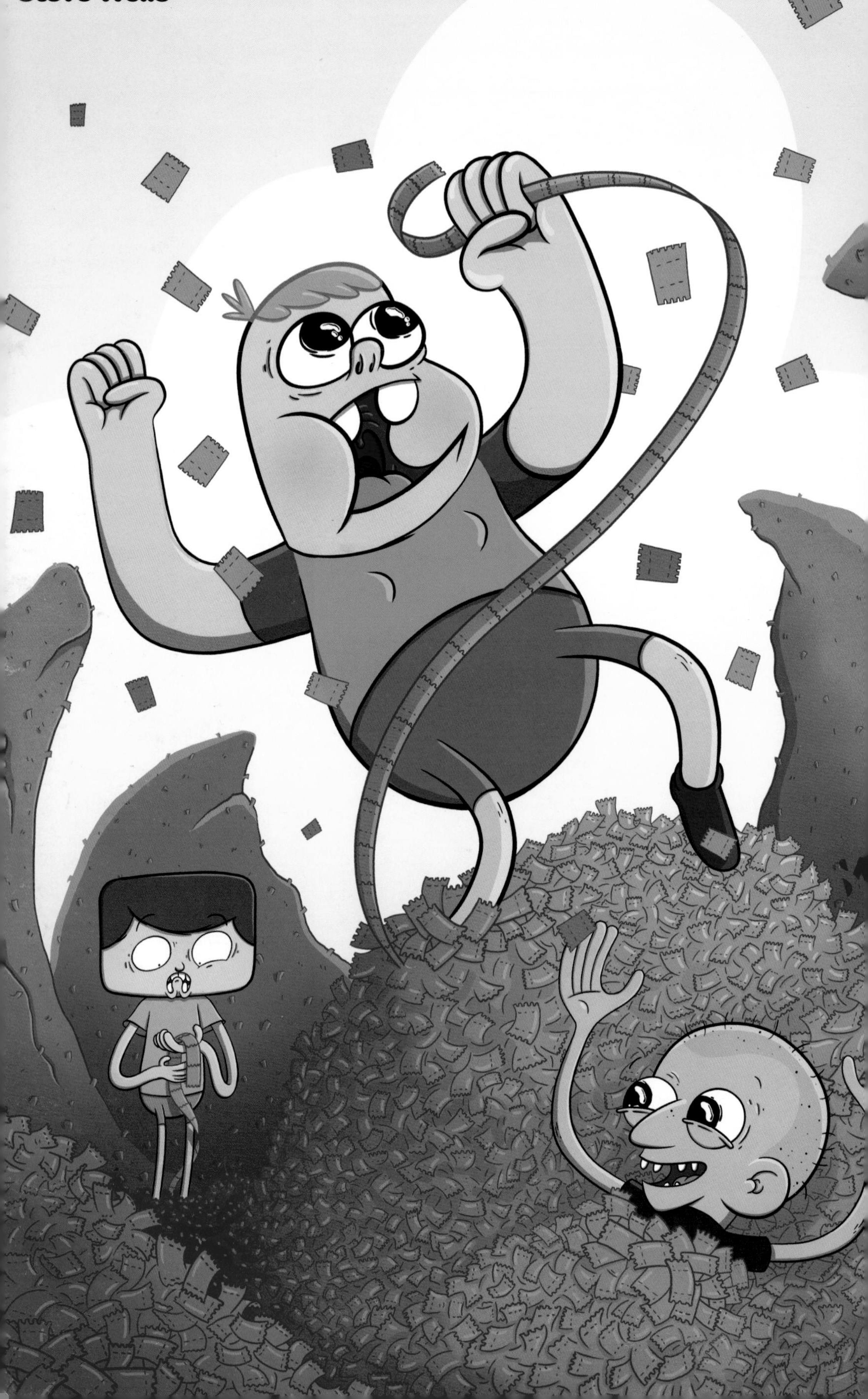

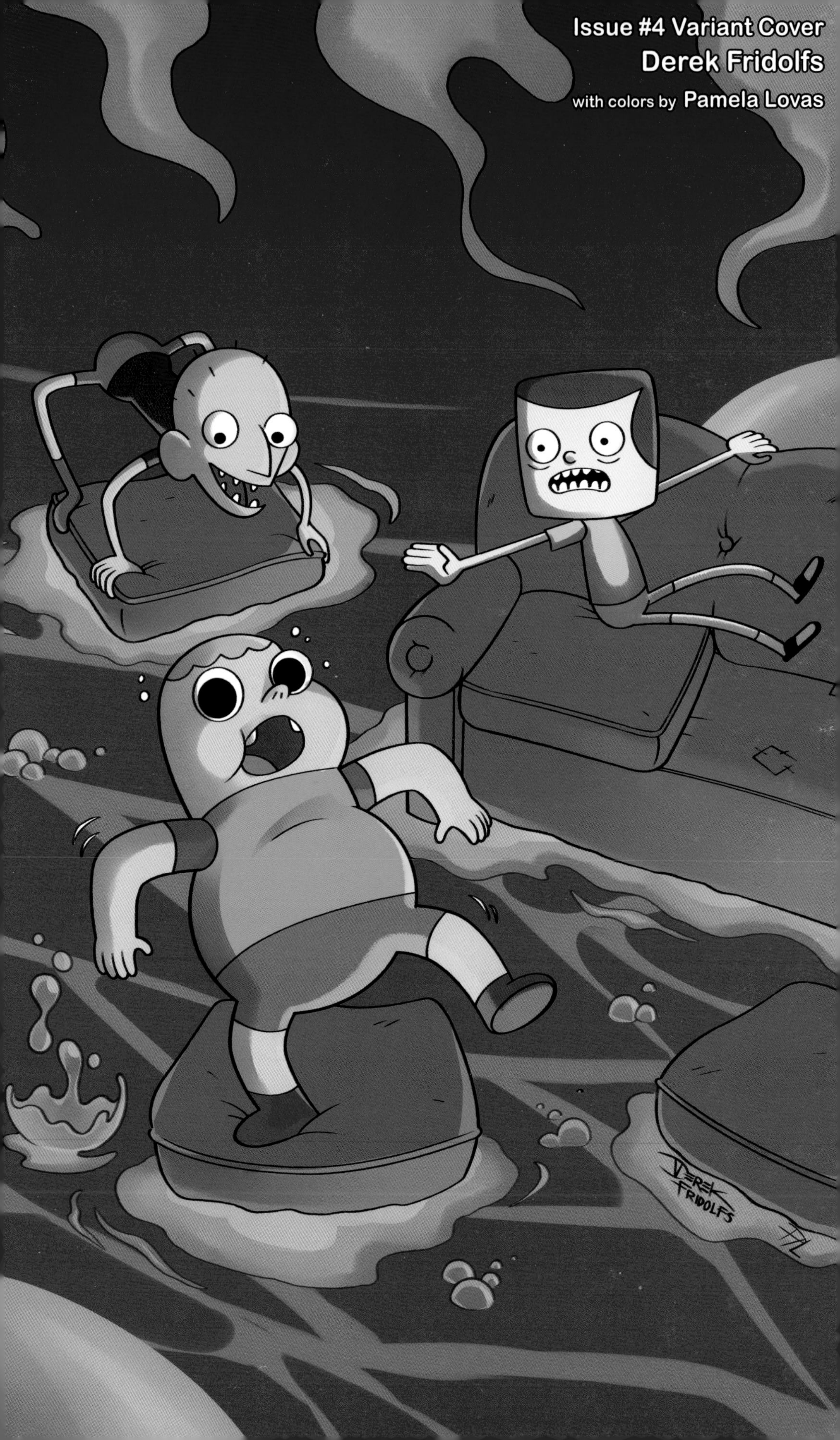
DEREK
FRIDOLFS

Issue #4 Variant Cover
Derek Fridolfs
with colors by **Pamela Lovas**